4

THURSDAY

E. L. TODD

CHAPTER ONE

Something Old, Something New

Axel

"Dude, I love Christmas time." I hopped out of Hawke's truck and landed on the sidewalk.

"Really?" He shoved his keys into his pocket as he walked around the hood. "I don't see what all the fuss is about."

Probably because his parents ditched him to go to Hawaii. Who does that? "There's no other time of year where it's perfectly okay to take off two whole weeks. Everything shuts down, every office and every business. It's the best thing ever."

"Actually, I don't think it works like that." Hawke walked beside me across the lawn. We were picking up Francesca on the way to Yaya's. "Maybe our office is closed but most of them aren't."

"Well, they should be. Where's their Christmas spirit?"

Thursday

"You don't have any Christmas spirit. You're just lazy and don't want to work."

"And you do?" I stopped when we reached her front door.

Hawke shrugged then rang the doorbell.

I tightened my jacket around my torso as we waited, feeling the sting of the cold. Frost had formed on the grass and the rooftop. I loved the winter but wasn't a fan of the chill. I preferred summertime because chicks wore short sundresses. Sometimes they blew up if it was windy enough.

Francesca opened the door. "Hey." Her eyes immediately went to Hawke, ignoring me completely.

He stared at her without blinking, looking intense and insufferable. "Hey."

Hawke said he didn't have a thing for my sister but I constantly caught him staring at her. "Get your shit and let's go." I pushed past her and walked inside, wanting some respite for the winter weather.

Francesca sighed before she walked down the hallway toward her bedroom.

I hardly ever came to her place, and if I did it was because she needed something. And she never stopped by my apartment either. The smell in the air hinted of some baked good so I walked into the kitchen to explore. On the table was a warm pan full of fresh muffins. "My lucky day." I grabbed one and felt the warmth in my fingertips.

"Those aren't for you." Marie slapped me on the wrist with her perfectly manicured fingertips. "You can wait until you get to Yaya's."

"Oh, come on." I stopped peeling the wrapper and looked at her.

Her blonde hair was long and in loose curls. It framed her face perfectly, looking voluptuous and soft. Her lips were painted with a light pink color, highlighting the curve of her mouth and her pristine white teeth. Dark make up was around her eyes, making their green color stand out and get my attention. Her fair skin was flawless, perfect like a porcelain doll.

She wore a dark green dress with sleeves, and dark pantyhose covered her legs. It looked like she was going to a Christmas party. Her long legs looked even longer in her black heels, and her petite frame was highlighted in the skin-tight fabric. One question came to mind.

Did she have a boyfriend?

I don't remember Marie ever looking this damn fine. Growing up she always had ratty hair that never looked brushed. She wore bright red lipstick that didn't suit her skin tone whatsoever, and she drowned in clothes that were obviously too big for her.

But now...day-yum.

She grew into her frame well, having a slender waist and neckline. Her hair looked like it was just done at the beauty parlor, and her dress couldn't be any tighter. Whatever baby fat she once had was gone.

She was a woman.

When did this happen? When was the last time I saw her? Why didn't Francesca mention this to me?

Marie put one hand on her hip while she gave me the stink-eye. "Hello?"

Her voice brought me back to the conversation. I didn't realize we were still having it until my haze was shattered. "What's up?"

"Put that back."

"This?" I held up the muffin and took a big bite. I chewed it slowly, my eyes on her the entire time. While the muffin was good I wish I were eating her instead. "Delicious."

She narrowed her eyes on me, looking frightening but cute at the same time. "Frankie made those for Christmas."

"Then it must be Christmas."

She snatched the pan off the table and carried it to the counter.

It was perfect. Now I had a great view of her ass. It had beautiful curves and contrasted against the deep arch in her back. I'd love to watch her twerk any day. I'd love to stick my dick between those cheeks.

Marie looked over her shoulder.

I took another bite of the muffin.

"Would you stop checking out my ass?"

"Depends. Will you let me touch it?"

She closed the muffin tin then walked past me again. She stopped when she was right beside me, her perfume washing over me. Her confidence was through the roof. She used to be hesitant, uncomfortable in her own skin. But now she knew exactly what she was worth. "In your dreams." Her lips were directly next to my ear, and the sound of her voice made me hard.

Damn, when did she get so hot?

***

After we were in the truck I looked out the window and stared at the house. "Marie has plans for Christmas?"

"Yeah," Frankie answered from the passenger seat. "She's going to her parents' place."

"So...she wouldn't want to tag along with us?" I asked hopefully.

Frankie fastened her safety belt then crossed her legs. "Doubtful."

Hawke pulled onto the road, the heater running at full blast.

"So...when did Marie get so hot?" I blurt. "Like, when did that happen?"

"Shut up, Axel." Frankie looked out the window.

I leaned forward over the center console. "I'm serious. When we were growing up she was a skinny little nerd."

Frankie elbowed me in the stomach. "Don't talk about my best friend like that."

I leaned back and gripped my stomach, feeling sick for a few seconds. "I didn't mean it in a bad way."

Hawke chuckled and glanced at me in the rearview mirror. "Then you should have phrased it better."

Thursday

"So, is she seeing anyone?" I rubbed my stomach until the ache passed.

Frankie held her silence and looked out the window.

"Oh, come on." I was getting this information one way or another. "Spill it."

"Axel, she's off limits. She's not some girl you can just screw and never see again. She's going to be in our lives forever."

"She might be down for casual sex."

Frankie cringed, her expression noticeable in the side mirror. "Just stop talking. I'm going to throw up."

"Just tell me if she's seeing someone." With legs like that and an ass to boot she had her pick of the crop.

Frankie didn't say a word.

I started poking her in the shoulder, over and over. It annoyed the shit out of her. I remembered, because I used to do it to her when we were kids. "If she seeing someone?"

She tried to elbow me again and missed. "No."

"She's single?" *Perfect.*

"Leave her alone, Axel," she said. "I mean it."

"Why? You think I'm going to break her heart?" I played the field a lot but I never misled women.
"No. I think she'll break yours."

CHAPTER TWO

Back To Reality

Axel

Christmas break came and went, and now the real world commenced. I was working as an intern for an investment company. It was my job to make portfolios for clients, determining what market was right for them. I put my brain to work but didn't reap any of the benefits.

And I barely got paid for it.

But it was just a stepping-stone. When I was finished with this internship I'd find a better gig somewhere else, probably in Manhattan. Wall Street never sleeps, and neither do I.

I hooked up with a few women over winter break, and when I came back home my mojo was worked up again. But instead of going on the prowl in search of tail I thought about Marie.

Seriously, when did she get so fine?

Thursday

It was like the story of the ugly duckling. She wasn't much to look at when we were kids, but when she became an adult she blossomed into an elegant swan. Now she was a fantasy. I'd be lucky if I could get her to notice me.

I wanted to see her but I wasn't sure how to go about it. If it were anyone else, I'd just flirt a little then ask her out. But she seemed a little more complicated than that. She already blew me off when I tried to get her into bed the first time. Maybe she wasn't into me, but I was too good-looking to be brushed off forever. Maybe a gentle touch would get her to change her mind.

But how would I see her?

I'd try to run into her when I was out but I didn't know what she did in her spare time. And if I asked Francesca I would just get slugged in the stomach. That wouldn't get me anywhere. And if I showed up to her house that would be straight up creepy ass shit.

***

I dug through my stuff and found something that once belonged to Francesca. It was an old bundt baking pan. I couldn't figure out how it ended up at my apartment because she never came over, but somehow it migrated into my cupboard. Returning it to her seemed like a legitimate excuse.

I put on my best jeans and my favorite t-shirt before I styled my hair perfectly. Then I left my apartment and drove to the house on the other side of town. If luck were on my side, Marie would be there alone. I could do some flirting, invite her out to dinner, and hopefully we'd be rolling around on my sheets by the time the sun went down. I wanted those legs wrapped my waist. Actually, I *needed* those legs wrapped around my waist.

I parked at the curb then walked to the door. I purposely left my jacket in the truck because I wanted my arms to be noticeable. Women always liked my body, and right now I was using it to my advantage.

I rang the doorbell and waited.

Frankie's car wasn't in the driveway but that didn't mean anything. It could be in the garage, staying safe from the cold. Marie's Toyota was parked outside so I knew she was around.

Yes.

The lock turned and then the door was pulled open. Marie stood there in a black t-shirt that said *The Grind* on it. Her dark jeans were skin tight, and her hair was pulled over one shoulder.

Shit, she was leaving for work. I had the worst luck.

"What's up?" She eyed me and the pan in my hands.

"Frankie left this at my place. I was in the neighborhood so I thought I'd drop it off."

She didn't invite me inside. She stood with one hand on her hip. Her t-shirt was skin-tight and showed all of her curves. The V-neck in front showed a graceful amount of cleavage from her tits.

I tried not to stare.

Thursday

"She's not home." She took the pan out of my hands. "But I'll tell her you stopped by."

My plan was backfiring. I couldn't find another excuse to come back here so I needed to seal the deal. "So, I was—"

"Bye." She shut the door.

I stayed on the doorstep, my jaw still open. Did she just shut the door in my face? What was with this woman? Was she totally immune to my charms? All the other girls wanted me. What was her problem?

Now I wanted her even more.

I rang the doorbell.

Her feet echoed on the hardwood floor before she answered. "What?" She returned her hand to her hip, as she always did when she spoke to me.

"You shut the door in my face."

"Aren't we done here?" Her blonde hair trailed down to her chest. It looked softer than silk. I wanted to run my fingers through it, grip it while I thrust inside her. Getting laid always came easy for me, but Marie was a difficult conquest.

"No hi? How are you?"

"Hi. How are you?"

"Great. How are you?"

"I'm fabulous." She shut the door again.

I wanted to scream in frustration. A smart guy would just give up and leave, but the more she turned me down the more I wanted her. Her confidence was seriously sexy.

I rang the doorbell a third time.

Marie opened the door. "Dude, get a hobby."

This time I walked inside without being invited. I pushed the door shut and backed her up with my proximity. If she wanted to play rough, then we'd play rough. I walked toward her while keeping my eyes trained on her. "Can I take you out to dinner?"

She crossed her arms over her chest, her eyes hiding every thought deep inside that pretty little head of hers.

"I haven't stopped thinking about you since Christmas." I laid all my cards on the table and folded. I didn't want to play games anymore. I wanted this woman—badly.

"Yeah?" Her cattiness dimmed. The fight wasn't obvious in her eyes anymore. Now that I was being honest, she was being honest too. "I think you're cute too."

She thought I was cute? Awesome. "Then we definitely should have dinner together."

"I guess we can do that."

"What are you doing right now?"

"Just got off work."

"Are you hungry?"

"I think so."

I came closer to her, my excitement burning my own skin. "I'm hungry too." I stopped just inches from her lips, wanting to skip to dessert.

"Just let me change and we'll go." She turned around and walked into the hallway.

My eyes immediately moved to her ass, hoping I'd get the chance to squeeze it later.

Thursday

***

We didn't talk much over dinner. Looks were exchanged, the sexual attraction sizzling like a hot pan. All I was thinking about was kissing her, feeling those soft lips against my own. I wanted her to whimper into my mouth, to moan when I hit her in the right place. Every time I tried to start a conversation I kept getting distracted by the thought of her being naked.

And I was hard.

"I'm surprised you don't have a boyfriend." Our dishes sat in front of us, hardly touched. We took a few bites but were too busy watching each other to really eat.

"Why is that surprising?"

"Look at you."

"I was seeing this guy a while ago but it didn't work out."

"What happened?" I sipped my wine but kept watching her.

"I just didn't like him anymore. I stayed at his place while my house was being remodeled. But once that was over, I ended it."

"That's a little cold," I said with a chuckle.

"Not really," she said. "We weren't in love or anything. And he got a lot of sex that week, so there's really nothing to complain about. When I broke up with him, he was fine with it."

"How long did you guys see each other?"

"For two months."

So it wasn't serious at all. "Well, if you ever need a place to crash, my apartment is always available. And I take sex as payment."

She chuckled. "I'll keep that in mind. What about you?"

"What about me?"

"Any serious girlfriends?"

"Nope." The thought never crossed my mind. I assumed if I met the right girl I'd settle down, but she hadn't walked into my life yet. I'm sure when I saw her I would know she was the one. Until then, I was playing the field.

"Terminal bachelor?"

"I hope not. But for now, yeah. What about you?"

"I haven't had a serious boyfriend in...forever." She picked at her pasta. "I'm picky when it comes to relationships."

"You never settle."

"I guess you could put it that way. But I don't mind having fun."

Fun worked for me.

"You like your job?"

"It's okay. The pay is horrendous."

She chuckled. "So is The Grind."

"Honestly, I probably make as much as you do. And I have a master's."

"That is horrendous."

"But it's temporary. I'll find something better once this internship is over."

"I'm sure you will." She took a long drink of her wine then pushed her plate away.

If she was done, I'd love to move this date elsewhere.

"You know, I used to have a huge crush on you in high school."

I grinned from ear-to-ear. "Yeah?"

"Yep. But you never noticed me."

I stared into her eyes, seeing the playfulness there. "I notice you now."

She sipped her wine again, her eyes on me the entire time.

When the tab arrived I shoved cash inside and left it on the table. "Are you ready to go?"

She downed the rest of her wine then set the empty glass on the table. "Yeah."

***

After we got into the truck I started the engine. "So, should I take you home? Or...do you want to see my apartment?" I didn't know what Frankie was doing tonight but I assumed she would come home and see my truck at the curb. I didn't care what my sister thought of Marie and I, but I didn't want her involved in it either.

"I'd love to see your apartment."

Yes. "Let the tour begin." I put my arm over her shoulders and pulled her into the middle seat. Her hair fell over my arm, and I loved the way it felt against my skin. My body temperature went up a few degrees when I knew what was going to happen. My dick was already hard and ready to go.

I drove to my apartment then walked with her to my front door. After I got it unlocked we walked inside. I turned on the lights so she could see it in all its glory. It was pretty small, with just the basic necessities. Right now, it was all I could afford.

"It's nice," she whispered.

"You want to see my bedroom?"

"Very much so."

I grabbed her hand and guided her down the hall to my bedroom. My room was plain. All it had were two dressers and my bed. All I did was sleep and screw in here so I didn't bother dressing up the place.

I turned around and prepared to kiss her, to do what I've wanted to do all night.

But she made the first move. She pushed me gently, guiding me back on the bed.

My back hit the mattress, and I propped myself up on my elbows, surprised by her forwardness.

She reached for the bottom of her blouse and slowly pulled it over her head, taking her time and swaying her hips slightly. Without music, she danced. Slowly, the fabric moved over her head, pulling her hair with it. When it was gone she stood in a pink bra, the push up kind that made her tits look amazing. She tossed the shirt aside then fingered the straps.

I lay there, mesmerized by the private show I was getting. My eyes were honed in on her tits, and I wanted to see the bra fall. She had the perfect body, with wide hips and a petite waist. I desperately wanted to touch her.

She unclasped the bra and let it fall to the floor.

I took an involuntary breath when I saw her tits. They were perky, round, and firm. Her nipples were hard, and I wanted to run my tongue across both of them. I wanted to grab her slender waist and squeeze.

Marie stripped the rest of the way and removed her jeans and then finally her thong. When she pulled it down I stared at the nub between her legs. I wanted to be inside her so bad, to stretch her and make her scream.

Her legs were perfect. She had slender thighs that stretched on for days. She was delicately manicured down below, making me even more turned on.

She climbed on the bed then moved on top of me, placing her chest against mine.

My hands immediately went to her hips, feeling the softness of her skin. My fingertips dug into her body because she felt so good. I stared at her lips and desperately wanted them against mine. Never in my life had I been this turned on.

My hand dug into her hair, and I pulled her mouth to mine. The second we touched, my entire body lit on fire. The heat between our mouths burned us, but it felt too good to stop. I brushed her lips with mine, and when her tongue entered my mouth, I released an involuntary moan.

My arm hooked around her waist, and I gripped her against me, grinding with her and breathing hard. I explored her body with my hands, feeling her slender back and that gorgeous ass. Feeling her naked on top of me while I was fully clothed was a turn-on in itself. I'd been with forward women who knew exactly what they wanted but it was nothing compared to this. Marie's confidence was the sexiest thing I'd ever seen. Without taking any further steps, I knew she would be one of the greatest lays I've ever gotten.

Marie ended our kiss slowly then moved down my body.

My lips immediately felt cold when hers were gone. I wanted to kiss her forever, to fuck her mouth with mine and never stop.

She slid to the edge of the bed then unbuttoned my jeans.

My dick throbbed in my pants, unable to handle the sight in front of me.

Marie pulled my jeans down along with my boxers and got them to my ankles. She flipped her hair over one shoulder, her tits shaking in the process, and then removed my shoes and socks. When my bottoms were gone she sat up and leaned over my crotch, her tits close to my balls.

She grabbed my dick by the base and pointed him toward the sky. She licked her lips slowly as she stared at him, like there was nothing more she wanted than to suck me off.

Holy motherfucker.

Thursday

Without realizing it, I was breathing hard. My entire body was tense in preparation. I'd gotten head plenty of times but not like this. She did it in such a sexy way.

She kissed my tip softly before she moved him into the back of her mouth. She started off slow, taking him inch by inch. And then she moved quickly, getting into it.

I closed my eyes because it felt so good. The view was just as amazing as the sensation but my body automatically responded to the pleasure she was giving me. I loved feeling her tongue moved over my cock. It was the best feeling ever.

She pulled him out of her mouth and rested him against my stomach. Then she moved for my shirt. Together, we got it off and tossed it aside.

I was high in the clouds and existing on a different plane of reality. My body and mind were combined into a single entity, and I no longer thought about my actions before I did them. They just happened.

I rolled her to her back and moved my face between her legs. I never went down on women because I never cared for it, but I desperately wanted to do it to her. I wanted to taste her, feeling the wetness I provoked between her legs.

I rubbed my tongue against her clitoris and felt her tighten in my arms. Her back arched slightly and musical sighs escaped her lips. Her fingers dug into my hair, and she panted, enjoying everything I gave her just as I enjoyed everything she gave to me.

She tasted like strawberry and that aroused me even more. My dick was still harder than ever and desperate to be inside her. I wanted to keep eating her out but now I was impatient. I wanted to move with her, to feel our bodies grind together in the throes of passion.

I opened my nightstand and grabbed a condom from the pile then quickly rolled it on. I made sure there was plenty of room at the tip because I knew I was going to make a big deposit.

I positioned myself on top of her and pinned my arms behind her knees. My tip found her entrance and it rested there, partially inside her.

She looked up at me with desire in her eyes. She was in the cloud too, drifting at a heightened level of reality. She was lost in me just the way I was lost in her. Her hands moved up my arms until they cupped my neck. She gently pulled me toward her, wanting me inside her then and there.

I slowly slid inside her, feeling my cock stretch her with every inch. I moved until I was completely inside her.

Marie released a loud moan, her nails digging into my skin. Her head rolled back slightly as if she wasn't prepared for how good it would feel. "Axel..."

My spine shivered. I thrust into her slowly, wanting to take my time before we reached the finish line. I already knew I was going to make her come. She was delirious in ecstasy just the way I was.

Her nails scratched down my back, leaving marks that would linger for days. She used my body as an anchor to thrust into me from down below. Her tits shook with every thrust I made. Redness had spread across her chest and the area surrounding her nipples. She bit her bottom lip in the cutest way.

"Just like that." She pressed her head to mine and breathed hard with me, feeling every sensation burn our bodies from the inside out. "God, yes. Just like that."

Goddammit, she was going to make me explode. I increased my pace slightly, pounding into her to give her the best climax she ever had.

"Yes." Her head rolled back, and she arched her back. "Yes, yes, yes." Her nails almost drew blood they were cutting into me so deeply.

I wanted to keep going but I couldn't after that performance. My entire body burned white-hot before the explosion happened. My cock twitched just before it released, filling the tip of the condom.

We went to another world together, using each other to get the biggest high we've ever felt. My body was covered in sweat and so was hers, but the pleasure made all the work worth it.

I stayed inside her and never wanted to leave. That was the best sex I've ever had and I hoped she felt the same way. It was so organic and easy. The chemistry was right and we fell deep into each other. It was the way sex was meant to be.

I cupped her face and gave her a slow kiss, satisfied but innately aroused.

She kissed me back, sweat on her upper lip.

"That was so good."

"I know." A sleepy haze came over her eyes, like she was drifting off to sleep after that intense orgasm.

I rolled over and disposed of the condom before I came back to her. I pulled the sheets back and tucked us in before I spooned her from behind. I was covered in sweat and so was she but I didn't mind. Unlike most of my dates, I actually wanted to hold her.

I liked it.

Thursday

CHAPTER THREE

Hit and Run

Marie

When I woke up the next morning I was in Axel's arms. Just as the sunlight filtered through the blinds of his window, the memory of what happened last night came back to me.

Axel was my biggest crush in high school. I'd always pictured us getting married and living happily ever after, but I knew he didn't notice me. I was just his sister's ugly friend. He didn't think twice about me before he chased after a cheerleader.

But now I finally had him.

He was great in bed, like I expected. He was a fantastic kisser. I could kiss those sexy lips all day. And he was even a good cuddler.

It was definitely a good time.

Thursday

But now I had to get back to reality. I had class in an hour, and I needed to hit the road. I slipped from his arms and quickly dressed myself before I called an UBER. I got a ride back to my house and hoped Francesca was either still asleep or never came home the night before. Otherwise, it would be a really awkward conversation.

I hadn't had a good lay in a while, and Axel fit the bill. I understood last night was just a friendly screw and would never happen again. Since Axel wasn't the kind of guy I was looking for it was fine by me. My happily ever after was out there and he certainly wasn't it.

When I got home I unlocked the door as quietly as possible then crept inside. But I stopped dead in my tracks when the distinct smell of breakfast entered my nose. "Goddammit."

"Marie, is that you?" Frankie called from the kitchen.

Why did she have to be awake at the crack of dawn? "Yeah. You're awake early." I came around the corner and hoped she wouldn't notice my wrinkled clothes and messy hair.

Frankie turned away from the stove and looked at me. "Yeah, I—" She shut her mouth when she realized I was right in the middle of a walk of shame. "Someone had fun last night..."

I tossed my purse on the table. "It wasn't a big deal."

Frankie scooped the pancakes onto a plate and set it at the table for me. "Spill."

"There's nothing to talk about." I wasn't going to talk about screwing her brother. That was the weirdest thing ever.

Frankie set her own plate down. "Since when did you stop telling me about your conquests?" She poured herself a cup of coffee and sat down. "Even when I don't want to hear about it you still gush about all the details."

I sat in the chair and drenched my pancakes with syrup. "Just trust me on this. You don't want to know." I gave her a firm look. "No questions asked."

Frankie stared at me as she cut into her pancakes. Her mind was working behind her eyes, trying to figure out why I would say such a thing. She took a few bites before she connected the dots. "Ew."

"Told you."

"Axel? Seriously?" She was thoroughly repulsed. "I thought you were over him."

"I was over him. But then he came by and said pretty things…"

She shook her head and kept eating. "Gross."

"It was a one-time thing so let's just move on."

"Thank god." She sipped her coffee and looked out the window. "Do you feel different now?"

"What do you mean?"

"I know you were really into him when we were younger. Like, obsessed. Was it what you pictured?"

It was hard to answer that question without going into detail. "I guess it was nice to have something I've always

25

wanted. But it wasn't the magical experience I pictured. The only reason why he noticed me was because I toned up, learned how to use make up, and starting wearing nice clothes. His attraction to me is totally superficial. If you ask me, he still doesn't really notice me. Does that make sense?"

Frankie abandoned her half eaten pancakes and considered my question. "I think I do. You have to be spiritually connected to someone to have a true relationship. It can't all be physical..." Her eyes drifted away like she was thinking of someone else.

"Hawke?" I smiled because my friend's happiness was infectious.

She didn't deny it. "A physical attraction is important but it's definitely not everything. Whatever connection we have...is beyond physical appearance. I think it's important when it comes to love."

"I think I know what you mean."

"If it was so meaningless why did you do it?"

She was naïve sometimes. "Your brother is hot. And I haven't had a good lay in a while."

She cringed and tried not to spit out her food. "I'm just glad this was a one-time thing. Will it be weird between you two?"

"No, not at all," I said. "Besides, we never see each other anyway."

Frankie finished the last of her pancakes. "Thank god for that."

***

Within a week I stopped thinking about Axel entirely. The night was fun, and the sex was awesome, but it was quickly forgotten. I didn't call him and he didn't call me, which was fine because it was clear we both understood what that night was.

I focused on school and worked on a term paper I'd been dreading. I spent most of the week locked up at home with my laptop. When I was finally finished with it, Mike asked me out on a date. We went out and had a good time, but it didn't lead anywhere. He wasn't my type, and I didn't want to lead him on so I said goodnight at the door.

I was home with Francesca when the doorbell rang three times in a row.

Francesca looked up from her textbook. "Expecting anyone?"

"No. Is it Hawke?"

"No. He doesn't ring the doorbell like that." She stood up and headed to the door. "Actually, he hardly even knocks." She opened the door to reveal Axel on the other side.

And he didn't look happy. "Do you have any idea what you're doing?"

Frankie gave him a bored look. "Do you?" She walked back to the table and sat beside me, returning her focus to the textbook.

Axel followed her, his chest puffed up like he had something to say. "You really think being with Hawke is a good idea?"

Thursday

It was only a matter of time before he figured it out. I wanted to excuse myself from the table but I was right next to them. Not moving or speaking was probably less distracting than if I left the room.

"Stay out of my business, Axel." Frankie turned the page.

"I can't stay out of your business," Axel snapped. "Hawke is the biggest womanizer I know. I'm not letting you get dragged through the mud like that."

"He's not like that with me," she argued. "Axel, we have a relationship, not a meaningless fling."

"He's still not good enough for you."

I admired Axel for looking after his sister, but I wish he would understand she was capable of taking care of herself.

"Axel, just butt out," Frankie snapped. "Hawke and I come as a set. You just need to accept that."

Axel didn't seem to realize I was there until that moment. He looked at me and held my gaze for a few seconds before he looked at his sister again. "It's my job to look after you—"

She threw her banana at him. "Get over yourself, Axel."

The banana fell on the ground with a loud thud.

I covered my mouth and tried not to laugh.

Axel kept a stoic expression on his face but it seemed like he was about to snap. "Fine. Be a brat." He walked out and slammed the door behind him.

E. L. Todd

"Wow...talk about an overprotective brother," I said with a laugh.

Frankie rolled her eyes. "He needs to grow up."

A second later the door opened again. "Hi, Marie." He walked out again, slamming the door a second time.

I laughed after he was gone. "Well, at least he's polite."

"I love my brother and everything, but damn, I hate him."

Thursday

CHAPTER FOUR

Egg Shells

Axel

I didn't speak to Hawke for weeks because I was pissed. He broke the Bro Code and went for my sister. I didn't care if he loved her or wanted to spend the rest of his life with her.

He crossed a line.

The second my dad shot himself in the head Francesca became my responsibility. He wasn't man enough to stick around and look after her, but I was. I'd take care of her just the way Mom would have wanted.

And Hawke was a player.

The biggest one I ever met.

At work I ignored him and refused to speak to him, but I kept my eye on him at the same time, seeing if his eye would wander to the other women in the office. To my surprise, they didn't.

Thursday

He tried talking to me a few times but I always brushed him off. What kind of friend went after my sister after I specifically said she was off limits?

But as more time passed, I realized their relationship—or whatever it was—wasn't going away. Three weeks had come and gone and they were still together, spending every waking hour together.

Maybe it was serious.

The longest I'd seen Hawke with anyone was two weeks—and that was an exaggeration. He was just like me, hit-it-and-quit-it type of guy. No one held our attention long enough to stick around. He'd sworn off relationships while I just wasn't interested in them.

But whatever he had with Francesca was clearly different.

So I ended the war.

"Hey." I met up with him outside the building after work.

He turned to me in surprise, clearly not expecting me to speak to him ever again.

"I'm sorry about the whole...you know. Frankie is pretty much all I have left, and I have to make sure she's okay. Sorry, it's nothing personal."

Instead of arguing with me or telling me off, he let it go. "I understand."

"It's pretty clear that you two are serious."

He nodded. "We are."

"Then...you have my blessing."

His eyes turned cold. "I never asked for it. But I hope you understand I would never hurt Francesca on purpose. And I would never hurt someone you love."

"Yeah, I get it."

He extended his hand.

I took it. "Friends again?"

He smiled. "We were always friends, man."

"Want to go out for a beer?"

"Let's do it."

***

"What have you been up to?" Hawke leaned back in the booth with his fingers wrapped around his beer on the table.

The place was crowded despite the early hour. A few cute girls were in the place but I stayed in my seat. "Nothing much."

He drank his beer while his gaze remained focused on me. "Frankie mentioned something happened with Marie."

"Oh yeah." I grinned at the memory. "Something did happen with Marie."

Hawke patiently waited for the tale.

"Dude, she's awesome in bed. I mean, like, wow."

"Really?" His tone remained the same, like he was only partially interested in the conversation.

"She's the best I've ever had."

"Sounds like a keeper."

"I don't know about that. I woke up the next morning and she was gone."

"Ouch." He chuckled. "Doesn't feel good, does it?"

"I guess I was a little disappointed. I haven't stopped thinking about that night since it happened."

"Why don't you ask her out again?"

"I don't know...I don't do back-to-backs."

"Has she called?"

I shook my head. "No. It seemed like she wanted the same thing I did—one night."

"Sounds perfect. You didn't have to have the talk with her. I can't count the number of times I couldn't get a girl to get off my back. "

"Yeah, I guess." When I woke up the next morning I expected her to be there. We could have some great morning sex and breakfast before she took off. But she was gone before my eyes opened. And we hadn't spoken since. I still thought about the way her lips tasted and the way her legs felt wrapped around my waist. All the sensations washed over me like they were happening again.

Hawke studied me, silent as a statue. He took a drink of his beer, his eyes still on me.

"What?"

He shrugged.

"Why are you looking at me like that?"

"You have a funny look on your face."

"No, I don't."

He chuckled. "Yes, you do. And I can tell you're thinking about Marie."

"Am not." I felt like I was having a child's argument.

"If you like her, why don't you just ask her out again?"

"That'll make things complicated."

"I don't know...she seems pretty laid back. Have you seen her since that night?"

"I was at Frankie's house a few weeks ago." Screaming at her and telling her to move on from Hawke.

"Was she there?"

"Yeah."

"And...?"

"She didn't look at me differently. It was like nothing happened."

"If you ask me, it doesn't get less complicated than that." He surveyed the bar, his eyes lingering on the TV in the corner.

Weeks had come and gone, and I hadn't stopped thinking about her. It never took me this long to forget about a girl after I screwed her. How much longer would it take? A few more weeks?

Thursday

CHAPTER FIVE

The Shit Hit The Fan

Axel

We sat on Hawke's couch and watched the basketball game. Our beers sat on the coffee table and a bag of chips sat alongside them.

"Dude, I hate to say it but I'm on the Curry train."

Hawke nodded from the other couch. "I've never seen anyone shoot like that."

"Not since Michael Jordan." I shoved a handful of chips into my mouth. "He's going in the Hall of Fame, for sure."

"And he'll be the MVP this year."

"I wish I played professional basketball. That'd be sick."

Hawke redirected his stare to me. "You're not even good."

"Excuse me?" I held the beer in my hand and stopped myself before I took a drink.

"I'm just saying you aren't the next Stephen Curry."

"I never said I was. That's why I said I *wish* I could play professional basketball. It's not a contact sport, they don't have to run very far, and the games are always inside. I'd never want to play football in the snow."

He brought the beer to his lips and whispered under his breath. "Because you're a pussy."

I grabbed a handful of chips and threw it at him. "Asshole."

He wiped the crumbs onto the floor. "Dude, don't make my house a mess. Francesca will try to clean it."

"Is she your maid now?"

"No. But she always cleans and organizes things when she's over here." He turned his gaze back to the screen. "It's pretty awesome, actually."

I wished I had a maid, a hot one that could give me sex. "What's she doing tonight?"

"She went to that sports bar with Marie."

Both of my eyebrows rose in interest. "She and Marie went out?"

"Yeah. I guess Francesca is acting as Marie's wingman. Didn't realize women needed those." He kept staring at the TV.

The game no longer seemed interesting in light of that information. If Marie was out drinking I could bump into her, start a conversation, and maybe she would come home with me. It was the perfect idea. "You know what? This game is boring. Let's go out."

Hawke turned to me, surprised. "What?"

"Let's stop by and say hi."

Hawke didn't leave his seat. "I'm not doing that."

"Why the hell not?"

"If I go down there it looks like I'm spying on her—which I'm not."

"Who cares?" I asked. "She wouldn't be happy to see her man?"

He set the beer down and sat up. "We got into a fight the other day about this guy she used to see..."

"And?"

"I got a little jealous and said some things I shouldn't. If I go down there it'll seem like I don't trust her—which I do."

"Whatever," I said. "Tell her I wanted to go out."

"Why do you want to go out anyway?"

I shrugged. "I guess I feel a little claustrophobic in here."

He regarded me for several seconds before he figured it out on his own. "You want to pick up on Marie?"

"Maybe..."

He didn't bother hiding his irritation. "Why don't you just text her?"

"No. It must seem organic. We just swing by and play it cool. I'll talk to her for a few moments and see if the chemistry flares up again. Then I'll take her back to my place." I wiggled my eyebrows.

Hawke sighed like he wanted nothing to do with it.

"Come on. I need you. If Francesca asks, just tell her the truth."

"You aren't going to stop bothering me until you get your way, huh?"

"Yep."

He set his beer down then stood up. "Alright. Let's do this."

***

We walked inside the bar and moved through the crowd. When I pictured Marie I imagined her wearing a short dress that showed off her endless legs. Even if she wore a pantsuit she'd still look amazing. How did I not notice this woman until now? Where had she been hiding?

When we got further inside I scanned the crowd. A lot of people were there that night, probably to watch the game and find dates at the same time. My eyes finally found Marie at a table. She was standing next to some pretty boy, and judging their proximity, they were hitting it off.

That wouldn't last.

Francesca was standing beside her and kissing some guy.

Whoa, what? Why is she kissing some guy? "Hawke—"

He was already charging at full speed. He came around the table and grabbed the guy by the neck. Like a bear he took down his opponent then mauled him with his massive hands. His fist collided with his face over and over with such brutality it even made me flinch.

"Hawke!" Francesca stepped back and screamed.

All thought of Marie evaporated. Some serious shit was going down, and I needed to stop it. I jogged to the fight and came around the table. Hawke had him by the throat and pinned to the ground, wailing on him without any mercy.

Francesca couldn't stand back anymore. She rushed in to make Hawke stop.

"Frankie, no." I grabbed her and pulled her back. "Hawke, enough. You taught him a lesson."

Like he was in a trance he kept going, beating the shit out of the guy even though he wasn't even fighting anymore. He was barely holding onto consciousness.

Shit, he was gonna kill him.

Frankie twisted in my grasp then sprinted to Hawke. She grabbed him by the arm and tried to pull him off.

Hawke slammed his arm into her and knocked her back, sending her sliding across the tile until she finally stopped under the table.

Everyone stopped.

A collective gasp spread through the crowd at the accident.

Francesca slowly got to her feet, seeming unharmed.

That's when Hawke stopped, realizing what he'd done. He turned around and stared at her, his eyes hopeless and defeated. Blood was on his hands, and he slowly stepped back, leaving his first victim on the floor.

Thursday

I didn't know what to say because I wasn't sure what was going on. But at least no one was being beaten to death anymore.

Then Hawke turned and left the bar. He pushed past everyone and got to the exit before he disappeared. The music didn't come on the loud speakers. It was deadly silent.

A few guys rushed in and helped the dude on the floor. He was totally out of it and unconscious.

I turned to Frankie. "Are you okay?" When I examined her body it didn't seem like anything was broken or bloody.

"I'm fine. He didn't hurt me."

I put my hand on her shoulder, awkwardly giving her affection. "What happened? Why were you kissing him?"

"I wasn't. He's a friend from school, and he drank too much. He literally just kissed me when you guys walked in."

"He didn't know about Hawke?"

"No, he did. But he did it anyway."

Then I didn't feel about for him. If he kept his hands to himself none of this would have happened. "You want me to hunt down Hawke?"

"No," she said quickly. "He needs space. Just let him be."

"Alright. Do you need a ride home?"

"I came with Marie."

"Well, I can take you both back." I looked over her shoulder and saw Marie talking to the pretty boy. They had a quick exchange before he left her side and helped his fallen friend out of the bar. I wanted to ask Francesca if Marie was in a relationship but I knew now wasn't the best time. "Come on. Let's go."

***

I took the girls home and walked them inside. "Are you sure you don't want me to swing by Hawke's place and check on him?"

"No, just leave him alone." Francesca tucked her hair behind her ear and looked exhausted. It didn't seem like she just went out for some fun with Marie. She somehow aged ten years since we came home. "He'll come around when he's ready."

She had a lot more patience than I did. "Is there anything else I can do?" Despite how calm she was being I knew she was upset.

"No, I'm okay. Thanks for taking us home." In a daze she walked down the hallway and immediately went to bed. The door shut behind her and the rest of the house was silent.

Now it was just Marie and I.

I'd wanted to be alone with her all night, but now that I had her it wouldn't work. Too much drama happened in just a few hours.

Marie dropped her purse on the table then removed her jacket. "What the hell happened? One minute I'm talking to Cade, and then the next minute, Hawke is beating the shit out of Aaron."

"When we walked in he was kissing Frankie. And Hawke lost it." It was hard to talk to her about something serious when all I could think about was how pretty she looked in her dress and heels.

"What?" She crossed her arms over her chest. "Frankie kissed Aaron?"

"No. She said he kissed her the second we walked in. He had too much to drink."

"Wow."

"Honestly, I don't blame Hawke. If some guy kissed my girl even though he was perfectly aware of the fact she was taken I'd beat him senseless too." I'd never had a girlfriend, at least a serious one. But if I did, I knew I'd be protective of her. "Hawke could go to jail for this."

I shook my head. "I doubt it. The guy would have to press charges first. Since he was the one who provoked the whole thing it would be really shady if he did."

"I guess." She walked into the kitchen and poured herself a glass of water. "You want anything?"

"No thanks." I knew it was time for me to leave but I was trying to find an excuse to linger. "So...was that guy you were with your boyfriend?" I prepared myself for the worst possible answer and tried to keep my face stoic so she wouldn't see my disappointment.

"Cade?" she asked. "No. I've seen him around campus a few times but that's it."

My mouth wanted to smile but I managed to stop it.

She took a long drink of water before she set the glass on the dining table. Her hair was in loose curls, and it trailed down her back in an elegant way. I wanted to place kisses on the skin between her shoulder blades. I wanted to taste the area between her legs again. I wanted another night of unbridled passion.

She stared at me and waited for me to leave.

"We never really had a chance to talk after...you know." When I woke up she was gone, and the sheets were cold.

"What did you want to talk about?"

I didn't really know. "I just don't want it to be awkward between us."

"It's not," she said. "I had a great time, and it was fun. But it was a one-time thing. There's nothing to be weird about."

Did that mean she didn't think about me? She didn't replay that night in her head when she was alone? Did she want to see me again? Sleep with me again? It didn't seem like it. "Great..."

She took another drink of her water. "I don't mean to be rude but I'm really tired." She glanced at the door.

"Oh, sure." I quickly turned to the door, feeling like an idiot for overstaying my welcome. Marie clearly didn't value that night the way I did. Did she get incredible sex like that on a daily basis? Did it mean more to me than it did to her? "Have a good night." I walked over the threshold and turned around.

Thursday

"Goodnight." Like all the other times in the past, she shut the door in my face.

CHAPTER SIX

Heartbreak

Marie

I knew something was wrong when Francesca didn't come home for two days. If she didn't sleep at the house she was usually with Hawke. But she always checked in at least once a day. Two days had come and gone, and I didn't hear a word from her.

I started to freak out.

I called her but it went straight to voicemail. It didn't even ring.

I called again because I assumed the line was just busy. But it went straight to voicemail again.

I started pacing in the kitchen, about to explode in fear. I thought about calling 9-1-1 but I didn't know if that was too presumptuous. Maybe she and Hawke were making up from their fight and they'd been in bed for two days.

But it's still unlike her not to call.

Unsure what else to do, I called Axel.

The phone rang three times before he picked up, and when he answered, he sounded different. "Hey, I was just thinking about you."

Both of my eyebrows rose. "What?"

He paused for nearly ten seconds. "What?"

"What do you mean you were just thinking about me?"

"Uh, sorry. Thought you were someone else..."

This was the weirdest conversation ever. "I'm worried about Frankie. I haven't heard from her in two days and her phone is off."

"She's probably just with Hawke."

"Maybe. But she always checks in with me, even if it's just a text. But now her phone is off, and I'm freaking out. I can't even think right now because I'm so terrified."

"Alright. I'm sure everything is fine but we'll look into it."

"Can you call Hawke?"

"Yeah, that's a good place to start."

"Call me back."

"Alright." He hung up.

I paced in my kitchen with the phone held tightly in my hand. I kept waiting for it to ring, needing some kind of news. Frankie was my best friend, and I couldn't picture my life without her.

The phone rang and I accidentally threw it in the air because I was jolted with adrenaline. I caught it before it hit the ground and answered. "What did he say?"

"His phone is off too…"

Now I was really freaking out. "Axel, I'm scared."

"It's okay, baby. I'm sure they're both fine."

I didn't like the baby comment but I was too upset to care. "What do we do?"

"I'll go to his apartment and check it out. They have to be there. If not, we'll call the cops."

"I'm coming with you." I could barely wait for him to call me back. There was no way I was going to stand around and wait for him to investigate Hawke's apartment.

"I'll pick you up in five minutes."

"Just hurry."

***

I sat in the passenger seat of his truck and gripped the armrest in fear. My worst nightmare was playing in front of my eyes. Francesca and Hawke were butchered into indefinite pieces across the apartment. Some criminal robbed them then decided to have some fun.

Axel glanced at me from the driver's seat. "I'm sure they are both fine, Marie."

I bit my nail, something I never did.

He grabbed my hand and held it on his thigh.

I let the touch linger because I was numb anyway.

We pulled up to the building then ran to his apartment. He was on the second floor and at the end of the hallway. Hawke's truck wasn't in the parking lot so that wasn't a good sign.

Axel got to the door first and stopped when he realized it was cracked. He eyed it before he looked at me, the fear finally entering his eyes. He held up his hand and told me to stay back before he kicked the door in.

The apartment was completely empty. There was no furniture in sight. It was just bare carpet and walls.

What the hell? "Is this the right apartment?"

"Yeah." Axel stepped inside and looked around. "Frankie!"

The second he said her name I was in the apartment, not caring if there was a serial killer in there with her. My best friend needed me, and I'd kick some serious ass if someone even touched a hair on her head.

Axel kneeled on the floor where Frankie lay. "Frankie?" He shook her arm. "Wake up."

I stopped when I reached them and stared at my best friend. She was lying on the ground in the same clothes she'd been wearing two days ago. Her hair was oily from not showering and she looked thin, like she hadn't drunk a glass of water in days. "Frankie?"

Axel forced her to sit up. "Frankie?"

She opened her eyes, looking dead inside.

"Are you hurt?" I examined her forearms, searching for bruises and cuts. "What happened? Are you okay?"

Frankie opened her mouth to speak but her voice came out raspy. She cleared her throat but that didn't help much. "I'm okay..."

"You don't look okay." I placed my palm against her forehead but she was cool like ice.

"He left." When she said those words I noticed the tear stains on her face. They formed tiny valleys in her skin, dried up riverbeds.

"Who left?" Axel asked.

I already knew the answer.

"Hawke." It pained her to say his name. Her face contorted like she was about to cry again but didn't have any moisture in her body to form tears. "He packed his things and left."

"Where did he go?" Who does that? Who just gets up and leaves like that?

"New York." She stared at the door like she expected him to walk back inside. "He's gone, and he's never coming back."

I stared at Axel, silently having a conversation with him.

He met my look with a blank one of his own, just as bewildered as I was.

I had so many questions but I knew I wouldn't get answers. Right now, Francesca needed to get home and have plenty of fluids and food. If not, she would shrivel up and die.

Axel adjusted her so he could lift her.

"No." Francesca pushed him off. "I can get up by myself." She climbed to her feet and swayed on the spot for a second. Then she walked forward, moving slow like a child taking its first steps.

I watched her move, feeling my heart break for her. I knew their relationship was rocky the moment that fight erupted in that bar. But I didn't understand why that would make him leave and move so far away. Francesca clearly didn't understand it either. Why else would she be lying on his floor for two days? "Axel, I'm so worried about her."

"I know." He kept his voice low. "I'm worried too."

***

Francesca sat at the table, her hair pulled into a greasy bun. She rested her chin on her palm and stared at the table. Her eyes were endlessly open, and she stared blankly at her fingertips. She didn't move or make any sign of life.

I made macaroni and cheese with breadcrumbs and pita bread with hummus, her favorite things to eat. She finished the glass of water I placed on the table so I refilled it. "Look. It's your favorite." I placed everything in front of her.

"Thank you, Marie." Her voice was lifeless. "But I'm not hungry."

I immediately snapped. "You're going to eat this whether you like it or not. Now do it." I sat in the chair across from her. Axel was sitting beside her, glancing at her every few seconds.

I had my own plate of food and so did he. If we ate with her, maybe that would encourage her to eat.

Axel picked up his fork and took a few bites, clearly forcing himself to take it down.

I wasn't hungry either. But I was doing it for Francesca.

Francesca did as I commanded and ate a few bites, moving at a sloth's pace. She had three glasses of water inside her, and now she was getting some desperately needed nutrition. If we hadn't found her, how long would she have stayed there? Until she died?

This wasn't normal behavior for Francesca. She was always so strong and fearless. Nothing could ruin her day because she never allowed that to happen. Men weren't worth her tears so she never cried over any guy. She always held her head high, refusing to let anyone pull her down.

But now she was weak. "Frankie...what happened?"

She picked at her macaroni and cheese, only taking a few small bites. "Hawke said it wouldn't work out between us. He got a job in the city and said he was leaving. I asked him to stay but he refused...he walked out."

This wasn't adding up. All I'd been hearing for the past year from her was Hawke was her soul mate. Whether they were lovers or friends he needed to be in her life in some way. Francesca wasn't a hopeless romantic, and she never talked about any other guys in this way, so I believed her. Hawke was really the one, the guy she'd spend the rest of her life with. But if that were the case, what would make him leave like that? And so suddenly? There was no way Francesca cheated on him so that wasn't it. And I didn't expect him to cheat on her either.

So what the hell happened?

"Why?" Axel asked. "Did you have a bad fight?"

"No." She dipped her pita bread into the macaroni and cheese instead of the hummus. "He has some personal issues that he can't...let go."

"Personal issues?" I asked. "What does that mean?"

Francesca kept her eyes glued to her food. "I can't say. But he's had this problem for a while. Now he's let it consume him."

Problem? Like, drugs? Alcohol? Hawke never struck me as an addict.

"Tell me." Axel watched his sister closely, the brotherly concern in his eyes. "I'm going to get a hold of him eventually, and we're going to talk about this. So you may as well give me a heads up."

"Axel, just leave him alone. He's made his decision and he's not going to change his mind."

"But that doesn't mean I'm not going to give him an earful." His temper flared, burning in his eyes.

I gave him a look that told him to back off. Getting worked up wouldn't help Francesca in the least. What she needed was our support and nothing else.

Somehow, Axel read that in my eyes. "Just talk to us, Frankie. We want to help."

She set her fork down and released the most depressing sigh I've ever heard. Then she stood up and left the table. "I'm going to shower…" She walked down the hall and got into the bathroom. A moment later, the water started to run.

Axel stopped eating and rubbed his temple, dropping his calm façade now that his sister wasn't in the room anymore. His eyes were glued to the table, his thoughts elsewhere.

"I've never seen her like this."

"I know." Despite his relation to Francesca he didn't look anything like her. He had the same dark hair but his eyes were blue rather than green. He had a strong jaw with soft lips. His cheekbones were fair, giving him a masculine face that Frankie simply lacked. He took after his father in every way imaginable, while Francesca was the spitting image of her mother. Axel was handsome in high school, that was why he was my biggest crush ever, but he had become a million times more desirable. He hit the gym every day and had nearly doubled his size. Anytime I saw him in a suit he filled it out perfectly. Even in his depressed state he was oddly beautiful.

"Even when your parents…" I didn't finish the sentence because it was too hard. "She kept it together."

"I know." His eyes were still on the table. "Nothing can break that woman…except him."

"I wonder what happened."

"I don't know. I've never understood them so I doubt I'll be able to figure it out."

"Whatever it was must have been pretty devastating."

"I guess." He grabbed his fork again and pushed his food around.

"I'll have to keep an eye on her. I know she's not…insane. But, I don't like the idea of leaving her alone."

"Neither do I."

"I'll figure something out—a way to be around her as much as possible."

"I'll take care of it," he whispered. "She's my sister. It's not your problem."

"She's my best friend," I argued. "She is a sister to me."

"Then we can work something out," he said. "We should both be around her as much as possible, distract her. We can play board games, watch movies, go do stuff…whatever helps."

"I think that's a good idea." I hadn't eaten in hours but I wasn't hungry. I was too miserable to have an appetite. I pushed my plate away, not even wanting to smell it.

Axel did the same thing then looked out the window. His blue eyes were unreadable, but the sadness was unmistakable. Hair started to come in around his chin because he hadn't shaved in a few days. He normally kept it clean but he seemed to have forgotten. The look suited him well, made him look a little older and wiser. He wore a black jacket with a white t-shirt underneath. A nice watch was on his wrist, something that looked too expensive for an intern to be able to afford. "Hawke promised me he wouldn't hurt her." The hurt in his voice was unmistakable.

"We don't know what happened."

"I don't care what happened. Packing your shit and leaving my sister on the floor is unacceptable." He spoke quietly but his threatening tone was unmistakable. "She's been through enough as it is. I warned him of that. But he fucked with her head anyway."

I watched him, feeling my heart ache for him.

"Both of my parents are dead, and she's all I have left. And then he had to fuck with her." He rested his fingers against his lips, his knuckles turning white.

"I don't know what happened, but I really don't think Hawke would purposely hurt her. I was there, Axel. I saw what they had. Whatever it was, it was real."

He shook his head slightly. "She and I are finally in a good place in our lives. Our parents left, and we bonded close together. That tragedy is finally in the past, and then this shit happens. Now we have to start all over."

"You'll get through it. And I'll be there too."

He looked out the window, his mind elsewhere. "My mom would be so disappointed in me."

My eyes watered.

"You want to know the last thing she said to me?" His eyes were glued to the window, watching the light fade from the sky. He was reliving a distant memory, thinking of something that happened long ago.

I stared at him in silence.

Thursday

"She was sitting in hospice, looking too small in a normal size bed. Her skin was falling off and her head was bald. My dad was in the cafeteria getting something to eat. Francesca was asleep in one of the chairs, sleep deprived from being there night and day. My mom was struggling to breathe as the darkness took her. Her body was shutting down, giving her just a few minutes before the end." He interlocked his fingers and squeezed them tightly, like the memory was too much for him to bear. "She asked me to look after Francesca. She didn't mention my father, and I never wondered why until he shot himself. I think she knew what he would do the second she was gone. I told her I would always be there for Frankie, being whatever she needed. And then she said Francesca would be there for me too. As long as we had each other, we would be okay."

My eyes welled with tears that could hardly be contained.

"And now I've let her down. Frankie is in the worst shape of her life. I could have prevented it, done more to keep Hawke away from her. But I didn't. I stepped aside and let it be."

"That doesn't mean you let her down, Hawke. Every woman goes through heartbreak."

"This isn't heartbreak." He lowered his hands to the table, his eyes still trained on the window. "Whatever this is...it's something else. Francesca wouldn't get worked up over a break up. I don't know what it is...but it's something neither one of us could ever understand."

CHAPTER SEVEN

Begin Again
Marie

When Francesca didn't wake up at her usual time the next morning I knocked on her bedroom door. "Hey, Frankie. It's time to get up." She had class in an hour. She wasn't in any shape to go to school and actually learn but she couldn't stay here and do nothing. Getting back into a routine was the best thing for her.

"Muh."

"I'm coming in." I opened the door and walked inside.

Frankie was lying in bed, her hair a tangled mess on the pillow. She washed her hair the night before then immediately went to bed without drying it. Now it was a mess of seaweed.

"You should get in the shower or you'll be late for class."

She turned over and faced the opposite wall.

Thursday

"Frankie, come on. It's the last semester. You can't quit now."

She didn't move.

I sat at the edge of the bed then rested my hand on her shoulder. "Frankie, it'll be a good distraction. You can't just shut down because something bad happened."

"I have my history class today. And I've never cared for history."

"You should still go."

"Its just lecture. And I won't pay attention anyway."

I rubbed her back gently. "You might miss something important."

"I couldn't care less."

Frankie was never passionate about school but she didn't hate it either. It was unlike her to drop everything and lay around doing nothing. "I know you're going through a hard time, but lying here isn't going to change anything. Are you really going to let a guy run you down like this?" Appealing to her fiery side might work. When it came to stuff like this, she was always feisty.

But it didn't work. "I guess so."

I wanted to stay here all day with her but I couldn't abandon my classes. "I have to go to class today. I'm sorry."

"You should go. Don't stay here just because of me."

"I'll be back in two hours. Do you need anything?"

"No."

"I'll leave some pancakes on the table for you."

She pulled the blanket over her head.

I had absolutely no affect on her and I felt useless. I never suffered from a broken heart before so I couldn't relate. "Love you." I didn't expect her to say it back but I wanted her to know how I felt.

"Love you too."

***

I just pulled into the driveway when Axel called me. "Hey."

"Hey." His tone was exactly the same as it was the other day. "How is she?"

"No improvement."

He breathed a quiet sigh into the phone. "Did she go to school?"

I wish I had a different answer. "No."

"I tried tracking down Hawke but had no success. His phone is still off."

"I say you forget about him. Even if you talked to him you won't accomplish anything."

"We'll see about that." The threat was palpable.

"I just went to the store. Maybe if she sees a bunch of baking supplies she'll start working in the kitchen."

"Maybe. It's worth a shot."

I leaned back into the chair and stared at the house. There didn't seem to be any life inside. It was completely dead. "I should go."

"I'm coming over. I got a few bored games she might like."

"Okay. I'll make dinner."

Thursday

He was quiet for nearly a minute. "I want her to get better but I don't think talking about it is making any difference. I think we should try to cheer her up, make her laugh, stuff like that."

"I agree."

"Glad we're on the same page."

***

I was cooking on the stove when Axel knocked on the door. "Come in."

He walked inside with board games stuffed under his arm. He set them on the table before he removed his black jacket. Underneath was a gray t-shirt that highlighted his ripped arms. They were cut, showing the distinction of every muscle. His veins popped when he moved. "Smells good."

"Chicken and Rice-A-Roni."

"Perfect." He walked to the refrigerator and grabbed a beer. "Do you need help?"

"No. I'm done." I turned off the stove and the oven.

He glanced in the living room and looked disappointed when he didn't see Francesca sitting on the couch. "Where is she?"

"In bed."

"Has she left the bed?"

"No." I grabbed three plates and served the food.

He set the beer on the table and glanced in the hallway. "No shower?"

"No."

"Well...I'll make her eat with us."

"Good luck with that."

He disappeared down the hallway.

I set the table and lit a few candles to change the atmosphere. I left *The Jimmy Fallon Show* on in the background, hoping it might make her laugh or even chuckle. I sat there quietly and waited for Francesca to appear.

Axel pulled her by the arm and guided her into the chair. "Sit."

She plopped down, looking lifeless and bored.

He sat beside her, acting as a parent to a disobedient child.

Her messy hair was pulled into a bun, and her skin was pale like milk. She stared at the food in front of her. "I'm not hungry."

"Too damn bad." Axel grabbed a fork and handed it over.

Francesca eyed it before she took it.

I looked down at my food and ate quietly.

Francesca picked at her dinner and only took a few bites.

Axel glanced at her every few minutes, making sure she was complying with his demands. "How was your day, Marie?"

I tried not to flinch at the question. It felt like Axel and I were married with a crazy teenage daughter. "Good. Just had school."

"What classes?" Axel ate everything like he was starving.

Thursday

"Journalism and photography." My major was literature and journalism. My dream was to be a writer for a publication—any publication. I didn't care if it was sports, music, or bird watching. I'd take anything.

"Cool." Axel looked up from his food like he was genuinely interested. "What career are you pursuing?"

"Writing. I want to be a reporter in some capacity." I sipped my wine and stared at his chest, noting the way it looked in his t-shirt. I'd already seen him naked and understood just how glorious he was, but he was still sexy as hell in clothes.

"That sounds like a fun job. A lot more interesting than putting portfolios together all the time."

"If you don't like your job why did you choose it?" I asked.

He shrugged. "I don't know. I've always wanted to be an entrepreneur. Understanding money is the best way to do that."

I sipped my wine again, realizing the conversation only centered on Axel and I.

He realized it too. "What did you do today, Frankie?"

She kept eating like she hadn't heard a word he said.

He eyed her for a few more seconds before he repeated the question. "Frankie?"

"Hmm?" She stopped in mid-bite and looked at him.

"What did you do today?" Axel watched her closely.

"Oh..." She tucked her hair behind her ear. "Nothing much."

"Marie told me you didn't go to school today." Axel was the biggest joker I knew. He could never take anything seriously. But the second things got tough he changed. Now he was a different person, a guardian.

"I didn't feel like it..." She ate most of her rice but didn't touch her chicken.

"Well, you better feel like it tomorrow," he said. "You shouldn't be laying around the house all day. It's not good for you."

Francesca didn't argue with him but it was clear she wasn't planning on leaving the house anytime soon.

Axel dropped the subject, knowing he pressured her enough. "Marie, this is good. Thank you."

"Thanks..." Right now I should be focusing on my friend but when Axel was near I started to notice the pretty color of his eyes and the deepness of his voice. The childhood girl inside me returned and I relieved the sensations of my teenage crush. When we slept together, I enjoyed it, but I was immune to his other charms—until now.

***

After dinner I had to talk Francesca into taking a shower. "You need to shower. And dry your hair this time."

She ignored me and headed to her room.

"Whoa, hold on." Axel got in her way. "You aren't going into your bedroom until it's actually time to sleep."

"Axel, get out of my way." Her old fire came back but it was dim.

"You can pass if you're taking a shower. If not, you're going to stay out here and play a board game with us."

"I appreciate you guys looking after me but this is unnecessary." Francesca tried to walk around him. "You guys have your own lives to get to. Just ignore me."

Axel blocked her path again. "Shower or board game. Pick."

She crossed her arms over her chest. "Just leave me alone."

Axel wouldn't budge. "Shower or board game."

Francesca looked like she wanted to murder him.

"Shower or board game." He crossed his arms over his chest, looking formidable with his large size and threatening gaze. "Those are your only two options."

"Whatever." Francesca stormed into the bathroom and slammed the door. A moment later the water began to run.

I was surprised Axel could handle her so well. She could be stubborn until the sun burned out. "Good job."

He shrugged. "I grew up with her. I know how to work her."

I'd been living with her for years and I didn't know how to work her that well. "What game do you want to play?"

"I don't care," he said. "Do you have a favorite?"

"Well, her favorite game is Monopoly."

"Because she dominates that shit."

I chuckled. "Whatever makes her feel better, right?"

"I guess you're right." He grabbed the box and set it up on the table. "At least I don't have to let her win. She'll kick my ass all on her own."

***

I tried to cover Francesca's shifts as much as possible but my attempts were coming to an end. Most of the time we worked together at The Grind, so I couldn't cover her shift if I was already there.

If she didn't come in soon she'd lose her job.

"Frankie, come on." I shook her vigorously. "You need to work."

She lay there like a dead body.

"I mean it. How are you going to pay bills?"

"I have my savings."

"That's for your bakery—and only your bakery." She wasn't giving that up because she couldn't get out of bed.

"Whatever…" She turned over.

"Francesca, it's been weeks. You need to snap out of this."

"I can't," she whispered. "I would but I can't…"

I pitied her deeply but I was also disappointed in her. Times got tough but we had to push on. She loved Hawke with everything she had but she was happy before he came along. She'd be happy now that he was gone. "I've covered for you as much as possible, but if you don't work today Tony is going to fire you."

"Good call."

Thursday

I wanted to scream. "I can't cover all of the bills, Frankie. I don't make enough money."

"Like I said, I have my savings."

When she was unreasonable like this, I couldn't talk to her. I stormed out of her bedroom and slammed the door. I loved Frankie like family but her depression was really taking a nosedive.

I called Axel, someone I spoke to on a daily basis now. "Hey, can you talk?" I assumed he was at work.

"Yeah, I'm at my desk. You can call me whenever you want. What's up?"

"Frankie..."

"What did she do now?"

"She refuses to go to work. I've covered her shifts as much as possible but my manager said he'd fire her if she doesn't come in today. I don't know what to do...I can't pay all the bills on my own."

"Don't worry about that," he said. "I've got her covered."

"What...?"

"If she's not going to class, then she's definitely not going to work. I can cover her bills as long as she needs it. Right now, we need to focus on getting her back to class. That job doesn't matter. She won't need it when she graduates anyway."

Gratitude washed through me in waves. The last thing I wanted to do was ask my parents for money to cover

Frankie's expenses. I'd resort to anything else before that. "Thank you."

"Don't thank me. I'm not going to let my sister's break-up ruin your life."

"It's not ruining my life...but it's nice to have one less thing to worry about."

"When is your rent due?"

"The first."

"Alright. I'll write you a check when I come by."

"Okay."

"How is she today?"

I didn't even want to answer.

"Nevermind." He sighed into the phone. "Forget I asked."

"That'll probably be best."

***

My photography class just ended and I was walking to the parking lot when Cade came to my side.

"Hey. Haven't seen you in a while."

I hadn't spoken to him since that horrific night in the bar. Actually, I hadn't thought about him either. "Hey. How are things?"

"They're okay." He walked beside me with his hands in his pockets.

"How's Aaron?"

"He's back on his feet and going back to school. But he was pretty messed up."

I can imagine. "I'm glad to hear it." Cade was the next guy on my list. I thought he was really cute and smart. He had a nice body, the athletic type. I was really into him until recently—when Axel started coming around.

"So, when are we going to go out?" he asked. "Now that the dust has settled."

I didn't know how I could make that happen. What kind of friend would I be if I went out on a date with Cade while my best friend stayed home and sulked in silence? I'd probably spend the night, which would make things worse. "I'm not sure but now isn't the best time."

"Why not?"

I didn't want to tell him about Francesca. I wanted to protect her privacy as much as possible. When people asked why she wasn't in class, I said she was sick. "Francesca is really under the weather and I should probably keep an eye on her."

"But you can't keep an eye on her all the time, right?" He nudged me in the side playfully.

"I guess not..."

"Then I'll text you with a time and a place." He walked with me to my car then stopped at the driver's door. "I'm thinking dinner—something romantic."

"That sounds nice." I wanted to go out with Cade but now Axel was in the back of my mind. I wasn't going to date Axel. Our relationship already went as far as it would go. A month had come and gone and he didn't bring up our night together. He got what he wanted out of me and returned to seeing me as his sister's friend. I needed to make sure I didn't get sucked into that childhood crush again. "I look forward to it."

Thursday

CHAPTER EIGHT

Betrayal

Axel

After weeks of trying, I finally got a hold of that motherfucker.

"You have some serious explaining to do." It was the first time I called and the phone actually rang. The rest of the time it'd been off.

Hawke was quiet over the phone, taking his time before he finally responded. "I know I do."

"Then you better get to it." I fell onto my couch and put my feet on the coffee table. "Because last time I checked you promised me you wouldn't hurt her."

"I know it doesn't seem like it, but I kept that promise."

"What?" I blurted. "No, it doesn't seem like you kept that promise at all."

Hawke held his silence.

"Do you care to explain that?"

"I can't say. But trust me when I say I did the right thing for her."

Hawke had been my best friend for years but I still didn't fully understand him. "What the hell are you talking about?"

"I love Francesca. I really do. But I can't be with her."

"Why?" I demanded. What reason could there possibly be to abandon her like that?

Hawke fell silent.

"You aren't going to tell me why?"

"It's between she and I."

"I don't think so, pal. You don't screw with my sister and not expect to be called out for it."

"Axel, you have every right to be mad. I don't blame you. I never should have gotten involved with her in the first place. I thought I could make it work with her, and then I was painfully reminded that I couldn't." He breathed heavily on the phone. "For what it's worth, I'm miserable. I'm going through the motions day-by-day but it's just a blur. Without her...I don't know who I am anymore."

"Then come back."

"Axel...I can't."

"She's a total wreck over here. I can't even get her to go to class. She just lays in bed all day."

Hawke didn't say anything but his hurt seeped through the phone. "Don't make this worse..."

I never understood their relationship and even after all this time I still didn't understand it. Whatever secret they shared wasn't going to come out. Both of them refused to tell me what it was. But it must be pretty compelling because Francesca understood he wasn't coming back. She didn't have hopeless fantasies of him returning. She's accepted the fate like its etched in stone.

"I know this puts us in an awkward position. But I really want to keep your friendship, Axel. You mean a lot to me, more than you know."

Would I be an ass if I said I still wanted to be his friend? Despite what he did?

"I know you need some time to process what's going on but I hope to hear from you…when the dust settles."

I was actually afraid the dust would never settle. Francesca was exactly the same as she was before. She was a zombie that aimlessly walked around the apartment with no clear direction. She still wasn't eating or going to class. She was…dead.

"Axel?"

Maybe in time I'd be able to let this go. Maybe I wouldn't. Hawke was my closest friend but Francesca was my sister. She was my family. If I had to choose, I'd always choose her. "We'll see."

***

I walked in the door and saw Francesca and Marie sitting on the couch. They were watching a home improvement show, where they purchase houses, fixed them up, and then flip them.

It seemed safe.

Thursday

"Hey." I removed my jacket and set it on the chair.

Marie looked at me over the back of the couch. "Hey."

I came closer and examined Francesca, who was tucked a under a blanket with her eyes barely open. With every passing day she became thinner and thinner, and she was beginning to look unhealthy. "How was your day?"

Francesca ignored me.

Marie knew Francesca wasn't going to speak, she said something. "I got back a paper from my journalism class. Got an A." She eyed Francesca, hoping that would motivate Francesca to go back to class.

"Good for you," I said. "I'm sure you worked hard."

Marie shrugged.

I sat on the couch beside Francesca and eyed her warily. "Marie, could you give us a second?"

"Sure." She left the living room and retreated to her bedroom.

When it was just she and I, I spoke. "I talked to Hawke today."

It was the first time Francesca reacted since I walked through the door. She turned to me slightly, her eyes holding emotion deep within.

"I asked why he left but he wouldn't tell me. But he said it was the best thing for you...whatever that means."

She pulled her knees to her chest. "What else did he say?"

"That he's miserable. Doesn't know who he is without you..."

She closed her eyes because they welled with tears.

"Frankie, help me understand what happened. Why did he leave?"

She shook her head.

"Did he hurt you?"

"No." Her voice came out strong as she spoke, for the first time. "He would never hurt me. That's what he doesn't understand."

"Doesn't understand what?" I pressed.

Francesca didn't give me any more information. She closed off from me all over again. "I hope you can stay friends with him, Axel. You guys have been close for a long time. I would hate to see you lose a friendship over something that has nothing to do with you."

"Frankie, I told him to stay away from you but he did it anyway."

She rested her chin on her knees, her cheeks wet. "Hawke and I are supposed to be together and it's a shame Hawke won't let that happen because of his fears. Even though he's hurt me so much I don't regret what happened. I don't regret what we had. If I'm never happy again for as long as I live, I still won't regret it. Because...it was beautiful."

Her words replayed in my mind over and over. I tried to understand it but couldn't. "I want you to get back on your feet. I hate seeing you this way."

"I know...I hate it too."

"Then buck up and do it. You've never been this type of person, the kind that falls apart so easily."

"I haven't fallen apart because he's gone."

I stared at her, feeling the confusion.

"I've fallen apart because...he was it. He was my one true love. He took a piece of me I'll never get back. Maybe one day I'll be happy again but I'll never be the same."

"Don't say that..."

"But it's the truth." She wiped her tears away on the back of her forearms. "Don't lose him, Axel. You need each other."

I wasn't sure how I could be friends with someone that hurt my family so much.

She reached for my hand and patted it slightly. "I wouldn't want you to ever lose each other."

***

I sat at the table and Marie dropped the pile of papers in front of me. "We have to get all of this done—by Friday."

I eyed it like it was Mount Everest.

"If we don't, she'll fail all of her classes." She sat across from me and opened her laptop.

Francesca was in her room, either sleeping or staring at the wall.

"Well, I graduated college once. I can do it again." I pulled the first assignment toward me, a history paper.

Marie looked through the stack and pulled out an assignment.

"Marie, I know you have your own things to focus on. I can handle this."

"I don't mind." She skimmed through the paper before she turned to her laptop. "She would do it for me."

"But I don't want you to fall behind on your studies. The only thing I'm losing out on is TV and chicks—" I stopped in mid-sentence when I realized what I just said. Talking about other women in front of her was weird, but I couldn't explain why. I didn't make eye contact with her and stared at the history paper.

The only response she gave was the sound of her fingertips hitting the keyboard.

The subject of dating shouldn't make her uncomfortable. In fact, our night together meant less to her than it did to me. I'd never met a woman who was so detached. Most of the time the girls wanted something more—at least a few more screws.

But Marie acted like it never happened.

She sighed as she looked back at the assignment. "Please tell me you took bio in college."

"Yeah."

She traded assignments with me. "I've already taken this history class so I should be able to do it. But science…I'm not even going to try."

I looked at the paper and realized it was a write-up for a lap report. I'd have to bullshit everything, from the data to the instructions, and hope for the best. "I can do this."

"Are you sure?"

"I liked science."

"Really?" Her head automatically cocked to the side.

I tried not to take offense. "Why is that surprising?"

"I don't know...you just don't strike me as the academic type."

"Well, I liked ever major besides math. That's never interested me. It doesn't possess any soul."

"I know what you mean."

"But everything else is cool. My favorite class I ever took was philosophy."

She spun a pen in her fingertips as she stared at me. "Why?"

"I don't know. I guess I like the fact there's endless possibilities to any given question. And everything is subjective. Depending on how the view holder sees something, anything is possible. It was the course that made me realize I can be as happy as I choose. I just have to choose it."

She stopped spinning the pen and just stared at me.

I held her gaze, feeling my heart speed up automatically. Her blue eyes were almost scenic, two paths down a forest road. Her eyes shifted slightly depending on her emotion, and I was beginning to understand her reactions to certain stimuli. The night we slept together was permanently ingrained in my mind but I was beginning to see her as a different person, a different woman than the one I'd already been with.

She didn't withdraw her gaze, still watching me like she was searching for something.

I wanted to save face and wait for her to look away first but I was struggling. Those eyes were getting to me, making my body burn from inexplicable heat. I swallowed the lump in my throat because the intensity was becoming too much. I clenched my toes in my shoes, needing something to do that she couldn't see. Seeing her look into my eyes was turning me on in a way I could never explain. It was the kind of intimacy I'd never had with a woman. It was stronger than anything else I'd ever felt. My entire body burned for her desperately. My jeans tightened around my crotch to the point where they were uncomfortable. Now I couldn't even remember what we were talking about.

She broke the contact first. "I didn't realize you had so many layers."

"I'm a lot more than what I project."

"Why is that?"

I didn't like to be serious as much as possible. Whenever I dealt with my emotions head-on, they crippled me. After all this time I still hadn't forgiven my father for the cowardice way he left Francesca and I. Just because he was dead didn't make him a saint. He would always be a pussy in my eyes. I was angry then and I was angry now. "It's easier to be as emotionless as possible."

"Without emotions what's the point?"

"It's a lot easier, if you ask me." I looked away from her gaze and flipped through the lap report.

Thursday

"Because of your father?" The second she said it she regretted it. The hesitance was loud in her voice, like she knew she crossed a line but chose to do it anyway.

I slowly turned my eyes back to her. "I'm guessing Francesca has already told you every little detail."

"Actually, she doesn't talk about it much. She told me what happened but...she didn't go into the specifics."

"I was the one who found him. Let's just leave it at that." It was hard for me to talk about, and I knew deep down inside it was because I feared I was just like him. One day I would become a coward just like him, unable to handle the stress of life. Maybe I wouldn't kill myself but I'd let my family down in some way, just the way I let Francesca down.

"I'm sorry that happened to you. I can't even imagine..." The apology seemed sincere even though she had no reason to apologize.

"Thanks." I refused to look at her, feeling uncomfortable by her stare. Something formed between us but I couldn't describe what it was. She wasn't just my sister's roommate anymore. But she wasn't my friend either. All I knew was, we were on a different level now. The intimacy was arousing but also frightening. I'd never had a connection with anyone like that before.

And I wasn't sure if I wanted it.

I changed the subject before we went any further down this road. "What's your family like?" Francesca mentioned them in passing but I didn't know anything real about them.

"My mom and dad live by the beach. Mom is a nurse and Dad is a realtor."

"Cool. Siblings?"

"I have a sister—Jessie."

"Is she older than you? Younger than you?"

"She's younger than me. She just started college, actually."

They were exactly the years apart as Francesca and I. I never knew that. On paper it sounded like she had a pretty normal family life. I hated to admit it, but I was a little jealous. I loved Yaya and she was a great guardian, but she would never be my mother. "That's nice."

"She's the 'pretty' one. I'm the smart one."

I laughed because her words were absolutely ridiculous.

She froze and stared at me, clearly not seeing the humor in my words. "What?"

"She's the pretty one?" I'd seen a lot of beautiful women in my life, brunettes, blondes, redheads…you name it. I've been with every size and shape out there. I had a good understanding of beautiful. "Marie, if she's 'prettier' than you then she wouldn't be real."

"Excuse me?"

"I just don't believe your sister could possibly be considered the pretty one, no offense."

"Well, she is."

"Yeah right. You're the hottest chick I've ever—" I shut my mouth once I realized my foot was inside. But the damage had already been done and I couldn't go back on what I said. So, I just rolled with it. "Been with."

Instead of taking that as a compliment she seemed hurt. When she turned back to her computer, she didn't look back at me again. She put on her headphones and listened to music as she got to work.

What just happened?

CHAPTER NINE

Escape

Marie

I didn't know why it bothered me so much.

It just did.

My entire high school career, I took every opportunity to get Axel to notice me. I was at Francesca's house every chance I got, and I did my best to look cute. But no matter how I did my hair or batted my eyelashes he was totally immune to me.

After I started working out, hitting the weights every single day, did my womanly figure come in. I toned my ass and thighs, and I sculpted my hourglass figure. My legs didn't get longer but I toned them as much as possible, giving the illusion they were longer than they really were.

After all that hard work, he noticed me.

Thursday

I was still the same girl, sweet and funny. I still had the same laugh and personality. But that didn't mean anything to him.

Only when I grew into my figure did he care.

I was beginning to realize that Axel wasn't just a crush from the past. There was something more there, a connection more powerful than a simple physical attraction. Somehow, as crazy as it sounded, I think I loved him at one point.

Why else would I be so insulted?

A night of passion was absolutely everything I could have asked for. I enjoyed every moment of it, living out a fantasy I never thought I could have. Walking away without any heartbreak seemed easy at the time, but I was clearly wrong. I wanted him to want me in the way I wanted him all those years ago—to actually care about me.

It was wrong to hold it against him when he had no idea what I was thinking but I couldn't contain my disappointment. As soon as he got what he wanted from me he returned to viewing me as a meaningless conquest.

I shouldn't let it bother me.

And I wasn't going to.

***

Cade texted me. *Can I buy you a drink?*

I'd forgotten about Cade in light of Hawke and Francesca. While I felt obligated to stay home and keep an eye on her, I knew I couldn't stop living my life because of it.

Besides, Axel would be there to make sure she didn't do anything stupid. *Yes. Several, please.*

LOL. Now we're talking.

You free tonight?

Free as a bird.

Great. Pick me up at seven.

Bossy. I like it.

I didn't know if I should tell Francesca I had a date tonight. It might make her think of Hawke and all the times he used to come by. But I didn't want to lie about it either. She would see right through that eventually.

I showered and got ready, putting on a black cocktail dress with silver heels. I put on the diamond earrings my father got me and borrowed one of Francesca's clutches. I knew she wouldn't care.

When it was almost seven, there was a knock on the door.

I walked into Francesca's room and saw her lying there, like usual. "Hey. I'm going out for the night."

"Okay." She was disinterested, like always.

"Remember Cade? He's taking me out for a drink."

"Cool," she whispered. "Have fun."

How long would she stay like this? It'd already been a month and she was still lifeless. I hated seeing my friend this way. She always had such a backbone, but when she met her match she crumbled like a pile of bricks. "Well, I'll see you when I get home."

She stared at the ceiling.

Thursday

I shut the door behind me then walked down the hallway, feeling down. Now I wasn't excited for the date. What I really wanted to do was fix my best friend. I wanted to wipe her memory clean of Hawke. She was so happy when they got together, but she was also happy before he came around. I missed that person.

I opened the door and expected to come face-to-face with Cade. It was ten till seven so he was probably picking me up for our date.

But it was Axel.

He held up a lab report and was about to say something until he saw me. He looked me up and down, eyeing me in my cocktail dress. His eyes were frozen in place and he forgot to shut his mouth. "Uh...wow."

I felt warm at the compliment but insulted at the same time. All he saw was my figure but not the girl underneath. I needed to stop expecting him to notice me as a person rather than a woman, but that was obviously never going to happen. "Is that the lab report?"

"Oh yeah." He held it out to me. "I got a B. Can you believe it?"

I took the papers and flipped through them. "No, actually."

"The professor must have been busy and just flew through them without paying much attention."

"I'll say..."

"Looks like Francesca is going to graduate college after all." Axel walked inside and shut the door behind him. "I'll just have to stay on top of her assignments."

"What about exams?"

He set his satchel on the dining table. "That...I don't know. I'm going to have to force her to go. If she fails every exam she should still get a C because all of her work is being submitted."

I still couldn't believe this was happening. She was so devastated over Hawke that she lost her job, and if it weren't for us, she would have flunked out of college. "She's lucky to have us."

"I know." He pulled out his laptop and sat down. "I haven't had any time to do anything besides work and schoolwork, but I know she would do it for me."

"Yeah, she would."

He eyed me in my dress again. "So, you going somewhere tonight—"

The doorbell rang.

"Excuse me." I opened the door and saw Cade on the other side. "Hey, right on time."

"Wouldn't be late for this." He eyed my dress with appreciation. "You look...awesome."

"Awesome?"

"It's a fitting compliment."

"Just let me grab my clutch." I walked back to the dining table and snatched it.

Thursday

Axel stared at me with a new expression. His playful attitude had disappeared and now he seemed morose. His fingertips touched his lap report but with a weak grip. "You have a date tonight...?"

Now that he asked me face-to-face my answer was difficult to give. I thought I could detect the disappointment in his voice, the sadness. But that could just be wishful thinking. "Yeah."

"Oh..." He fidgeted with the papers.

I stood there awkwardly, expecting him to say something else. When the silence lingered, I thought I should say something but I couldn't think of anything.

"Well...have a good time." He cleared his throat and turned his gaze to his assignment and studied it like he'd never looked at it before.

"Good night." I turned back to the doorway, my heels clanking against the hardwood floor.

Axel didn't say anything back.

Cade was waiting on the doorstep, wearing jeans and a t-shirt. A black leather jacket covered most of his build from view. "Ready to go, beautiful?"

"Yeah." I shut the door behind me and wondered if Axel heard that last comment.

***

Cade and I had a great time.

We went to a sports bar and ordered greasy food with tons of beer. We made small talk about school and sports.

Cade was getting his degree in business with a concentration in sports management. His dream was to be a sports agent.

I told him about my dream to be a writer, and he seemed interested. A few hours went by until we were both stuffed and couldn't eat anymore. We got into his truck and headed back to my place.

Despite how well the night went, I couldn't stop thinking about Axel. Did it bother him that I was on a date? Or was I seeing stuff that wasn't really there? He'd probably been with tons of girls since we slept together, so I doubted I was on his mind in any capacity.

Cade jerked the wheel a few times on the way home, and when he rounded the corner and he almost hit the curb I started to be concerned. "Cade, are you alright?"

He stopped in front of my place and killed the engine. He had a sleepy look in his eyes, like he was halfway in dreamland. "You know…I think I had too much to drink. It kicked in on the way home."

At least he acknowledged it before he drove back to his place.

"I know this is a terrible way to end our date but would you mind dropping me off? You can keep my truck and I'll come back and get it tomorrow."

That was a lot of unnecessary work. "Why don't you just sleep here and drive home in the morning?"

He turned to me with a lazy grin. "There's no way I'm saying no to that."

"I'm inviting you to sleep—nothing else." I wasn't sleeping with a drunk guy. I definitely wouldn't be satisfied by the time we were done, and he'd probably fall asleep on top of me.

He shrugged. "Whatever. Sharing a bed with a beautiful woman still sounds awesome to me."

"Then let's go." I hopped out of the truck and noticed Axel's truck in the driveway. I was hoping he already went home but that was wishful thinking. He probably wouldn't leave until I returned from my date to look after Francesca.

I got the door unlocked and we walked inside.

Axel and Francesca were sitting on the couch.

"Hey." I tossed my purse on the counter.

Francesca hardly waved.

Axel was the only one who turned around. He clearly expected me to be alone because his face fell when he realized Cade was with me. "Hey…"

"We're going to bed. Good night." I walked down the hall with Cade close behind me.

"I'm Cade, by the way." He waved to Axel and Francesca before he followed me. "Nice to meet you."

We got into my bedroom and I changed into my pajamas in the closet. When I came back to bed, he was already stripped down to his boxers. He had a nice body, compacted with muscle. But it didn't compare to Axel, not that I should be comparing.

"I normally sleep in the nude," he said. "So, you're getting an upgrade." He lay in my bed then closed his eyes like he couldn't keep them open for a moment longer.

I got on my side of the bed then set an alarm. My legs touched his under the sheets but that was all the affection we shared. The TV from the living room reached my ears and I could hear it distantly playing. Axel and Francesca didn't speak at all, which made me sad. Axel was pretty much alone because Francesca was a warm body beside him.

"I'm sorry I drank too much…"

"It's okay."

"Next time, I'll be totally sober."

"But will you be as much fun?" I teased.

He chuckled. "Probably not. But I'll kiss you goodnight."

"Alright. We'll see." I closed my eyes and felt my body drift away.

Cade turned over and spooned me from behind. "This is okay, right?"

"You aren't quite as good as my teddy bear but I'll take it."

He chuckled into my ear. "Then I'll keep practicing."

Thursday

CHAPTER TEN

Beach Day

Axel

I carried the groceries into the house and stored them in the cabinets and the refrigerator. Francesca didn't eat much, only when I threatened to break her neck when she refused, but most of the food was for Marie and I since we ate like normal people.

I bought the things that Francesca loved to eat, including lots of baking ingredients. She never seemed happier unless she was making a new creation. Maybe having these things lying around would inspire her to get back into the kitchen.

The front door opened and Marie walked inside. Her bag was over her shoulder, and she wore skin-tight jeans with brown-heeled boots. She wore a white cardigan, looking like a winter snowflake.

Thursday

Anytime she walked into the room my eyes roamed over her figure. I've had her once before but now it seemed like a lifetime ago. And she seemed like a different person—in my eyes. Whenever she was near me, I could feel the static in the air, like our presence in each other's space manipulated the world around us. When I moved, she registered it. And when she took a step I was completely aware of it.

She set her bag down. "Hey. Got some good stuff?"

"Stuff that Francesca won't eat." I put the milk in the refrigerator then grabbed a carton of almond creamer. "I got vanilla flavor. Is that okay?" I spotted the empty carton before I left the store. I knew Francesca wouldn't be caught dead drinking almond milk so it had to be Marie's.

Marie had grabbed the mail off the table and started to sort through it. "What?"

I held up the carton.

She eyed it in my hand for nearly five seconds before she processed what I was asking. "How did you know I drank that...?"

"I saw the empty carton in the fridge."

She continued to stare at me blankly.

Since she wasn't going to say anything I set the carton on the shelf.

"Thank you...that was sweet of you."

I shrugged and continued to unpack the groceries. "I got you some coffee too. I noticed you were low."

She tossed the mail on the table and came to my side. She grabbed the bag of coffee from my hands. "It's whole bean."

"Isn't that what you like?" I wasn't usually here in the mornings but I noticed the grinder on the counter. Francesca drank coffee but she wasn't picky about it. I assumed it belonged to Marie.

"How did you know that?"

I shrugged again. "I just deduced it." I set the beans on the counter.

Marie stared at me for a few more seconds before she helped me unload the groceries. Quietly, we worked together and placed everything where it belonged. Her arm brushed against mine when she passed and I got a draft of her scent. "You're a sweet brother."

"And friend, I hope." The words left my mouth without being considered. They just flew out like word vomit. I set the bag of chips in the cabinet before I met her gaze.

She nodded. "Yes. A good friend."

When I stared at her like that, I felt the tension deep in my gut. Being this close to her made me feel things I couldn't explain. The energy flowed through me like an electric wire. Whenever I looked at her, I was always aware of my unnatural breathing. It was always a little faster than normal.

She held my gaze without speaking, her thoughts a mystery.

Thursday

We stood there for nearly a minute and nothing happened.

She crossed her arms over her chest, succumbing to the pull that affected both of us.

I finally found something to say. "Let's take Frankie to the beach. Maybe some fresh air will lighten her spirits."

"Yeah." She tucked her hair behind her ear, something she'd never done before. "That could be fun."

"Alright. I'll get her up."

***

Like always, it was a struggle to get Francesca to do anything. By pure manipulation I managed to get her showered and ready for the day. I got her in shorts and a tank top, her hair done and her teeth brushed. I couldn't get any make up on her. It was a pointless attempt.

We drove to the beach then set up our stuff in the sand. It was a nice day, sunny and bright. The breeze kept us cool and protected us from the summer's heat. I wore swim trunks and a t-shirt, but I probably would take a dip eventually.

Marie wore a sundress, and the straps of her bikini peeked out through the translucent fabric. I wanted to see her pull her dress off, showing off those gorgeous curves that she should flaunt every single moment of the day.

Francesca stuck her feet in the sand and stayed quiet, like always. I made small talk about the weather and the size of the waves. Since our conversation, I never brought up

Hawke. It seemed to please her but also destroy her when I did.

After an hour Francesca left the blanket and walked along the shore, her eyes downcast for seashells that washed up on the sand. Her dark hair blew in the wind, the slight curls becoming straight.

Marie watched her go, concern in her eyes for her friend.

It was getting warm so I removed my t-shirt and felt the sun's rays right on my skin. I glanced at her in my peripheral to see if she would look.

She did.

"Good idea." Marie pulled her dress off then lay back on the towel, her flawless skin glowing in the sunshine.

I wanted to look but I controlled myself. I leaned back on my elbows and stared at the ocean.

"I wish I could wipe her memory."

Like always, her voice washed over me like a soothing bath. She had a distinctly feminine voice that was also strong. It belied her strength and power underneath. I liked listening to it. And like always, the memory of her saying my name came back to me. The hair on the back of my neck stood up. "I know what you mean."

"I still don't understand why he left. They were so in love."

"I know. I don't get it either."

"He hasn't said anything to you?"

"He won't tell me why. But he said it had nothing to do with cheating or anything like that."

"Then what could possibly be the reason?" She crossed her ankles, her perfectly manicured nails reflecting the light. They were turquoise, playful and bright.

"I haven't got a clue." If two people loved each other they should be together—end of story. "But she seems to understand he's never coming back. But yet, she continues to mope around."

"It's not like her at all. If someone pushes her down she gets right back up. She's a fighter."

"I know…it scares me."

"We'll just have to wait and hope things get better."

But how long would the wait last? I'd been spending all my free time with my sister. I didn't mind because I knew she needed me, and I also didn't mind because I liked spending time with Marie. I was beginning to see the layers she possessed. She was smart, ambitious, and funny. There were many more traits that I never paid attention to, besides her obvious beauty. The fact she was so loyal to her friend, standing beside her no matter what, was what I noticed the most. Good friends were hard to find, and I was glad Francesca had someone who had her back until the end of time. "It will get better. I just don't know when."

She lay back on the towel and looked up at the sky.

I glanced at her and realized her eyes were closed. That's when my eyes took her in, focusing on her face. She had thick eyelashes that were black and beautiful. It heightened the shape of her almond eyes. She didn't wear make up to the beach, but the gleam of the sunscreen was obvious. There were a few streaks across her cheek, difficult to see but noticeable all the same. Her lips were shiny like she just put on Chap Stick. Her hair was in loose curls but they were starting to fall out from the ocean breeze.

Without her make up I could see the small freckles that marked her face. They were tiny and almost invisible but I could see them when I sat this close to her. They reminded me of distant stars in the sky, and I wondered why she covered them up at all. If anything, they were cute.

I never really paid attention to the structure of her face, but then again, I'd never seen her face bare like that. Her eyebrows were light just like her hair, and her cheekbones were prominent, making her have a slender face. I began to notice every little detail, every little feature.

I forgot about her body in her bikini because I was more interested in her face. Now I wish she would open her eyes so I could see their beauty. They were green, I knew that. But what other details would I be able to see under the bright sun?

When I realized I was gawking at her like she was a painting, I looked away. To any passerby, it looked like I was staring at her in her bikini. Technically, I was. But I'd only been paying attention to her face. "So...that guy you brought back the other night is your boyfriend?" I hadn't realized she was seeing anyone, and when they went into her bedroom I felt a little sick.

Thursday

"He's not my boyfriend." She opened her eyes then grabbed her sunglasses from her bag. "We're just seeing each other."

And sleeping together? I held back the retort because I knew I'd be a huge ass if I actually said that out loud. "So, it's casual?"

"Yeah. We've only been on one date."

I think I recognized him from the bar that night Hawke flipped out on Aaron. "I think I've seen you with him before."

"We have mutual friends but he didn't ask me out until recently." She spoke quietly like she didn't want to have this conversation at all.

I realized I was interrogating her, asking a bunch of questions I had no right to ask. I wasn't even sure why I was asking them at all.

"Are you seeing anyone?"

"No." Now that I thought about it, I realized Marie was the last woman I slept with. When Francesca crashed and burned, my sex life was put on hold. I'd been spending so much time with her that everything else took a backseat. "Haven't been out in a while."

"I've never seen you with a girlfriend."

It wasn't a question but I took it that way. "I've never been into relationships."

"You like to play the field?"

"I guess." She seemed to be the same way, if she slept with Cade on their first date. It was a sexist thing for me to think but it still happened. Or maybe I thought I was the only guy she ever had casual sex with. When she told me I used to be her high school crush, I actually thought she was making an exception for me. But now I realized she wasn't. I couldn't describe what I was feeling, but I knew one thing.

I was confused.

"What about you?" I asked. "You've been in any serious relationships?"

"Not really. The longest I've been with the same person is a few months."

Marie could have whomever she wanted. Obviously, she was hot. But she was also smart. She was going to college and working a part-time job at the same time, so she was motivated to make something of herself. On top of that, she was loyal to those she loved. And she was confident—her sexiest attribute. She could have any guy she wanted—as long as she wanted him. "Any reason why?"

"None of them fit the bill."

I didn't understand her expression. "What does that mean?"

"I didn't see it lasting forever. I didn't want to lead them on longer than necessary. Heartbreak is a terrible thing." She propped herself up on her elbows and looked at Francesca, who was still walking along the beach quietly.

She was considerate—another attractive attribute.

I worked hard to get where I am now. I put myself through college just the way Francesca did. I got my degree in finance then continued onto my master's. Right now I was an underpaid intern but one day I'd make real money. Marie was the exact same way. "That's the right thing to do."

"There's nothing worse than falling for someone who doesn't feel the same way. If a guy weren't into me I'd like to know. Saves us both some time."

"True."

She looked out to the water then uncrossed her legs. She dug her feet into the sand and watched them disappear. She sat up then got her hands involved, playing in the sand.

I watched her and immediately thought of a child building a sand castle.

I sat up and rested my arms on my knees, staring at her every move. "You think Cade is going to turn into something serious?" I needed to holster my questions but I couldn't stop them from coming out.

"If I could predict the future my life would be boring."

Her vague response shut me down. I clearly wasn't invited to ask anything else. "Where would you like to work someday?"

She drew her fingers in the sand then erased it. "Anywhere that will take me."

"I meant your dream job. If there's one place you could work where would it be?"

She drew Francesca's name in the sand. "Well, I've always been a fan of Maximum Shot. He's the biggest fashion guru in the world. I would love to write articles for his magazine. If I could combine my two loves—writing and passion—I'd be a very happy woman.

I wasn't into designer clothes but I knew who he was. "Is their office in Manhattan?"

"Yeah. I'm going to apply after college but my hopes aren't very high. I know they get a zillion applicants every week—most of them from IV league schools."

"That doesn't matter."

"When all you are is a resume, it makes all the difference in the world."

Maybe one day I'd be able to pull some strings for her. If I had the right clients I could make anything happen. "It doesn't matter where you go to school. It doesn't reflect your intelligence."

"I don't know about that..."

"Well, I know you'll be smarter than every other applicant."

She stopped writing in the sand and looked at me, hesitance in her eyes. She was trying to read me, to understand if I had a different meaning than I projected. I wasn't trying to come onto her. I said what I really thought— that she was talented. She eventually turned away, not getting an answer to her unspoken question. She wrote my name in the sand.

I eyed it. "You have nice handwriting."

"Thanks." She smeared the sand across the letters, wiping them out.

I looked down the coast to make sure Francesca was doing okay. She was sitting in the sand far along the beach, her hair flapping in the wind. She was probably crying to herself, just as she did in her bedroom when she thought I couldn't hear her. If this break up happened over another guy I would tell her to get over it. But Hawke's departure really screwed her up.

Marie followed my gaze. "How long do you think this is going to go on for?"

"I don't know…" If it lasted more than a few months I'd go crazy. I could only handle Francesca's depression for so long. "I might have to get her a prescription for Prozac."

"I don't think that would do anything. She's not clinically depressed."

"Her brain chemistry is still out of whack."

"We'll just have to keep distracting her until she moves on."

We took her to the beach for the afternoon but she still managed to wander off and mope silently. There was only so much Marie and I could do. "She's lucky to have a friend like you."

"She's lucky to have a brother like you."

Francesca and I weren't close. Typically, I only saw her a few times a year. We usually got together around the holidays and sometimes for birthdays. Even though we lived in the same city we didn't bump into each other at the bars. But when disaster hit, I was there.

Just the way she would be there for me.

***

After we came home Francesca immediately went into her bedroom, barricading herself inside for the rest of the night. She didn't talk anymore or announce what she was doing when she was doing it, but I'd come to learn from her actions.

Marie set her beach bag on the couch and tossed her sunglasses inside. "Well, I had fun even if she didn't."

"Yeah, me too." I sat on the couch and stared at the blank TV, unsure what I should do. It was okay for me to go home but something kept me there. Marie's presence soothed me. If I went home I'd just be alone in my empty apartment. But if I stayed here...Marie was there. "Maybe we can try to get her to bake tomorrow."

"Maybe."

"We can have football on and make something that goes with the sport." I didn't know anything about baking but Francesca always found a reason to throw something together.

"Yeah, we can give it a try."

I wished Mom were still around. She would know exactly what to do. I couldn't even begin to understand Francesca's feelings. I'd never been in love before, and I certainly had never experienced heartbreak—at least in a romantic way.

Marie spotted my unease. She was beginning to read me more clearly. "It'll be alright, Axel."

"I keep telling myself that..."

She eyed my hand sitting on my thigh but didn't take it.

Thursday

"I wish my mom were still here—especially at times like this. She would know what to say."

Marie listened to my every word, her eyes locked to mine.

"Francesca was closer to her than I was. They were more like friends than mother and daughter."

"I remember…"

"Are you close with your mom?"

She stared down at the ground. "Not really. But I love her."

I nodded even though I wasn't agreeing to anything.

Marie looked down at herself, seeing the sundress that had tightly specks of sand stuck to it. "I'm going to shower. I guess I'll see you tomorrow."

That was my invitation to leave and I couldn't reject it. "Yeah. I'll be here in the morning." I put my hands in my pockets and walked to the front door.

She walked with me, her face slightly tinted from being in the sun all day. Her nose was the darkest part, probably because it was the flattest surface on her body. The sunblock was still smeared on her face distantly. Soon, it would disintegrate altogether. I stared at her face repeatedly, memorizing it.

She stopped when we reached the door and waited for me to walk out. "Have a good night."

"You too." I didn't reach for the door. Instead, I stood there.

She held my gaze like always, refusing to back down from any type of engagement.

I found myself wanting to stand there and stare all day.

She kept her arms by her sides, hardly blinking as she met my look.

These strange things kept happening with her. Inexplicable moments happened where we just stared in silence, but had a conversation that wasn't communicated with words. I could feel the hum in the air, the distant chime that hugged inside my brain. These moments were both addicting and uncomfortable.

I turned away first, letting her win the round. "Good night, Marie." I let myself out and stepped onto the threshold. The door closed behind me, but I stayed on the stoop and waited for a sound I needed to hear. Never in my life had I stood like that, waiting for something I never paid attention to.

The lock turned and snapped into place.

Then I left.

Thursday

CHAPTER ELEVEN

Bromance

Axel

After a lot of convincing I agreed to make the drive to New York to see Hawke. The only problem I had with that was Francesca. I couldn't tell her where I was going, but I also couldn't leave her alone.

I called Marie.

"Hey." Her voice was a lot perkier than it used to be. It seemed like she looked forward to talking to me, enjoying our conversations as much as I did. "Are you coming over?"

I didn't want this conversation to be heard. "You alone?"

Her tone changed when she knew this talk would be a serious one. "She's in her room."

"I'm going to New York to see Hawke. You think you can handle her over the weekend?"

"Absolutely."

"If she asks, tell her I had a work thing. I don't want her to know where I really went." I didn't need to give her more of an explanation than that.

"Okay. Are you trying to patch things up with him?"

"No. He's pestered me about coming to visit him and I caved."

"Well, hope you guys have fun."

All I could think about were her plans for the weekend. Was she going to see Cade? Would she see him if I wasn't there to keep an eye on Francesca? Would I be a dick if I hoped that was the case? "Hope you have a good weekend too. I'll see you when I get back."

"Alright." Instead of hanging up she stayed on the line.

Whatever affection I felt for her, I think she felt it for me too. I was always a little bit nervous around her, but in a good way. When I first made a move on her, I wasn't nervous in the least. But now...I watched what I said and the way I behaved. I could sense every moment of tension in the air. Whenever we spoke to each other, it was different than it was with everyone else. "I'll text you when I get there." *Whoa, what? What the fuck did I Just say?*

"Okay." Her response was automatic, like she'd been expecting that answer before I even gave it.

What the hell was that?

***

I walked inside his apartment and took a look around. It was small—really small. And I suspected he was paying three times what he was paying in South Carolina. "It's nice…"

"I know it's a dump." He grabbed a beer from the fridge and handed it over. "But it'll do."

I sat on a dark green couch in the center of his living room. An old TV sat on a plastic chair against the wall. There was a tiny window that looked over the city. The drab walls made the place feel foreign, dusty. "How's your new job?"

"It's alright. It's better than being an intern."

"I bet." Anything was better than not getting paid. I took a drink of my beer and tried not to cringe when I realized how warm it was. Did his fridge work at all?

"Thanks for coming up. I would have made the drive down to see you but…" He didn't finish the sentence because he didn't need to.

"It's alright."

He sat on the opposite side of the chair, his elbows resting on his knees. The silence filled the air, and without saying anything I knew what he was thinking. It was only a matter of time before he asked about her. "How is she?"

Francesca wanted me to keep her struggles a secret, and I understood why. But I also wanted to lie to make my sister look better. Hawke left her for whatever reason, but I didn't want him to know how much he destroyed her. "She's okay. Just focusing on school and work."

He couldn't hide the surprise on his face. "So, she's back into a routine?"

"Yeah. For the first two weeks she was a little lost but after that she was fine. There's this baking contest at the college and she's been preparing for that." I even wanted to go as far as to say she was dating someone but I knew it wouldn't be believable.

He picked at the label on the beer. "Good for her."

"How about you?"

He shrugged. "I've been better. Just work and come home."

"Made any...friends?" Even though he wasn't with Francesca anymore it would tick me off if he were already sleeping around.

"No. I haven't really spoken to anyone except for a few coworkers—and you." His skin was deathly pale and he seemed a little thinner. His facial hair was unnaturally thick because he hadn't shaved in weeks. His eyes looked hollow, like they would never light up again. His despair wasn't as obvious as Francesca's but it was clear he was suffering underneath the skin. Knowing that made me dislike him less. "I'm glad she's doing better...I want her to be happy."

It didn't seem like she'd ever be happy without him. "She's a fighter. She bounces back from everything."

"I know. That's why I love—" He cleared his throat and took a long drink.

I stared out his pitiful window because I didn't know how else to brush off his final words. Even though I didn't understand why they went their separate ways I understood one thing.

They really did love each other.

***

We watched the game at a bar. It was better than sitting in his tiny apartment with his TV that looked ancient. Plus, the beer was cold.

"What's new with you?" Hawke's eyes lingered on the TV for a moment before he looked at me.

Nothing. I spent all my time at Francesca's in a futile attempt to put her back together. "Just work."

"Seeing anyone?"

I didn't have time for that either. "No. I've had to work a lot of hours at the office since you left." It was a lie and it was cruel, but I didn't care.

Hawke didn't seem to care either. "Nothing else happened with Marie?"

The mention of her name made me tense involuntarily. "Why would anything else happen with her...?"

He watched me with a raised eyebrow. "Because you said she's the best sex you've ever had..." He held his glass on the table but didn't take a drink. He was scrutinizing me, reading every reaction my face made. "Why are you being weird right now?"

"I'm not being weird."

Hawke didn't look at the TV again. "If you hunched any further you'd look like the Hunchback of Notre Dame."

I turned my attention to the game and tried to ignore him.

But he didn't look away. "Axel…"

"What?" I barked. "I haven't slept with her."

"Well, *something* happened."

"Dude, nothing has happened. My dick has been in my pants—the zipper shut tight."

Hawke wasn't buying it. "When your voice gets high and you squirm like that, I know you're hiding something. We tell each other everything. So, what's up?"

"I haven't slept with Marie." It was the truth and nothing but the truth.

"You've said that already, but something else must be going on."

"There's not."

"You have feelings for her?"

"Psh. Hell no." I looked out the window, doing anything to ignore his gaze.

"Are we in second grade right now?"

"You tell me." I didn't have a single comeback up my sleeve so I blurted out the first thing that came to mind.

Hawke didn't say anything else but he didn't need to. He stared me down, silently interrogating me.

I cracked. "I've been seeing her a lot lately and…I don't know. I notice I pay a lot of attention to her."

He didn't touch his beer or look at the TV.

"Like, I notice all the tiny freckles on her face when she doesn't wear make up. Whenever she's in the room, I recognize her scent before I even see her. When she laughs,

I immediately think of a summer day. All these weird things… I don't know what to make of it."

The corner of his lip turned up slightly.

I didn't like that look at all.

"You're into her."

"Am not." I sounded like a child even to my own ears.

"Big time."

"Dude, no." I rubbed the back of my neck even though there wasn't a kink.

"What's the big deal if you are?" he asked. "Marie is pretty cool."

"I'm just not into her, okay? She's pretty, sweet, and funny but that's it."

He raised an eyebrow.

"She hums under her breath in this cute way when she cleans the house but I hardly even notice it."

Hawke started to smile again.

"I don't have feelings for her."

"Axel, I don't see what the problem is. If you like her, go for it."

That had disaster written all over it. "I'm not ready for that." I looked out the window and recalled a memory that would scar me for life.

"Ready for what, exactly?"

"Anything serious. I'm just not into it."

"Why?" he pressed.

I took a drink of my beer to avoid the question.

"Axel, you can talk to me."

Thursday

I didn't like heart-to-heart talks with dudes. The only person I had a somewhat serious conversation with was Marie. "I'm not boyfriend material. We both know that."

"How do you know? You've never tried."

"I just do. Let's leave it at that."

Hawke hadn't touched his beer in a long time and didn't seem like he was going to. "I felt the same way before...her." He never said her name anymore, only referring to her passively. "But when I fell in love I just knew what to do. It comes naturally."

"I'm not in love with her, Hawke."

"Whatever. When you find someone you like, you'll know how to behave."

I didn't agree with that. I'd been doing a lot of stupid stuff lately, like texting her when I got here, like we were something more than friends.

"Just ask her out on a date."

"No."

"Why?" he pressed.

"I just..." It was hard to explain in words. I understood my feelings but not well enough to describe to another person. "I'm still bitter and angry about what my dad did. I know it's been years but I'll never really get over it."

Hawke's face fell in sadness, clearly not expecting me to bring it up.

"He's the biggest coward I've ever met in my life. I'm actually ashamed to call him my father. He deserted Francesca and I without looking back. I'll never be able to understand what he could have possibly thought to justify putting a barrel in his mouth. But whatever the case…I'm afraid I'm just like him."

He didn't blink as he watched me, his blue eyes glued to my face.

"What kind of husband will I be?" Now I was talking to myself more than anything else. "When things get difficult, will I just turn my back like my father did? If I am in a relationship, will I take off the second we hit a bump in the road? I still have nightmares about what I saw when I walked into that house. I'm not emotionally stable enough to have any kind of intimacy with someone. Just looking at Marie makes me uncomfortable sometimes."

Hawke remained silent, just watching me.

I stared at my beer because I was too awkward to look at him. I just dumped a bunch of emotional bullshit on him. "Forget I said anything…I should have kept my mouth shut."

"Axel, you're nothing like your father."

"How would you know?" I said bitterly.

"Francesca." It was the first time he said her name, and he swallowed the lump in his throat after he said it. "You always look after her—no matter what. Even when it annoys the shit out of her you're there for her. You're just her brother and her well-being isn't your problem but you always take care of her. That's more than enough reason."

"It's not the same thing…"

"It is," he said firmly. "I understand your doubts and your emotional insecurity but if you find someone you really love it fixes all of that."

"I don't love Marie."

"Well, if you gave her a chance you might."

I wanted to throw his words back in his face. He talked about love like he knew it so well, but here he was in New York City while Francesca was sobbing in her bedroom.

"My point is, just keep an open mind."

"I've never done the boyfriend thing. I doubt I'm good at it."

"Just take it slow."

"I don't know how to treat her..." I shook my head. "It's just too complicated for me."

"You always said you would commit to a woman if you found the right one."

"Well...maybe Marie isn't the right one."

"Or you're a pussy."

I glared at him.

"Prove me wrong." He held my gaze without backing down.

I quickly realized what he was doing. "Not gonna work, man."

"Let me put this into terms that you'll understand." He leaned over the table and lowered his voice. "Marie is a pretty girl. She's smart, sophisticated, funny, and loyal. If you've noticed these characteristics someone else is bound to as well. So, get in there before someone else stakes a claim."

I was already too late. "She's seeing this guy…"

"Are they serious?"

"She says they aren't but I know she's sleeping with him."

"That doesn't mean anything."

It does to me. "I already missed my chance so there's no point in talking about this."

"If she says they aren't serious you can still make a move."

I didn't want to compete with anyone. And I didn't want to disrupt her happiness—if that's what she felt. "No." Sometimes I felt something between us, some kind of hum in the air, and I was pretty certain she felt it too. But that could just be a figment of my imagination.

Hawke sighed in defeat, irritated with my response. "Don't wait until it's too late."

"You're acting like I'm in love with this girl. I'm not."

Hawke leaned back in the booth and stared me down. A question or statement was about to escape his lips, but it wasn't clear which one it would be. Nearly a full minute passed before he opened his mouth. "Axel, have you slept with anyone since Marie?"

I refused to meet his gaze because my heart just fell into my stomach. On display, my emotions burned like a fire. I wanted to crawl under the table and hide. For the first time I actually felt ashamed for an answer I was about to give.

Thursday

"Axel?" He pressed the question on me even though he already knew the answer.

My throat felt dry like I hadn't had a glass of water in years. When I swallowed, it actually hurt. Like a dog that couldn't look at his owner after pissing all over the carpet, I avoided his gaze. "No."

CHAPTER TWELVE

Sorrow

Marie

Like always, Francesca was a living corpse. She didn't want to do anything, go anywhere, or eat anything. If I didn't pester her to get out of bed, shower, and eat something, she probably would have died by now.

It was a type of sorrow I couldn't understand. I was there when both of her parents passed away. She was devastated, but what she felt now was completely different.

I wish I could fix this.

On Sunday night, I tried to convince her to go to school the following day. "Frankie, you've been moping around for too long now."

"I don't care." She lay on the couch, wearing the same pajamas she'd been wearing all week.

"Axel and I can cover for you but we can't do everything."

"I never asked you to do that." Her voice always held the same tone, one of pure boredom.

"Well, I'm obligated to do that. You're my best friend."

She slowly got off the couch, like her body was failing her. "You aren't obligated to do anything, Marie. Don't let my misery ruin your life." She walked down the hall and shut her bedroom door.

I stayed on the couch and stopped myself from screaming. I missed my best friend, the feisty and badass chick I used to know. Nothing could bother her. She was like a concrete wall that an army could never break through.

But now she was as good as dead.

My phone rang and I looked at the screen.

It was Axel.

Anytime I saw his name on my phone my heart did a tiny somersault. I suddenly grew nervous, feeling my mouth go dry. A tiny burst of excitement exploded inside me. When the nerves faded away, I answered it. "Hello?"

"Hey." Static sounded behind him, like he was driving.

"Hi." I already said that but I said it again. I listened to the sound of his moving car, wondering where he was and if he was coming by.

"Hey…" Now he listened to the static over the line, probably listening to my voice over the speakers of his Bluetooth.

"So…how'd it go?"

"Fine. I'm on my way home now."

"How far away are you?"

"About an hour."

So he wasn't coming by. Disappointment flooded through me.

"How is she?"

I kept the bitterness out of my voice. "The same."

He sighed into the phone. "Come on, Frankie..."

I was disappointed too, even though I would never actually tell her that. "How is he?"

"He's upset too. But he's better at hiding it."

If they were both so miserable why weren't they just together? "I hate them both."

"I know what you mean."

I sat on the couch and listened to the static again.

He didn't say anything for a long time, but he didn't try to get off the phone either.

I didn't have these kinds of conversations with Cade. Was that a good thing? Or a bad one? Actually, we didn't talk on the phone at all. All we ever did was text.

"Well, I should go. I just wanted to check in."

"I'll see you tomorrow."

"Alright. Good night."

"Drive safe. Good night."

He didn't hang up. The background noise still played. He waited for me to hang up first.

I listened to the sound for a moment longer, taking it in as comfort.

Then I hung up.

***

While juggling my classes, I took care of picking up Francesca's assignments from other students in her classes. I had to hunt them down and make copies of everything I needed. I already had enough on my plate, but I would do anything for my best friends.

After class I finally got into my car and headed home. There was a stack of papers sitting beside me that made me depressed just thinking about it. Axel and I would spend all our free time working on it before submitting it online. My life had suddenly become extremely boring.

I stopped at the stoplight then eyed the papers beside me. Thankfully, Axel was smart enough to take care of most of it on his own. Personally, I didn't know anything about science. And I definitely didn't know anything about business or mathematics.

The car behind me honked.

I looked up and saw the green light. Then I gave the people behind me the bird before I drove through it.

BAM.

Out of nowhere a car collided into my door going at least fifty miles an hour. Before I knew it my car was spinning in the middle of the intersection, the momentum of the car throwing me back and forth. My airbag deployed and hit me in the face, the scent of latex accompanying it. I screamed even though no one could hear me, and I felt the seatbelt dig painfully into my skin, burning it like fire.

The collision happened so slowly, taking forever to come to an end. I feared another car would strike me and make me spin all over again. There was a weak sense of pain coming from my left arm, but since I was terrified of dying it didn't matter at the moment.

Finally, the car stopped.

Smoke erupted from my engine and my windshield was cracked all the way through. The seat belt was still biting into my skin, almost making it bleed. I breathed hard, feeling my lungs expand normally. I was alive.

I was alive.

When I looked down at my arm, that's when I realized the damage that had been inflicted. It was bent at an odd angle, and the reality sunk in.

My arm was broken.

How would I take care of Francesca with one arm?

I leaned back into the seat and closed my eyes, trying to remain calm. The sound of the ambulance reached my ears and I knew help was on the way. It would only be a matter of time before the police questioned what happened. It was such a blur that I honestly didn't know what happened.

I didn't know anything.

***

My parents were the first ones to arrive. Mom was terrified, crying hysterically. Dad yelled at every person who came into my room, demanding I get more pain meds and an extra blanket. When he was stressed out, he screamed at people because it kept him calm.

Thursday

"The doctor said you're going to be fine." Mom patted my hand as she sat at my bedside. "The orthopedic surgeon is going to come in here soon and pop your shoulder back into place."

Ugh, that sounded terrible. "Okay."

"I called Francesca but she didn't answer. I left her voicemail."

Which she would never listen to. "Do you have my phone?"

"Yes." Mom quickly fished it out of her purse and handed it over.

Without thinking twice about it I called Axel. He was probably at work but he said it was okay if I called him.

He answered almost immediately. "Hey." Now that we were spending more time together he said less than he used to. It was strange, but not strange at the same time.

Talking to him immediately made me feel better. I forgot about the pain in my shoulder. "Hi..."

Axel remained quiet, saying nothing but saying so much at the same time. A voice came over the loud speaker from the ceiling, calling a code red on a different floor. "Where are you?"

"At the hospital..."

"What's wrong? Are you okay?" The words flew out faster than ever.

"That's why I'm calling. I was in a car accident—"

"Shit, are you okay? Fuck, I'll be right there."

"Axel, wait—"

128

He hung up.

I didn't bother calling him back because I didn't want him to crash the way I did. I handed the phone back to my mom.

She took it and eyed me suspiciously. "Who was that...?"

"Axel—Francesca's brother."

"Oh..."

"He's just a friend, Mom. Don't get your hopes up."

She kept giving me that look. You know, the kind that mothers do. "Just a friend that happens to be your first call..."

"Francesca would have been my first call but you said she didn't answer."

She patted my hand. "Whatever you say, honey."

***

Axel darted into the room, out of breath. He wore a gray collared shirt with black slacks along with a black tie. He clearly darted out of the office and got here as fast as he could. "Marie." He ignored both of my parents and immediately came to my bedside. "What happened?" He eyed my arm in the sling. "Are you okay? What can I do for you?"

"I was driving through a light when a guy ran the red. He smacked right into me." It was scary at the time but now that I knew no one died it wasn't as big of a deal. "But everything is okay. My shoulder came out of the socket but the doctor is supposed to put it back in."

He eyed the sling again, the devastation written all over his face. "You have enough pain meds? Do you need something? I can hunt down a doctor and take care of it—"

"I don't feel a thing."

He breathed a sigh of relief and continued to stand at my bedside. He eyed my hand like he might take it.

I waited a moment, feeling my fingers tingle with need.

Axel stared at it for another moment before he looked at me, the same devastation still glued to his face.

I cleared my throat. "Axel, these are my parents. This is my mom, Dorothy."

He turned to her, and judging the surprise in his eyes he didn't see her sitting there when he walked inside. "Oh, I'm sorry." He extended his hand to shake hers. "I got caught up with Marie…"

"It's more than okay." She grinned from ear-to-ear as she shook his hand. "That's very sweet of you to care so much for my daughter."

"She's an amazing woman." He dropped her hand then turned to my father. "I'm sorry for my rudeness. I didn't see you either."

Dad stared at him affectionately, liking him before he even met him. "It's okay. Your heart was in the right place." He shook his hand and sized him up, noting his attire and perfectly styled hair. "What do you do?"

"I work in finance," Axel answered. "I'm an intern for Charles Schwab."

"That's great," Dad answered.

"Working for pretty much nothing isn't all that great, but I'm thankful for the experience." Axel put his hands in his pockets, clearly uncomfortable talking to my parents in a cornered environment.

"Dear, let's get something from the cafeteria." Mom rose out of the chair and grabbed Dad by the arm. "I'm starving..." She pulled him with her and gave me a mischievous look as she went.

I really hoped Axel didn't notice.

Axel turned to the bed and sat in the chair my mother had just been sitting in.

"You didn't need to leave work..."

"I know. I wanted to." He eyed my arm in the sling, disturbed by it. "You got the info from the guy who hit you?"

"Yeah. The police are taking care of it."

He nodded. "Let me know if you need any help with that."

"What do you mean?"

"If you were planning to sue or something."

"Oh, no. I'm sure it was just a mistake."

Axel clenched his jaw like I said the wrong thing. "A mistake is messing up someone's drink at Starbucks. This is completely unacceptable. You could have been killed, Marie. No, it wasn't some human mistake that we can just forget about."

I pulled my knees to my chest.

Axel realized his anger got the best of him. "Sorry...I shouldn't stress you out."

"It's okay."

"Where's Francesca?"

"Mom called her but she didn't answer."

He shook his head in disappointment. "She should be here right now."

"She doesn't know, Axel. If she did she would."

"I hope so. If not, I might have to knock some sense into her."

Even though my shoulder was in serious pain, I knew it was only a fraction of the agony Francesca felt.

"Your parents are nice."

"They're great. Annoying—but great."

He chuckled. "My mom used to be that way—really attentive. She would be in my business every second of the day. Now I miss it."

Now I wish I could take back what I said. I had two parents and Axel didn't even have one. I should never take them for granted. For all I know, they might not be here tomorrow. "I love my parents."

He looked into my eyes and gave me a slight smile.

"Well, thanks for coming down here but you didn't have to do that."

"I wanted to be here." He sat perfectly straight with his hands in his lap. "I can't go back to the office now."

"I don't want you to get in trouble."

"I'm pretty much free labor. They aren't going to get rid of me for any reason. Don't worry about it."

I was glad he was there. He was distracting me from the pain and making me smile. With him at my side I didn't think about anything else.

***

The orthopedic surgeon walked inside and prepared to return my shoulder to the socket. Even though my entire arm had been numbed I was nervous. Just the idea of returning a body part where it belonged made me nauseated. "I have to ask everyone to step out." He pulled on his gloves and set up the table.

My parents walked out and stood in the hallway.

Axel walked around my bed until he was on the other side, giving the doctor plenty of room. He pulled up a chair then grabbed my hand. "I won't get in your way."

The doctor eyed him as he adjusted his gloves. He obviously didn't see him as a problem because he returned to his work and ignored him.

Axel interlocked our fingers together and kept his eyes on me. "It'll be okay."

I felt his warm fingers in mine. His hand was much bigger than mine, and feeling his touch was comforting. Just a moment ago I was worried about the procedure but now it was barely in the back of my mind. "I'm not scared." I noticed the dryness of his skin and the way his veins popped out on his hands. His forearms were full of definition, every muscle highlighted like it was chiseled out.

"I'm going to begin." The doctor grabbed my hand with his then placed his other hand on my elbow.

"Look at me." Axel rested his other hand on my elbow, his fingers comforting.

I stared at him and tried to ignore what the doctor was doing.

"What did you do today?"

"I had class." I looked into his blue eyes and noted how different they were from Francesca's. Hers were green like moss while his were brighter than the tropical ocean.

"Did you get Francesca's homework?"

"Yeah. She has a lot of it."

"Great..." He gave me a smile.

I loved that smile.

The doctor twisted something, and that made me cry out.

Axel squeezed my hand. "Don't look."

Why didn't he want me to look?

"What did you do over the weekend?"

The pain was excruciating. The doctor twisted my arm in unnatural ways, and the image in my head was sickening. "Nothing. Just stayed home."

"Hawke took me to a bar downtown. The city was pretty cool."

There was a final snap and the pain was enough to make me throw up.

"It's in," the doctor said.

E. L. Todd

Within seconds the pain started to ebb away but it never fully disappeared. My arm was returned to the sling and the doctor removed his gloves.

"It's all done." Axel kept his hand in mine. "The hard part is over."

"It'll take a few weeks for it to get better," the doctor said. "You can go home in the morning."

"Thank you..." Or was I really thankful after the way he bent my arm like origami?

He walked out and shut the door behind him.

Axel never pulled his hand away. "It looks like I'll be taking care of both of you now." He chuckled slightly.

"I'll be fine," I said. "I have my other arm."

"You can't drive," he reminded me. "You definitely can't work."

"Shit..." I didn't even think of that. Without work I wouldn't be able to pay my bills. My parents would help me if I asked for it but I didn't want to resort to that.

"I've got you covered. Don't worry about it."

"I can't take your money." It was one thing to let him pay for Francesca's expenses but I wasn't letting him pay for mine too. I'd figure something out.

"You aren't taking it. I'm giving it to you."

"No." I could be stubborn just like Francesca. "You've said several times you don't get paid much."

"For the amount of work I do, no. But I do just fine."

"You have your own rent."

"You've seen my place. It's a hole in the wall and it's dirt cheap." Mentioning his apartment, the place where we hooked up, made him shut his mouth and fall silent. That night was just a fun evening but now we both seemed to regret it. A part of me wished it never happened, and I think he felt the same way too. "Marie, I really don't mind."

"I'll pay you back."

"I'd never take your money." The look in his eyes showed the truth of that statement. "Right now, you shouldn't stress out. I'm helping you and that's the end of the story." The determination was still in his eyes, glowing bright.

The door opened, and instead of seeing my parents walk back into the room I saw Francesca. I did a double take because I almost couldn't believe she was there. Her hair was a mess like it always was, and her clothes looked several days old. But there was emotion in her face. Her eyes crinkled with a different kind of sadness. "Marie..." She rushed to my bedside and grabbed my hand. "I just got your mom's voicemail."

Axel quickly pulled his hand away, ending our affection.

I felt cold the moment he was gone.

Francesca eyed my shoulder then stared at the bruises all over my face. "I'm so glad you're okay."

I squeezed her fingers. "I'll be alright. Just a few scrapes and bruises."

She squeezed my hand before she wiped her tears away with the back of her forearm. "I love you…"

"I love you too." She hugged me, making sure she didn't touch my injured shoulder, and held me there, like she needed it more than I did.

I held onto my best friend, seeing her for the first time in over a month. All she'd been was a zombie around the house. Her true self was gone, somewhere I couldn't follow. But now she was here—she was back.

Thursday

CHAPTER THIRTEEN

Recovery

Marie

It was good to be home.

The hospital bed wasn't very comfortable, and the constant beeping of the monitor made it difficult for me to sleep. I hadn't sat in one of the chairs but I knew they were uncomfortable for everyone.

I got settled on the couch, my arm still in a sling. I could still do things on my own but only having one arm made it difficult. I didn't realize how much I took my health for granted until that moment.

Francesca was still in her funk but she came out of her shell slightly. "Are you hungry? Can I make you anything?"

"No, I'm okay." I grabbed my tablet and downloaded a book. "I'm just going to read."

Francesca sat beside me on the couch. "Is there anything else you need? A blanket?"

"I'm not helpless. I can get it myself."

She still seemed worried.

"Really, I'm fine."

She leaned against the couch and pulled her knees to her chest. Her eyes glazed over again, like she was slipping back into her depression. The only thing strong enough to pull her back out was my injury.

Someone knocked on the door and made us both turn to the entryway.

"It's probably Axel." Francesca got off the couch, her jeans practically falling off her body, and headed to the door. When she opened it, it was clear it wasn't him. "Hey, what brings you here?"

"Is Marie around?" Cade's voice came to my ears.

"Yeah, she's on the couch." Francesca walked into her bedroom and shut the door.

I'd totally forgotten about Cade. He didn't know about the accident or my hospital visit. How could I forget to tell him?

Cade came to the couch. "Francesca looks...different." That was his nice way of saying she looked absolutely terrible. He stopped when he realized my arm was in a sling and I was beat up. "Whoa, what the hell happened?" He sat beside me and eyed my injuries.

"I got into an accident. No one else was hurt."

"Damn, you broke your arm?"

"My shoulder came out of place. They put it back in the socket and now everything is fine." I grabbed my prescription and shook it, hearing the pills rattle inside. "But I got some Vicodin."

"Holy shit. You're okay, right?"

"Yeah, I'll be fine. My arm will be in a sling for a few weeks, but after that it should be back to normal."

"Why didn't you call me?"

"Uh, I don't know. Everything happened so fast...it just slipped my mind."

He didn't seem angry, just concerned. "I'm glad you're okay. Is there anything I can do for you?"

"No. I have Francesca and Axel."

He nodded. "Well, you can call me for anything."

"I know, Cade." He sat beside me on the couch and turned on the TV. "I guess all I can do is keep you company."

"Yeah...it's better than nothing." Now that we sat side-by-side together I didn't feel the attraction I once felt before. If anything, he seemed like a friend. Cade was a nice guy with great looks, but I just didn't feel anything anymore.

And I couldn't figure out why.

***

Axel walked inside in his office clothes. "Ready for school?"

"You really don't need to take me." I placed my bag over my good shoulder.

"I don't mind. You really shouldn't drive with one hand anyway."

"Lots of people do it."

"Yeah, but they shouldn't." He guided me to his car and opened the door for me. Once we were inside he drove to the campus. "Francesca didn't offer?"

"She did but I don't trust her to drive right now."

"That's probably best."

"Besides, she's slowly crawled back into her hole. I thought my accident might keep her out of it for a while but it didn't last very long."

"At least she crawled out of it to begin with."

"I guess..."

He grabbed a Starbucks coffee from the cup holder. "It's medium roast with soy milk. I know it's not exactly what you drink but it was the best I could do."

I stared at it and tried to keep the emotion from seeping into my face. He did thoughtful things without me even asking. He paid attention to the things I liked and disliked. Axel had always been innately selfish but I was realizing just how wrong I was. When it mattered most, he was there. "Thank you. That was sweet of you..." I took a sip.

"I know I'm grouchy without my morning coffee."

"I've never seen you grouchy."

He chuckled. "Ask Francesca. She'll tell you." He parked as close as he could to my first class. "Need any help? I can walk you."

"I'm not handicapped." It was sweet Axel and Francesca were concerned but I still had two legs and one arm. I could get by just fine. "Thanks for the ride."

"Anytime. I'll see you at three."

"I can just take an UBER."

"Or you can get a free ride from a dashing guy like me." He wiggled his eyebrows.

I chuckled and felt my cheeks tint. "You make a compelling argument."

"Then I'll see you at three."

"Okay." I opened the door but didn't get out. I felt like I was missing something, forgetting to do something important. My body automatically wanted to lean in and give him a kiss goodbye, something I've never done before. I wasn't even sure where the urge came from. "Bye."

***

Axel took me home then started dinner in the kitchen.

I almost couldn't believe the sight. "You know how to cook?"

"A few things. Francesca taught me." He cooked the steak on the grill and warmed up the tortillas in the microwave. "My mom used to make tacos at least once a week. It was my favorite."

Francesca made tacos all the time, and now I knew why. "Well, thanks. Can I help?"

"No. Just chill."

"Chill?" I couldn't help but make a face.

"Yes. Chill." He gave me a playful look before he returned his attention to the stove.

I felt the pain in my arm begin to throb. It'd been four hours since my last pill and I needed another one. I was trying to take as few as possible because substance drugs could get addicting. But the pain was too unbearable and I caved. I swallowed a fat pill with a bottle of water.

Axel noticed my movements. "Still having pain?"

"Unfortunately."

"Give it more time. It'll be gone before you know it."

"I hope so." I glanced at the hallway and wondered if I should even bother trying to get Francesca to have dinner with us.

"Don't worry about her." Axel didn't look at me but he seemed to know what I was thinking. "I'll handle it."

"Don't you feel like she's our child?"

He chuckled. "I've always felt like she was a child."

"It makes me never want to have kids."

"I know what you mean. Too much work." He turned off the stove then prepared the food in the dishes. "Dude, I'm so hungry."

"Dude?"

"Sorry, you know what I mean." He set everything down on the table then prepared two tacos for me, sliding the plate in front of me. "I'll round up the little terror." He walked down the hallway and knocked on her bedroom door. "Dinnertime."

"I'm not hungry..."

I rolled my eyes and stared at my food.

"I don't give a shit," Axel snapped. "Get in here and eat like a big girl."

"Go away..."

"I'm sorry you're going through a hard time but you're totally pathetic. What would Mom think if she saw you like this? You remind me of Dad. Good thing there's not a loaded pistol in there." He slammed the door so hard the house shook.

I stared at my food in shock, surprised Axel snapped like that.

He came back to the table and fell into the chair, his shoulders tense.

I stared at him, speechless.

He started to eat like nothing happened.

Since he was in a bad mood I kept my head down and remained silent.

Axel ate with his elbows on the table, too angry to practice his usual manners. "I'm sorry, but I'm sick of her shit. When I saw Hawke, I lied and said she was fine. She's back at school and work like nothing happened. She's been moping around the house for over a month now just because he's gone. She was just as pissed with our father as I was, but yet she's doing the exact same thing. She needs to have some pride, for the love of god."

I ate quietly because I wasn't sure if I should say anything. Axel was upset for more than one reason.

"When our parents died, you know what I did?" He stopped eating and stared out the window. "I got off my ass and lived my life. I didn't just stop because they were gone."

"And neither did Francesca." She was heartbroken over what happened but she kept going. She went to school and took care of herself. After her parents left she wasn't the same but she was still strong. Maybe he needed to be reminded of that.

"Well, this is different. She's acting this way over a boyfriend. It's pathetic."

"We don't understand what she's feeling." I didn't think Francesca should stop living her life just because Hawke was gone, but I knew breakups had an impact on brain chemistry. It was just as real as any physical pain.

"If I got dumped I would get over it." He drank his beer, his eyes still glued to the window.

"I understand why you're frustrated. I feel the same way. But insulting her isn't going to get her out of bed quicker." There were other ways to go about it. Telling her she was pathetic wasn't one of them.

He picked up his taco again and took a few bites.

"She'll get better in her own time. We just have to be patient."

He shook his head in disappointment. "When I'm on my deathbed, she better be there to wipe my ass."

There wasn't any doubt in my mind she would be—whether he was there for her or not.

***

Cade texted me. *Hey, Beautiful. Can I take you out for a drink?*

I hadn't been thinking about him much. And that made me feel guilty. We weren't anything serious. In fact, we only went on one date—which didn't end well. But now I was beginning to think I was wasting his time. *Yeah. But I can't drink because of my medication.*

Then can I take you out for a cold glass of water?

I chuckled to myself. *Yeah. That sounds nice.*

Alright. You'll be ready in an hour?

I'm ready now.

Even better.

I did my hair the best I could with one arm and changed into something more appropriate for a date. I could have just told him we were done over a text message but I thought that would be cold. We could go out and have a good time and I would tell him how I felt at the end of the night. I wanted to be friends with him, and ending on good terms was essential for that.

He picked me up an hour later and we left for a small café downtown. It was better than any bar because it was quaint and small. He told me about school and his job for the county. Then he asked me about my arm.

"It's getting better. But I'm still having some pain."

"Did the driver's insurance cover everything?"

"Yeah. My car is totaled so the insurance company is giving me the value to replace it."

"Well, that's something to be thankful for. How have you been getting around?"

Saying his name made me uncomfortable, like I was hiding something. I fidgeted with my hair, feeling nervous for no particular reason. "Axel has been taking me around…"

Thursday

Cade finished his sandwich. "Sounds like a nice guy. That's Francesca's brother?"

"Yeah."

"Well, he seems pretty cool."

He was the coolest person I knew. "He's very thoughtful."

He drank his water then eyed mine. "Nice water, huh?"

I chuckled. "Best water I've ever had on a date."

"That's what I'm talking about." His basket was empty of the sandwich and chips he devoured.

Now that we reached the end of the meal I knew it was time to tell him the truth. He really was a nice guy so I felt bad for letting him go. But it didn't seem like he was really into me anyway so it should be okay. "Cade, you're a really nice guy and I like you but...I think we should just be friends."

"Just friends?" He wiped his mouth with a napkin and regarded me with complete bewilderment. "Why?"

"I just...I guess I don't feel a real connection between us. It's not you. I just don't want to lead you on."

"Well, we haven't really had a chance. Our first date wasn't that great because I screwed it up, but I promise nothing like that would ever happen again. Come on, give me a try."

Axel's face kept popping up in my mind and I wish it would stop. "I don't think I'm going to change my mind. It's either there or it's not..."

Cade looked disappointed as he stared at the table between us.

"I hope we can still be friends."

"Of course we can be friends." Cade looked up at me again. "I just wish you would give me another chance. With Francesca being sick and your car accident we haven't really had much of a chance to get things going."

He had a good point but I still felt deceitful if I kept seeing him.

"Maybe sometime down the road. But for right now, no."

Cade finally gave up because he knew I wouldn't budge. "If that's how you feel I respect it."

"Thank you…"

"Well, are you ready to go?"

I nodded and hoped the drive home wouldn't feel awkward.

***

He walked me to my door then faced me. "I had a great time tonight—even though I got dumped." He chuckled and put his hands in his pockets.

"You didn't get dumped."

"Pretty much."

"I'll probably regret this sometime down the road."

He shrugged. "I'm a pretty good guy but I'm nothing special. You're a ten and I'm like a five."

I busted up laughing because it was ridiculous. "You have those numbers flipped."

149

"Do not." He gave me a playful tap with his foot.

"Yes, you do. Or you're blind."

"Maybe you're delirious from the painkillers."

I looked into my purse and pulled out my keys. "I really don't think so."

He watched my movements until I met his gaze. Then he took a step toward me, his hand still in his pockets. "Kiss goodbye?"

"I guess." What was the harm in that?

He pressed his mouth against mine and gave me a closed mouth kiss. It was strictly PG but there was a hint of a spark there. But it was nothing like the fire I felt with Axel when we slept together, not that I should be comparing. "Good night."

"Good night, Cade." I watched him walk down the path to his truck. Most women would tell me I was stupid for kicking Cade to the side, but I had to stop the relationship before it became serious. If I didn't see it working out now, why would it work out later? It was better to save us both the heartache.

When I heard the sound of footsteps on the lawn, I turned around to see Axel standing there. He had a bag of groceries in one arm and a pale look on his face. He stared at me without reacting, every thought and emotion blocked off from me.

I assumed he went home by this time of night and hadn't expected him to show up at this hour. He usually had to work late on Wednesdays. And I definitely didn't expect him to appear out of nowhere. His car wasn't around so he must have borrowed Francesca's.

I stared at him and didn't know what to say. The guilt flooded through me, like I'd been caught doing something I shouldn't. I wanted to apologize but what do I apologize for?

He stopped on the grass and stared me down, the bag still in his arms. He didn't give his thoughts away in his eyes. Everything in his mind was a mystery to me. Then he started walking again, heading right to the front door. He walked past me without looking at me.

I felt like shit.

I followed him inside and watched him set the bag of groceries on the table. Even then, I had no idea what was going on between Axel and I. We never talked about anything romantic but I always felt it in the air. The chemistry was there, and the more time we spent together a connection formed. Somehow, I felt like I betrayed him. "Axel—"

"I just wanted to drop these off on my way home." His voice came out normal, like nothing just happened. "I've got to run."

"Axel, let me explain." He needed to know that I just broke it off with Cade. "I'm not seeing—"

"I have a date tonight so I really need to get going." He walked around me and headed to the door.

Wait, what? "You have a date tonight?"

He stopped on the doorstep and looked at me. "Not so much a date as friendly fucking." He walked down the steps and headed to Francesca's car. "I'm sure you and Cade just did the same."

CHAPTER FOURTEEN

Stupidity

Axel

I was sitting at a bar at eleven o' clock on a Wednesday night. My beer sat in front of me and I searched for a woman to bring back to my place. So far, I hadn't seen anyone I liked.

When I saw her with Cade, I snapped.

I assumed she stopped seeing him because he didn't come around anymore. I was by her side at the hospital the entire time and not once did he make an appearance. If he didn't show up for that, I just assumed he was out of the picture.

Despite the anger I knew I was overreacting—and being unfair. Marie never said a word to me about a relationship between us, and I claimed I didn't want one at all. We hadn't even had a conversation about it.

She didn't owe me anything.

But when I saw them kissing on her doorstep I was pissed. I'd been waiting on her hand-and-foot, taking her to school every day, cooking for her, and picking up her meds. I didn't mind doing those things and I certainly didn't expect anything in return but...I didn't like her being with someone else.

Was I the biggest asshole in the world?

A pretty brunette walked inside so I made my move. I left my beer on the table and engaged her in conversation. I did my usual moves, making a few jokes and giving her some sexy smolders. Within twenty minutes, she was down to get funky.

We stood together near the bathrooms and that's when I kissed her. I dug my hand into her hair and felt the strands. They were nothing like Marie's. They weren't soft and delicate. In fact, they were a little tangled. Our kiss didn't send shivers down my spine. I felt like I was having a dream, one where I couldn't feel anything in reality.

I realized I was just forcing it, trying to screw someone so I could forget about the way Marie screwed Cade. I was seriously screwed up in the head and I didn't know how to fix it.

But this wasn't the solution.

"I'm sorry." I broke apart and stepped back. "I just realized I have to be somewhere..."

"Uh...okay." She gave me an incredulous look, like I must be crazy to walk away from a guaranteed lay.

"Good night." I left the bar and felt the guilt on my shoulders. Marie was seeing someone else, and I wasn't even seeing her. So I didn't do anything wrong. There was no one to betray. But I felt like I did something terrible, something unforgivable.

I needed some serious help.

***

I didn't want to take Marie to school but I refused to flake on her. She was depending on me, and I was a man of my word. I picked up her morning coffee like usual then pulled up to the curb.

She spotted me through the window and she couldn't hide her look of surprise. She hadn't been anticipating me to show up.

That hurt.

She came to the car and got into the passenger seat. She was dead quiet, and she didn't look at me.

Once her safety belt was on I drove off. Thankfully, the radio was on so there was something to listen to. She and I didn't speak to each other. I didn't say anything because I didn't have a clue what to say. How did I explain my behavior last night without having a conversation I didn't want to have? She must think I'm pathetic, getting upset over something that I had no right to be upset about. I felt like a high school girl starting drama for no reason.

I arrived at her building and put the car in park.

She stayed in the seat like she might say something. But the silence lingered on eternally. She turned her face toward me slightly then turned away. The door opened and she stepped out, leaving her untouched coffee behind.

Then she walked away.

***

When I picked her up, I expected another round of silence. The car ride would be painfully awkward, probably worse than the first one. I pulled up to the curve and watched her get inside from my peripheral. Her arm was still in a sling but she handled it well.

She shut the door and hastened her safety belt. And just like before, she ignored me.

I drove back to her house and tried to focus on the music from the radio. If I paid attention to the purposeful way she turned her head the way, I felt my insides boil. Getting her home as quickly as possible was the priority.

I parked at the curb in front of her house and we both walked inside. Francesca was a pain in the ass but I had to check on her. With Marie's disability and medication she couldn't handle everything on her own.

Unfortunately.

We walked inside and I walked down the hall to check on Francesca. Like always, she was lying in bed doing absolutely nothing. "Let's go for a walk or something." She'd get a blood clot if she just sat there all day.

"Muh."

I wanted to rip her head off. "Do you have any idea how pathetic you are?"

She stayed silent.

"I've never been more disappointed in you in my life."
I shut the door and walked back into the kitchen.

Marie had just unpacked her laptop and notebook.
She stared at me coldly, judging me for the harsh things I just
said. "I know she needs to get off her ass but stop talking to
her like that."

"I can say whatever the hell I want." We were talking
about Francesca but it felt like we were talking about
something else.

She tossed her bag on the table then stared at me with
one arm on her hip. "You're an insensitive jerk."

"You're a whore."

Her eyes widened to the size of tennis balls. The fire
burned across her face and she was about to explode. She
gave me the fiercest look I'd ever seen in my life.

But I didn't need to see it to know what I said was
unforgivable. "I'm sorry. I take that back."

She still seethed quietly, her anger palpable.

"I didn't mean it." I lost my temper and did something
idiotic. I insulted someone I respected more than anyone
else. Whatever feelings I was experiencing...I wasn't
handling them very well.

"How was your date?" she sneered. "I mean, friendly
fucking?"

"It was great. Thanks for asking." I didn't sleep with
anyone but I did kiss someone. But I let the lie continue, not
wanting her to understand how I felt about her.

She shook her head and looked down. "I feel so stupid…" Her voice was hardly coherent because she was speaking to herself, not me.

"Sorry?"

"Nothing." She sat down and opened her laptop, dismissing the conversation.

"No. Tell me." I stepped closer to her, needing to know what she said. Somehow, I knew it was important.

She started her computer then looked up at me, giving me a look of sheer disappointment. "For some inexplicable reason I thought there might be something between us. I can't explain why. We've never talked about it but it didn't seem like we needed to. I felt guilty for seeing Cade knowing it wasn't going to go anywhere so I broke it off that night."

She dumped him?

"But if I'd known you were screwing around and had no problem calling me a whore, then I might have done otherwise." She pressed her lips tightly together and shook her head. Then she turned her gaze to the computer screen and ignored me. "It was a stupid decision…"

I was frozen in place, unable to believe what I just heard. "If you broke it off with him why did you kiss him?"

"A kiss goodbye. It was innocent."

Now I hated myself for flipping out. I stormed off that night without turning back. And then I made out with that chick in the bar… "I overreacted that night. I'm not even sure what happened. I just…snapped."

Her eyes were glued to her computer.

"I lied about having a date. I just said that because I was pissed off."

She slowly turned her gaze back to me.

I omitted the part about the girl. If she kissed Cade that same night then we were even. There wasn't any point in bringing it up. It wasn't like I slept with her. "I don't know what's going on between us either. But I know what you're talking about...I've noticed it."

Now her eyes were glued to mine.

I watched her and hoped she would say something.

She didn't.

I pulled out the chair then sat beside her, wanting to be close to her. She wore make up so the tiny freckles I once noticed were gone. Her eyes were still the same, lively and green. I was standing on a precipice of fear. I didn't know which way I wanted to sway, if I wanted to sway at all. I'd always assumed I'd settle down with a girl if I found the right one, but now that was a possibility I wasn't sure what I wanted. Could I really handle a relationship? Would I just screw it up?

"I liked Cade but when you started coming around...I thought about him less." She shut her laptop, and when it closed it made a quiet clicking noise. "Anytime I was with him I thought about you. It got to the point where I felt deceitful. Cade and I were never serious but I felt terrible for leading him on."

Thursday

Never serious? "You sleep with guys and still don't think it's serious?" My jealousy got to me again and I wished I could control it. I didn't even have a right to be jealous. "I'm sorry...I take that back too."

"So, you can sleep around but I can't? That makes me a whore and it has no barring on your reputation?" She shook her head slightly. "I'm not into bigots and I didn't realize you were one of them."

This conversation was taking another nosedive. "That's not what I said, and it's certainly not what I meant. When you brought Cade here a few months ago...it bothered me. That's all."

Marie narrowed her eyes on my face as she processed what I said. Her eyebrows relaxed when she realized something. "I never slept with Cade. He spent the night one time because he was too drunk to drive home. That's all."

Choir music began to play in my head.

"At the time I didn't think you cared either way."

"I didn't think I did either."

She eyed the table between us, her hands resting on her laptop. She cleared her throat then released a quiet sigh.

I stared at her and tried to think of the next thing to say.

She looked up at me, her green eyes intoxicating. They pulled me in time and time again.

I wasn't sure where we went from here.

"So...now what?"

"I don't know." I'd been battling my feelings for a long time. Every time I tried to convince myself my feelings for Marie were platonic I failed. Even when I tried to stop myself, I still noticed the curve of her lips and the softness of her hair. Details that I always considered irrelevant were somehow vital to my survival.

She stared at her fingers before she returned her gaze to me. "Well...maybe we should go out."

I wanted to take her out on a date. I'd wine and dine her and walk her to her doorstep. That seemed easy to go. When I thought about everything else a date would entail, it made me antsy. I'd already slept with her, but now it was different. That was a lifetime ago and she was a different woman. Now I couldn't wait to kiss those lips slowly, to treasure the way they felt against my mouth. I wanted to cherish her naked body and take my time. I wanted to really feel her, not rush through it to the finish line. I didn't want to fuck. I wanted to make love. And I wanted it so much it hurt sometimes.

But then I thought about everything else that entailed. She was my sister's best friend. If it didn't work out between us, and knowing me it wouldn't, it would affect their friendship. It would affect my relationship with Francesca. It had the capability of destroying everything around us. Marie was the definition of a real woman, and I was afraid I wasn't man enough to handle her. What if I became a coward and deserted her when she needed me most? Francesca already strayed down that path and she was the stronger one of the two of us. Would I succumb when things got difficult? Was I just as pathetic as my own father?

Marie kept staring at me, waiting for a response.

My mind flooded with thoughts and doubts. I liked Marie—a lot. But I wasn't sure if I could give her everything she wanted. Fidelity wasn't an issue. I hadn't been with anyone since we started spending time together. But there was so much more to a relationship and I knew I was lacking in every department. "I don't think that's a good idea..."

Marie tried to hide the hurt on her face but it was impossible. Her eyes crinkled in sadness, like I just said the worst thing imaginable. Her reaction was slow, as if she thought she misheard me. When she looked down and avoided my look altogether, I knew she'd been struck harshly.

"I really like you, Marie. That's not the problem."

"You enjoy your freedom too much?" She turned back to her laptop and opened it, dismissing the conversation.

"No, not at all." When Hawke pointed out I'd been faithful to a woman I wasn't even seeing, it freaked me out. "You're Francesca's best friend and I'm her brother. If things get messy...it could affect all three of us."

She nodded in understanding. "I guess you're right."

"If it doesn't work out...we could have more problems. And honestly, I don't know anything about relationships. More than likely, I'd just screw ours up. Then it would be awkward forever."

"I guess it's just as well." Her voice changed, coming out stronger. "Our situation isn't exactly what I'm looking for anyway."

Her meaning was lost on me. "What do you mean?"

"I noticed you in high school, and I didn't just think you were cute. I loved the fact you were funny and loyal to your friends. I loved the fact you picked on your sister but had her back at the same time. When your parents passed away, you took care of Francesca. There are so many qualities about you that I admire. But you only noticed me when I grew up and found my shape. You only noticed me when I became one of the pretty girls. Physical attraction is important, but you never noticed everything on the inside, the stuff that really matters. And even now you're still shallow." She looked at me again, this time her face emotionless. "I think you're right. This would never work."

A building collapsed on top of me and knocked the air out of my lungs. Her words broke me, killed me from the inside out. I never stopped to consider any of that, that I might he shallow and empty. "That's not how I feel..."

"I know," she said. "But that's what happened. And the fact you don't want to start up something now...just confirms you don't feel the same emotional connection I do. All you feel is the physical attraction, the hum in the air. You don't notice anything beneath the surface. And that's fine, Axel. I'm not judging you for it. But I agree that a relationship between us would never work. Neither one of us would ever be happy."

Thursday

My shoulders slouched and I felt sick.

She opened her bag and took out her homework. Some of it was hers and some of it was Francesca's. "Let's just go back to what we were before—friends." When she didn't look at me again, I knew the conversation was over.

I wanted to say something, do something to change her opinion of me. But I realized there was nothing I could do to change anything—because she was right.

CHAPTER FIFTEEN

Friendship

Marie

The physical therapist helped me move my arm, returning a sense of motion to it. We used light weights to build up strength, and he helped me stretch the tendons and return them to their previous vitality. Sometimes the actions hurt but they were necessary.

"You did a good job today." The therapist gave me a friendly smile before he walked with me to the lobby. "Just take it easy and leave it on the sling. You can't rush the healing part."

"Thank you." I signed out then walked to Axel, who was sitting in the lobby. He'd been helping me take care of errands since I still only had one arm.

He stood up, still wearing his work clothes. His collared shirt was blue, bringing out his eyes, and his tie was gray. "How was it?"

Thursday

"It was okay. I'm stronger now but it still hurts."

He eyed my shoulder like he could see through my shirt. "Don't worry. It'll get better."

My biggest fear was never being able to use it the same. What if I always had a pain there? What if I tried to move my arm but it just made it worse? What if it was never the same?

Axel picked up on my unease. "These things take time. It'll go back to normal eventually." He walked out with me then opened the passenger door.

"Thanks." I got inside then fastened my safety belt. Axel and I never brought up that conversation we had last week. I put myself out there and said I wanted something more, something meaningful, but he shot me down.

I was mortified.

Feeling rejected like that was brutal. I'd put myself out there a few times in the past and I recovered from the rejection, but this was different. Being with him was something I really wanted—something I thought he wanted too.

When he turned me down, it reminded me of the truth, that Axel had never changed. Sometimes, I imagined him as a different person. When we spent time together, it seemed like he'd deepened, grew more layers underneath his aloof attitude. But now I realized I was only imagining it. Axel was exactly the same person as before, looking for a good time without any commitment. He didn't change his ways when we became closer. I didn't mean as much to him as he did to me.

I'd have to move on.

He took me home then walked with me inside.

I tried to act as normal as possible around him, to pretend that awkward conversation never happened at all. But our relationship never returned to what it used to be. I used to be at ease around him, to feel comfortable in his presence—even comforted by it. But now there was a wedge between us.

Axel checked on Francesca before he came back to me. "I think I'm going to take her to a therapist."

She hadn't improved in nearly two months and we were both starting to worry. Break ups were hard on lots of people, but this was a whole new level. "That's not a bad idea."

"I don't know what else to do." He sat at the kitchen table and stared out the window. "If I could knock this senseless behavior out of her I would."

I took the seat beside him, sitting exactly as we did on that night we decided to go our separate ways. "Me too."

"So, you think I should do it?" He turned his eyes away from the window and looked at me. "I found someone in Myrtle Beach. He specializes in this sort of thing."

"Is it expensive?"

He shrugged. "If it's necessary I don't think the cost matters."

I wasn't sure what Axel's financial situation was but I didn't want him to blow his life savings on Francesca. "Maybe we can do one session and see how it goes."

"Yeah," he said in agreement. "Maybe if she talks to a professional she'll open up a bit more."

"It's worth a shot."

"Okay. I'll make an appointment." He left the chair then headed to the door. "I've got to run. I'll see you later."

"Alright." I watched him go, wondering if he had a date or something. I shouldn't care or even think about it. But I did care.

And I did think about it.

***

I got into bed beside Francesca and lay there.

She didn't say a word. She didn't even protest that I was in her bed.

"I miss you…" She was the one person I could talk to about everything. Right now, I wanted to talk about Axel. But since he was her brother I couldn't say anything anyway. Maybe being with her would comfort me.

Francesca was quiet nearly a full minute. "I miss you too."

"I want my friend back."

"I'm still here, Marie. I know I'm not the same as I used to be but I'm still me…deep underneath."

"When do you think you'll be better?"

Francesca shrugged.

"Axel and I are taking you to a therapist."

She immediately turned argumentative. "I don't need a therapist."

"Frankie, you're doing this whether you like it or not. Axel and I have been through hell while you've been decomposing in here. You're going to do this, not for you, but for us."

When I worded it that way, she couldn't refuse. "Okay."

I'd be surprised if she gave me any other response. "How's your arm?"

"It's getting better…"

"What's new with you?" It was sad she had to ask these sorts of questions. She lived with me but she was never truly around.

"Nothing much. I stopped seeing Cade."

"Why? I thought you liked him."

"I did. But I didn't see it going anywhere…" Francesca wasn't close to her brother but I doubt she wanted to listen to me talk about him in a romantic way. Maybe Axel was right. If we did date, it would be too weird.

"That's too bad. You'll find someone else."

"I'm sure I will." I'd just have to stop thinking about Axel to make that happen.

"I'm sure he's with someone by now…" The sorrow in her voice was soul crushing.

I didn't need to ask whom she was referring to. "Axel made it sound like he's just as miserable."

"That doesn't mean he's not with other people…"

Thursday

I didn't know what to say to make her feel better so I didn't say anything at all.

Francesca closed her eyes and didn't speak again.

I lay there with her to find comfort in her despair. I was sad as well, wishing I could be with the one man I couldn't have.

***

We took Francesca to the office and watched her walk through the doors into the therapist's office. Her clothes were loose on her, and she didn't look like herself at all. If Hawke saw her now he may not recognize her.

When the doors shut, we both took a seat and waited.

Axel rested his ankle on the opposite knee and drummed his fingers lightly. He couldn't remain still when he was anxious. Anytime he was expecting serious news he twitched in one way or another. Sometimes, he shook his knee or tapped his foot.

"I'm sure the session will go well." I rested my hand on his wrist and steadied his fingers. The usual jolt of emotion rushed through my body the second we came in contact. I noticed how warm his skin was. Flashbacks of that night we had together came into my mind, strong and powerful. That seemed like a lifetime ago, and it seemed like we were different people at the time.

His fingers stopped moving and he eyed my hand.

I pulled it away when I realized the touch had lingered for too long. I moved my hands to my lap and tried to pretend I didn't feel anything.

He kept his hand there but stopped drumming. "I hope so."

It was still awkward between us, and I was beginning to miss the friendship we once had. We used to have fun together, playing games or just talking. But now it was...stiff. "Are you seeing anyone?" I didn't want to know the answer but I wanted to make a step toward normalcy. Someone had to do it.

Axel turned my way, flinching at the question.

"I want to be friends again. You know, to be ourselves around each other. It's been so strained and...I miss you."

His eyes softened.

"I hate walking on eggshells around you. I want to go back to normal."

"We never talked about our personal lives..."

"I know. But maybe we can start." If we were never going to be romantic we may as well get used to seeing other people.

"Well...I'm not seeing anyone. I haven't seen anyone since..." He fell quiet as he tried to recall it. "Shortly after we slept together."

That was two months ago. He hadn't been with anyone since then? Or recently?

He pulled his hand away from his knee and rubbed his chin. "How about you? Been on any dates lately?" He asked the question like he didn't want the answer.

"No." I hadn't even been seeing my vibrator because I was too bummed.

He didn't hide his relief at that statement.

"What have you been up to lately?"

"I've been working on a portfolio for one of my clients. He's insanely rich—like stupid rich. He wants me to play with his money like a cheap toy. My boss has been micromanaging me about it."

"Sounds stressful."

"It can be. But I'm learning a lot, and that's what's important."

"Where do you intend to go next?"

"I don't know...I'd like to open up my own business someday. I'm not sure how that will work."

"If you put your mind to it I'm sure you'll succeed."

"Maybe..."

We fell into a conversation that was tense in the beginning but slowly began to relax. Soon, we were chuckling again, falling back in line to what we once were. While I felt our friendship return I also felt my heart slip away. For whatever reason, my body yearned for his. I cared about him in a special way, a way I couldn't explain with words. He wasn't my soul mate or even someone I found compatible, but my feelings rang true nonetheless.

***

Axel drove and I sat in the passenger seat. Francesca sat in the rear, her gaze glued outside.

"So...how'd it go?" I decided to do the questioning because Axel was a little harsh.

"It was okay." Francesca leaned her head against the window like she was trying not to fall asleep.

"What did you talk about?" It was unrealistic to expect Francesca to be fixed within an hour but I was hoping she had some progress.

"Just...stuff." Francesca was quiet like a teenager, unwilling to yield any information.

Now I never wanted to have kids.

Axel glanced at me from the driver's seat but held his silence.

"Did you like him?" I asked.

"He was nice," Francesca answered. "Soft spoken and patient."

"Will you go again?"

Francesca paused for nearly a minute. "If you want."

"Do you feel like it's helping?" I asked.

"I don't know," Francesca said. "I don't think anything can help. It's just something I have to deal with on my own."

Axel gripped the steering wheel. "But you aren't—"

I rested my hand on his thigh and gave him a gentle squeeze.

Axel fell silent and didn't make another outburst.

"I think you should keep seeing him," I said calmly. "It's always good to talk to someone."

"I guess," Francesca answered.

I looked out the passenger window and tried to figure out what our next move was. I didn't have any experience with this type of emotional disturbance, but since Francesca was my best friend I'd do my best to figure it out.

***

After a few rounds of Monopoly Francesca went to bed. She didn't say a word as she excused herself. She simply drifted into her bedroom and shut the door.

Axel threw everything in the box. The way he tossed all the money, houses, and pieces showed how irritated he was.

I pitied him. "Maybe you should take a step back and let me handle her."

"It's okay." He tossed the game on the ground.

"I know you have other things to worry about."

"I said it's okay." He sat beside me against the couch and rested his arms on his knees. "She's my family—and we always stick together."

I admired his commitment to his sister despite how crazy it drove him. It was hauntingly similar to what happened to his father, and I knew it was eating him away. "She'll get better, Axel. I promise."

"Don't make promises you can't keep."

"I can keep this one."

He turned to me, his blue eyes surprisingly different from Francesca's. He had a strong jaw like the men in those western movies, and he had the gentleness of a swan in his eyes. He possessed more contradictory traits than anyone I'd ever met. "I hope you're right." He grabbed his satchel beside the couch and opened it. "I got something for you."

"For me?" Axel did enough for me as it was.

"Yeah." He pulled out a handful of different color fabrics. They were an array of colors, from pink and blue to orange and red. "They are slings. I thought you could change them out depending on your wardrobe. You know, so it doesn't stick out as much." He handed them over.

I held them in my fingers and felt the soft fabric. "That was thoughtful..."

"I know you won't be wearing it much longer but at least you'll have some style."

I stared at them in my lap before I turned back to him. Axel always did so many thoughtful things for me. Actually, I felt like he was more thoughtful to me than his own sister. He paid attention to my needs and attended to them without waiting for me to ask for it. He just did it on his own. "Thank you."

"No problem. What color do you want to wear?"

I was wearing pink at the moment. "How about this one?" I held up the material that was similar to the one I was already wearing.

"Excellent choice." He held my arm as he removed the fabric and replaced it with the new one. He adjusted the length so it was exactly perfect for me. He leaned close to me, admiring his handiwork as he adjusted it. His cologne was noticeable and it washed over me like a gentle tide. I was aware of how close his mouth was. He hadn't shaved in a few days and I liked the hair on his chin. No matter what he did he looked handsome—in a painful way.

Thursday

My heartbeat sped up on its own when he was near me. Anytime he touched me my entire body was on fire. I was terrified he would notice, realize how much his presence affected me. Never in my life had I felt this kind of chemistry. Even when we first slept together I didn't feel it then. Everything was different now.

He perfected the sling then leaned back, but the look in his eyes was different. He was staring at me the way I was staring at him. Our heartbeats thudded together as one. I could feel the heat radiating from his body, almost burning me.

How could I keep doing this? How could I keep being his friend but feel something so much more?

He broke the contact then stared at the floor. "Well...it's getting late."

"Yeah."

"I should get home and get some sleep."

"Yeah, me too."

He got up and grabbed his satchel from the floor. He was rushing to leave, trying to get away from me as quickly as possible. "Good night."

"Good night." I wanted him to leave as much as he did. If I got too close to him I'd do something stupid.

He walked out the front door without looking back. When he locked it from the outside, I knew he was really gone and not coming back. With every step he took I wished he would return, come back to me.

But I knew that would never happen.

CHAPTER SIXTEEN

Shallow

Axel

I never forgot what Marie said to me.

I was shallow.

All I cared about was a girl's looks. She had to have the right hair, the perfect body, and she had to have an exquisite face. Without those things I would never pay attention to them.

It was true. And that fact hurt.

In high school Marie was a quiet, geeky girl. Whenever we were in the same room together, she didn't say a word. She was constantly nervous, practically terrified of me. There were a lot of reasons I didn't notice her, but her practical invisibility was the biggest reason of all.

When I saw her again, the first thing I noticed was her confidence. She walked into the room like she owned it, but she didn't seem arrogant about it. There was a fine line there, but she never crossed it.

But I did notice her appearance. In fact, it was the first thing I commented on.

Was I really shallow? Did all I care about was a woman's appearance?

The realization made me feel like shit. I didn't deserve Marie and I would never deserve her. She should be with someone who noticed her perfections right from the beginning. Now I felt like a jerk for coming onto her only when she changed her clothes and did her hair differently.

I was totally an ass.

But I couldn't stop thinking about her.

When I was at work, she came across my mind. When I went home, I was thinking about her too. I hardly went out because I had no interest in meeting women. All I ever wanted to do was be with her.

Damn, I was so confused.

If I was just into her looks why did I think about her all the time? Why did I wonder how she did on her photography test? Why did I constantly do stuff for her? Why did I notice the way her hair framed her face at any given time of day?

I didn't have a clue.

***

I picked up a pizza on the way then walked inside. The TV was on in the living room but no one was watching it. Marie sat at the kitchen table working on homework, and Francesca was nowhere in sight—like usual. "Hey."

She looked up from her laptop and took me in. "Hey."

That old way of communicating was coming back. We said so much with just our eyes and nothing else. I could feel the pressure sitting at the top of my spine, constantly weighing me down. My entire body froze when I was around her, making me feel cold and hot at the same time. She did strange things to my insides, making them contort and behave in the most peculiar ways.

I set the box on the table and grabbed a few plates.

"Frankie already ate."

"She did?" I couldn't hide my surprise. Frankie never ate.

"I made her some macaroni and cheese."

"And she ate it?" Anytime I tried to get anything down her throat it was another world war.

Marie nodded. "I think she's coming around—slowly."

"Halle-fucking-lujah." I fell into the chair and pulled a few pieces onto my plate. It would be a relief not to look after her every single day. I didn't mind helping her, but I hated the stress it placed on my shoulders. Never knowing if she would get better was the worst part.

"Yeah, it is a miracle." She tapped her pencil against her notebook as she read through her notes.

I noticed her arm hung freely by her side, no longer in a cast. "Looking good."

"Oh, thanks." She looked up and moved her shoulder. "The therapist said I didn't need it anymore."

"I told you it would go back to normal." I knew she was seriously worried about her shoulder, assuming it would never return to the way it used to be. Honestly, I was a little worried about it too, but thankfully that didn't happen.

"Now I need to go buy a new car."

"I can help with that. What are you thinking?"

"I don't know...a Toyota or something."

"Well, those are good cars. You can't go wrong with that."

"That's what I'm thinking. And the resale value is high."

"Are you planning on selling it in the future?" I moved onto my second piece.

"Well...my goal is to move to New York eventually. I probably won't need a car at all."

I nodded in understanding. "That makes sense."

"So, I just need something reliable for now."

"And practical." I placed a slice on the plate and pushed it toward her. "Hungry?"

"Thanks." She took a small bite before she set it down.

I rested my elbows on the table as I stared at her. Sometimes I got lost in her appearance. Whenever she was reading something, her eyebrows narrowed. Sometimes they moved depending on what she was thinking or feeling.

I noticed little things like that, even the slight rise of the corner of her mouth.

When she realized I was staring at her, she looked up.

I quickly turned my gaze elsewhere so she wouldn't know I was staring. "So...anything new with you?"

"I have a date later tonight. We're going to the movies."

I felt sick all over again. Somehow, I felt worse than I did when she was seeing Cade. The idea of her touching someone else, or even worse, letting him touch her was sickening. Now I couldn't tell if it was jealousy or rage that worked inside me. "That's great..."

"We met in the cafeteria. He was cute and nice so I decided to give him a chance."

I grabbed another slice of pizza even though I wasn't hungry.

"What about you?" she asked. "Have any dates lined up?"

Hell no. I wasn't even looking. "No."

She nodded then looked down at her laptop again.

I fell silent and seethed to myself. I couldn't be with her but I couldn't stand the idea of her being with anyone else. What was wrong with me? Did Marie mean more to me than I realized? I didn't deserve her but I still didn't want her to be with anyone else.

I didn't get it.

"Axel?"

"Hmm?" I took a bite of my pizza because I realized all I'd been doing was staring at it.

"Are you okay?"

Am I okay? No. Why would I be okay? "I'm fine. I just remembered I left a folder at the office. But I'll just have to get it tomorrow." I finished my pizza then met her gaze.

She didn't look sad at my response but she didn't look happy either. "Okay." She looked back down at her notes and wrote a few sentences.

When her gaze was averted, I returned to suffering in silence.

***

At seven o' clock her date picked her up.

Ugh.

Marie grabbed her jacket from the coat rack. "I'll be back later."

"I'm probably going to go home soon." I didn't want to be here when they got back. What if she invited him to stay over? What if I had to see them kiss on the doorstep?

"Okay." She opened the front door and greeted the guy before they walked to his car at the curb.

I immediately ran to the window to get a peek through the blinds. He was tall, about my height, but he wasn't built like I was. He didn't possess the right muscle mass. And his car was old, like twenty years old. "What a loser..."

"What?"

I jumped nearly ten feet into the air when Francesca walked up behind me. "Shit, don't do that."

"What?" She opened the fridge and grabbed a bottle of water. "What were you doing?"

"Nothing." I walked away from the window and tried to pretend I wasn't spying on Marie.

Francesca eyed me like she didn't believe me, but instead of asking questions like she normally would she walked back into her room.

I sat at the kitchen table and listened to the sound of his car as they drove away. They were probably watching a stupid chick flick and sharing a bucket of popcorn together. Maybe he would buy her a box of Snow Caps, her favorite candy. Maybe they would have a great time and she would forget about me forever.

***

Three hours came and went and I didn't move from my seat at the table. I sat in silence, not having the TV or my iPod for entertainment. The pizza went cold but the box still sat on the counter. Marie's things were still across from me. Her laptop was closed and her notebook was still open.

I should go home but I stayed in the same spot. When they came home, I didn't know what I expected to see. A part of me wanted to wait for her to walk inside and say the date went terrible. Another part of me wanted to be there so she wouldn't invite him to spend the night. And another part of me stayed there because I didn't know what else to do with myself.

Just when I was about to pull out my phone to check the time, I heard voices.

"That was a cute movie." Marie's voice came through the door. "I'd watch it again."

"My cousins saw Zootopia awhile ago," the guy explained. "I thought it would be a cute movie for a date."

"Well, you made a good call."

I rolled my eyes because I already hated this guy.

"Well, good night." Marie's voice was a little more high-pitched than usual, like she was nervous.

"Good night." The guy didn't walk away because there were no footsteps.

He was about to kiss her. I knew it. Somehow, I could feel it in the air.

My hands formed fists and my knuckles turned white.

My heart rate wouldn't slow down.

I wanted to scream.

Without thinking, I hopped out of the chair and stormed to the front door. Marie must have noticed my car in the driveway so she knew I was still at the house. No good would come of this but I wasn't the most reasonable guy at the moment.

I opened the front door. "Hey. How was the movie?"

Her date had just leaned in to kiss her but quickly stepped back when he saw me.

Marie stared at me in complete bewilderment. "Uh..."

"Marie, you have to tell me all about it." I grabbed her by the arm and dragged her inside. "But right now, Francesca needs our help. She's had an episode…"

"Is she okay?" Marie immediately became concerned for her friend.

Now I felt bad for lying. "She's fine. But we should go see her." I turned to her date. "Sorry, Marie has to go. See ya." I shut the door in his face and turned to her.

"So, what happened?" she asked. "Did she call Hawke or something?"

Now that I had her inside and away from her date I didn't know what to do. I always got to these moments then chickened out. "Actually…Francesca is fine."

"What…?"

"There's nothing wrong with her. I mean, there is. But it's nothing new."

She crossed her arms over her chest and stared me down.

"Look, I panicked. I knew he was going to kiss you and I freaked out."

"You freaked out?"

"I didn't want him to kiss you." That was the only explanation I could provide. I already saw Cade kiss her once and I wanted to die. I didn't want to go through that again.

Instead of being moved by that she seemed pissed. "Excuse me?"

"I'm sorry. I should have left you alone—"

"You don't want me but no one else can have me?" she snapped. "That's how it is now?"

"No, not at all. And keep your voice down." I didn't want my sister to hear this conversation.

"I will not keep my voice down," she hissed. "What the hell is wrong with you? What happened to being friends? Friends don't sabotage each other's dates like that."

"I know—"

"You're a jerk, you know that?" She walked around me and threw her purse on the table. "I will kiss as many guys as I want. You have no absolutely no right to interfere with that."

"I know but—"

"Obviously, we can't be friends. Maybe it's best if you just disappeared for a while and let me look after Francesca. I knew you were shallow and I knew you were committed to playing the field, but I had no idea you were this twisted." She marched down the hall to her bedroom. "Good night, Axel." She walked in and slammed the door behind her.

I stood in the entryway and felt my own anger rise. I wasn't shallow. Maybe I was in the past but I'm not anymore. I wasn't some asshole that controlled her every move and manipulated her. All I knew was something clicked inside me. I didn't want some guy touching her because she wasn't his to touch.

She was mine.

I left the house and locked the door behind me. Now all I wanted was to put as much distance between us. Ever since that terrible day all we'd been doing is butting heads nonstop. I was clueless and she was headstrong. We were like gasoline and fire. Together, we exploded.

I got to my car and unlocked it but didn't get inside. I stood there and leaned my forehead against the roof of the car, thinking about everything that just happened that night. Committing to someone terrified me for a million reasons, but I was already committed to her whether I would admit it or not. I wasn't seeing anyone and I didn't even want to see anyone. All I could think about was the one woman I kept hurting.

I listened to the sound of the world, allowing it to clear my head. One street over I could hear a truck passing by. The sound of crickets was in the air, the approach of spring calling their name. Birds stirred in the trees, rustling the leaves. I listened to all of that and felt my heart rate slow. It became so quiet that I could feel my own pulse in my ears.

I turned back to the house and stared at it, noting the dimly lit porch light. It was covered in dust and cobwebs and needed to be changed. Otherwise it wouldn't omit any light at all.

I'd never been more confused in my life. I didn't know what I wanted, but I knew what I didn't want.

I didn't want this.

I walked back to the house and got the door unlocked. When I walked inside, all the lights were out. Marie must have heard the front door when I left and closed up the house.

Thursday

I stared down the hallway and noticed her bedroom door was closed. So was Francesca's. I stared at it for several heartbeats before I approached it with light footsteps. My hand found the knob and I noticed how easily it turned.

I held my breath before I walked inside.

She was lying on her side facing the opposite wall. The sheets were pulled to her shoulder and she lied still, not hearing me come inside.

I shut the door behind me and approached her bed. I stared at her outline in the fabric, noting her slender waist and long legs. All I wanted to do was crawl into that bed with her, to pass the night with her in my arms.

I undressed and kicked my clothes away into a pile. When I was only in my briefs, I pulled back the covers and got into bed beside her. I expected her to jolt upright and scream. The intrusion would terrify anyone.

I placed my hand on her shoulder, silently telling her I was there.

She sat up and looked at me, clearly expecting to see Francesca instead. She took me in with her green eyes, taking in everything without giving anything away.

Now that I was here I didn't know what else to do. I didn't come here for sex. That was the last thing I wanted. All I really wanted, if she would allow it, was to hold her. "Marie, you were wrong about me."

She turned over and faced me head-on.

"I may not have noticed you all those years ago, but I notice you now—in a different way. When you were in the hospital, you didn't have any makeup on. And that's when I noticed all the small freckles on your face. There are twelve of them. I've counted many times."

She searched my gaze, her hostility slowly fading.

"You have thick eyelashes, the kind that don't need any mascara. I've never counted the strands but I know you have many." My eyes moved to her lips. "Your upper lip reminds me of a bow. You know, the kind Katniss Everdeen uses. Whenever you're sad, your eyes dilate in this special way... That's how I can read you sometimes."

Her lips parted slightly as she listened, her breathing increased.

"When I first saw you, I thought you were the hottest chick I'd ever seen. I wanted to fuck your brains out and never speak of it again. All I wanted was to hit the sheets and add you to my list. I'm not going to lie about that. We both know that night didn't mean anything—to either one of us." It was a fling I wouldn't have thought twice about if I didn't see her every day. "But I couldn't stop thinking about that night after it happened. And when you weren't there the next morning, I actually wished you were. I'd never felt that way before. And that's when everything changed.

"When you play Monopoly, you always have to be the hat. When you have your coffee in the morning, you can only use almond creamer. When you shower, you always hum. I can hear it even in the living room. And every time Francesca struggles, your heart breaks. You're selfless and loyal, one of the most amazing people I've ever met. For the past two months, I've begun to notice every little detail about you, from the way your hair falls after you tuck it behind your ear to the sound of your heartbeat when I'm close enough to hear it." I hadn't planned on saying any of this, but now that the words were coming out, they kept going. "I think you're beautiful because that's painstakingly obvious to anyone with eyes. But, I think your heart is more beautiful than anything else. I see the way you look at me, like I'm someone worth looking at. You understand my perfections as well as my flaws but it doesn't change your opinion about me. Despite what's happened in my life you don't think less of me."

Her eyes softened further, all of her grudges disappearing.

"You were wrong, Marie. I'm not shallow—anymore."

Her eyes took in my features, noting the sincerity in my eyes. They lingered on my lips for several heartbeats before they looked at me again.

"I don't want to be with anyone else, and I don't want you to be with anyone either. I don't know what I can offer you or where this will go but...I want to be here." I didn't want to sleep alone in my bed tonight, and I didn't want there to be a night when she slept with someone else besides me.

She slowly lowered herself back to the pillow, her eyes still trained on me.

I took that as an invitation so I lay beside her and hooked my arms around her. The second I held her it felt right. She was warm and soft just as she used to be, but feeling her skin alleviated all the pain I was carrying. Just touching her made me feel like I was in heaven. I'd wanted to do this for so long and now it was really happening. I pulled her to my chest and locked my arms so she could never escape. Feeling this kind of intimacy...felt so damn good.

Her hand glided up my neck until it cupped the side of my face. Her thumb rested on my bottom lip, feeling the invisible grooves of the skin. She stared at it before she leaned in and lightly pressed her mouth against mine.

I died and came back to life.

It was a closed mouth kiss but it felt incredible. It was better than any kiss I had before, that was including the one I had with her. Something about her drove me wild, made me feel things I didn't think were possible. My heart swelled to twice its size and burned from the emotion.

She pulled away and rested her face near mine on the pillow. Her hands glided over my body, feeling my definition of warmth.

I loved it when she touched me.

I wanted to kiss her all night, to feel those soft lips over and over. But I steadied myself because just looking at her was enough. We were wrapped around one another in this bed, becoming a single person.

Her fingers dug into my hair, fingering the short strands. Her legs were wrapped around my waist, keeping me anchored to her. "It's never felt so good to be wrong..."

Thursday

CHAPTER SEVENTEEN

Love Is In The Air

Axel

I'd never slept so well in my life.

I opened my eyes to Marie, a woman beautiful on the inside as well as the outside. The joy that rushed through me in that moment couldn't be explained to any sane person. At that moment, I was slightly out of my mind.

Because I was happy.

She looked back at me, her make up running from the night before. Her hair was tangled from all the times I ran my fingers through it. Despite all those things, I'd never seen a more beautiful image.

"Morning."

Her voice cracked. "Morning." She arched her back and stretched across the sheets.

"Sleep well?"

"Very." She ran her hand up my chest.

Thursday

"I guess I can't blame you. Sleeping with a sexy beast would make anyone sleep peacefully."

"A sexy beast, huh?"

"Yeah."

"And what am I?"

"A sexier beast." I rubbed my nose against hers and gripped her hip at the same time.

She chuckled then slid from my arms. "I wish I didn't have school today..."

Fuck, I had work today. I glanced at her clock and realized I still had some time—if I didn't shower and wore the same clothes as yesterday.

"Can I get a ride?" she asked. "I still have to buy my car."

Now I'd definitely be late. "Sure."

We both threw on our clothes then walked into the living area. I fixed my hair as much as possible but it was still messy. Everyone at the office would know I did something last year, but I guess there were worse things.

Francesca walked into the kitchen, wearing the same pajamas she'd been wearing all week.

The last thing I needed was for Francesca to figure out what was going on with Marie and I. It might send her off the deep end or do something worse. "Just waiting for Marie so I can take her to school." I straightened my tie and tried to act nonchalant.

Francesca opened the fridge and poured herself a glass of orange juice.

Was she onto me? "Just here to pick up Marie…nothing else. She still hasn't gotten a new car yet. I'm just trying to be a nice guy. That's it. Nothing else. Nope."

Francesca turned around. "Why are you being weird?"

"Weird?" I gave a high maniacal laugh like it was the funniest thing I've ever heard. "Me? Weird? No."

Francesca kept eyeing me like I was a freak. "Whatever…" She walked back into her bedroom with the glass in her hand.

I breathed a sigh of relief when she left.

Marie walked in, looking like she just stepped out of the salon. "Ready to go?"

"I think Frankie was onto us but I took care of that. She doesn't know a thing."

Marie grabbed her bag and shouldered it. "Why would she be onto us?"

"She's smart."

"But she's not a mind reader."

"She probably heard us arguing last night."

"Even then, that's not conclusive." She walked out of the house and I followed behind her. "Don't overthink it, Axel."

I wasn't sure how we were going to explain everything to my sister. Would she be freaked out by it? Supportive? Indifferent? We got into the car and I drove her to school, my former joy completely gone. Now I was stressed about Francesca and how to handle it.

Marie eyed me from the passenger seat, knowing something was up. "What is it?"

"Just worried about my sister."

"And us?"

I nodded.

"There's nothing to worry about. She'll get over it."

"Probably." I remember what she said to me when she and Hawke got together. My opinion was irrelevant in the matter. "But do you think it's a good idea for us to be together in front of her?"

"I don't catch your meaning."

"Well, she's depressed about Hawke, right? Would seeing us together just make her more depressed?" I wasn't the most sensitive guy in the world and I struggled to understand what Francesca meant most of the time, but I thought that might be a problem.

"I didn't think of that..."

"What do we do?" She was starting to come out of her room a little more, and she was eating more too. It would suck if she retreated and had to start over—because of us.

"I guess we can keep it a secret. Honestly, it won't be that hard. She's hardly around, and when she is she's pretty oblivious to everything around her."

"True."

"When the time is right, we'll tell her."

"Sounds good to me." I wasn't sure what Marie and I were, exactly. But I guess she was my girlfriend. I'd never had one before so I couldn't be sure. Is that how monogamous people referred to each other?

I arrived at the school and parked in the same place I always did. "I'll be here at the same time."

"Thanks for driving me around, dashing man."

I didn't understand her reference so I just stared at her.

"Remember...I offered to take UBER but you said a free ride with a dashing man was better."

Then it became clear to me. "Of course. How could I forget?"

She sat still and didn't get out. Instead, she looked at me.

I rested my arm on the center console and leaned toward her. "You want a kiss goodbye?"

"Why do you think I'm still sitting here?"

I chuckled then leaned closer to her, my eyes on her lips. When I kissed her last night, it set all my nerves on fire. It was too much stimulation for one man. I prepared for that same explosion, knowing she would blow my mind like always.

I kissed her softly on the mouth, feeling her lips move past mine. The kiss was gentle with restricted passion, but I immediately wanted to turn it up a notch once I felt her tongue. I wanted to kiss her forever and only stop when the world came to an end.

She pulled away before things could get too heated. "I'll see you later."

Why couldn't later be now? "Alright."

"Bye." She gave me a smile before she got out and walked to class. She had the cutest smile I'd ever seen. Her teeth were perfectly straight, and her eyes matched the happiness in that grin.

I missed it the second it was gone.

***

We walked inside the house and set our things down.

"What should we do for dinner?" Marie asked. She wore a teal blouse with gold hoop earrings hanging from her earlobes. She always dressed classy but looked sexy at the same time.

"How about I take you out?"

"Me?" She leaned against the table as she looked up at me.

"Yeah. You." I stepped closer to her, wanting to kiss her just like I did in the car. "I want to take you out on a date."

"That sounds nice."

"It'll be romantic as hell."

"Ooh...I like romantic."

I came closer to her, my chest almost touching hers. "So, you'll go out with me?"

"I would...but not tonight."

"Why not?"

She nodded toward the bedroom. "Frankie."

I rolled my eyes. "She won't even notice if we're gone."

"Maybe. But one of us is usually here with her."

I was her brother, not her babysitter. "Then how about a date here? We'll have some dinner and wine. Then I'll feel you up on the couch."

She chuckled because she knew I was joking. "So much for romantic as hell."

"Have you ever been felt up on the couch?" I asked. "It's a lot more romantic than you think."

She chuckled again. "Oh really?"

"Really." I wiggled my eyebrows at her.

"So, what's for dinner?"

"Depends." I walked to the refrigerator and took a peek inside. There wasn't much to choose from because I hadn't been shopping in a while. "How does leftover lasagna sound?"

She cringed.

"Frozen corndogs?"

"Those are delicious—but no."

I searched through the cabinets. "Well...this date is going well."

She came to my side and pulled out a carton of pasta and a bottle of marinara. "We'll have spaghetti."

"Perfect. Like the Lady and the Tramp."

Marie gave me a funny look.

I realized what I just said. "Hey, I grew up with a sister..."

"That forced you to watch it?" she teased.

"It was on in the background all the time..." I snatched the pasta and sauce away from her. "Now let me get to work."

"How about I cook?" She snatched it out of my hands. "You've been taking care of me every day. Let me do something for you."

I wasn't going to argue with that. "Perfect. I'll just sit down and watch you work it in the kitchen." I grabbed a beer from the fridge and took a seat, ready to gawk at her all I wanted.

She gave me a smile before she began dinner. "How was work?"

"Boring. What's new?"

"I know you like your job." She brought the pot to a boil and tossed the pasta inside.

"I like my discipline—not my job." Two very different things. "One day I'll move to the big city and find something better—with better pay."

"But you don't like it at all?"

I shrugged. "I'm an intern. People pile crap on me all day long."

When she moved around the kitchen, she swayed her hips in a sexy way. Her blonde hair trailed down her back, making her look even more beautiful. I'd always preferred brunettes to blondes, but Marie was a major exception.

When dinner was ready, she placed the dishes on the table.

"Mmm...this looks good." I eyed the steam coming from the noodles.

"It's no Mac and Cheese, but it'll be tasty." Marie walked down the hall to fetch Francesca.

I forgot about her altogether.

Marie returned without her.

Thankfully.

"She said she's not hungry."

"What's new?" I scooped the pasta onto her plate before I made my own. "Maybe she'll starve to death and end the problem altogether."

Marie kicked me.

"Ouch...right in the shin."

"Don't say things like that."

"What? It's true."

"No, it's not." She used her spoon to spin the pasta before she took a bite.

I forgot about our argument in light of what she was doing. "You actually eat pasta like that?"

"What?" She stopped and looked up at me. "This is how you're supposed to do it."

"But no one ever does anything the way they're supposed to. You're actually doing it."

"Well, I'm on a date. I want to impress you."

I chuckled. "You impressed me a long time ago."

Her foot moved to mine under the table and rubbed against it gently.

I smiled at the quiet way she apologized to me for kicking me earlier.

Francesca left her bedroom then entered the kitchen.

I quickly pulled my feet away even though she couldn't see them. "What brings you in here?" I tried to act casual but failed miserably.

Francesca gave me the same look she gave me that morning. "Just getting some water…" She grabbed it out of the fridge then retreated back to her room.

The second she was out of earshot Marie turned on me. "You need to chill out."

"She caught me by surprise. What if I were kissing you?"

"But you weren't."

"But if I was…?"

"But you weren't." She rolled her eyes and kept eating.

I sipped my beer but kept eyeing the hallway, wondering if she would reappear at any moment. Sneaking around might not be as easy as I imagined.

***

"Alright." I spoke loudly so Francesca could hear me in her room. "I'm going home now."

Marie rolled her eyes.

"I'll see you later." I was practically yelling.

Marie opened the door like I was leaving. Then she shut it when I was gone.

Thankfully, Francesca's door remained closed.

Marie took my hand and guided me into her bedroom. Once the door was shut I could breathe easy again. She wouldn't walk in here for any reason so I was safe.

Marie had the master bedroom so we went into her private bathroom and brushed our teeth. I stood at the sink and waited for her to finish before I snatched it away and brushed my gums.

"What are you doing?" She gave me a repulsed look.

"Brushing my teeth." I scrubbed my mouth then spit in the sink.

"But that's my tooth brush."

"You kiss me so what does it matter?" I rinsed my mouth before I dropped her toothbrush in the cup. "And you've done much nastier things..." I walked into her bedroom then stripped my clothes away until I was in my boxers.

"Bring your own over next time." She opened a drawer and pulled out a nightshirt.

"Why? I'd rather share with you." I came behind her and wrapped my arms around her waist.

She pulled her top off and unclasped her bra without breaking her stride.

I'd always seen her naked, but the action caused me to stop breathing. I stared at her back, seeing the definition of the muscle there. Her spine was noticeable, and the muscle around it popped. She was petite but built with muscle so she obviously hit the weights a few times a week. I stared at the individual grooves of her body, loving the way she looked. I wanted to sprinkle kisses everywhere.

Marie pulled on the new top and covered her flawless skin, hiding the steep arch in her back.

Thursday

I stopped the protest before it escaped my lips.

She removed her jeans and kicked them to the side. Her shirt was long enough to cover her ass and panties. When she turned around, she examined my chest, noting its hardness. I tried to hit the gym as often as I could, and I was glad she appreciated it.

Now that I was alone with her I didn't have to worry about Francesca catching us. I could just be with her—do anything I wanted. I guided her to the bed then moved on top of her. Even though we already had a passionate night together it didn't really count. It was meaningless and aggressive, and I didn't feel the way I did now.

I stared at her lips and watched them slightly part in excitement. Her thighs were pressed tightly together and she writhed for me. I'd already had her once and I wanted her again, but now I wanted something else.

Something more.

I separated her knees with my hips and moved directly over her, my hard-on in my boxers directly next to her panties. Using my arms as anchors I positioned myself over her and looked her in the eye. Then I leaned in and did the thing I'd wanted to do all day.

I kissed her.

My kiss was soft and slow, just the way it should be. I had nowhere to go and nothing better to do, so I treasured every second of it. There was no rush, no need to get to the physical stuff. Kissing her, feeling her like this, was all I wanted.

Her lips moved with mine, dancing together like they could communicate. When her warm breath filled my lungs, the air on the back of my neck stood on end. Kissing was something I hardly did, and when it happened, it didn't last long. I preferred the dirtier things. But with Marie, this was all I wanted to do.

Her arms wrapped around my neck and she kissed me harder, her passion guiding her forward. Her legs wrapped around my waist and she squeezed me gently.

I grinded against her gently, the definition of my cock giving her the right amount of friction. After a few thrusts I felt moisture between her legs seep through her panties and soak my boxers.

It was hot.

I knew she wanted me and I wanted her, but I was content doing this. I could kiss her forever, feel those soft lips until the end of time. Marie dragged her sharp nails down my back, cutting into me in a pleasurable way. Soft moans entered my mouth, and she writhed underneath me like she wanted more.

It was the hottest make out session I've ever had.

"I could do this forever." I sucked her bottom lip before I kissed her again.

She ran her hands up my back, feeling the muscle underneath the skin. "That sounds nice."

I kissed the area along her jaw then moved down to her neck, wanting to taste her everywhere. I'd already been between her legs and I wanted to revisit that magical place but I was fine where I was.

Marie's fingers played with the hem of my boxers before she pulled them down slowly.

I grabbed her hands and pinned them above her head. "I just want to kiss you."

She tried to get free but couldn't free herself from the restraints. "Why?"

"Because I love it." I brushed my nose against her before I returned my mouth to hers. Our tongues danced together, teasing one another as we received mutual satisfaction. Our bodies were connected just as much as our minds were. Somehow, it was better than sex.

I released her wrists and allowed her to touch me again. She felt the details of my chest and stomach, feeling the hard grooves that separated the masses of muscle. Her fingers traced the area like she was trying to memorize it.

My hips grinded against her, my cock moving over her folds through her lacey panties. The moisture was soaked into my body and I could feel it on the skin of my dick.

Fuck.

Her hands went to my ass and she gripped it tightly as she kissed me harder, breathing fast into my mouth. She was moaning with me, not bothering to try and remain quiet.

I rubbed against her harder, loving the way she was turned on. I wanted to make her come like this, without me touching her.

Her fingers dug into the fabric. "Axel…"

I remembered the way she said that before, on a night similar to this one. I loved hearing it again, bringing my body to a new level of heat. I was an inferno about to burn everything around me.

I rubbed myself against her harder, dry humping her in a way I never did as a teenager. The fact it was so amateur somehow made it sexy. We were so hot for each other we didn't need to have intercourse to get off.

She stopped kissing me and just breathed into my mouth, moaning loudly. "God, yes…" She clung to me tightly, spiraling out of control. Her nails almost drew blood because they were digging into me so deeply.

I didn't think I could find a release like this, but seeing her eyes roll into the back of her head as she continued to moan for me hit my trigger. With my lips pressed to hers I came inside my boxers, unable to recall the last time I ever did that. I filled the fabric and moaned the entire way. When I was finished, I remained on top of her, out of breath and satisfied.

She dug her fingers into my hair and felt the sweat that formed on the back of my neck. "I feel like an eighth grader."

I chuckled. "Me too. But I like it."

"I like it too." She kissed the corner of my mouth.

"Then I think we should keep going." I sealed my mouth over hers and kissed her slowly, starting all over. I hadn't kissed a woman like this since I could remember.

There was nothing else I wanted to do than feel her mouth move with mine. It felt right.

It felt like we should have started this sooner.

***

Alexia walked into my cubicle wearing a dress that was way too short for the office. "Hey, Axel."

I was reading through a portfolio when she stopped by. "Yo. What's up?" I lowered the folder and looked at her, trying to get Marie out of my head. She'd been circling there all day. I couldn't concentrate on anything.

"You doing anything later?"

I looked up at the question. Alexia and I had hooked up a few times in the past. Then she got a boyfriend because I wouldn't commit. From the sound of things they weren't together anymore. "Why?"

"Wanted to see if you wanted to get a drink." She had long brown hair, the kind that reached past her boobs.

"Didn't work out with Tom?"

"No...he wasn't right for me."

"What a shame." I tossed the folder on the desk. "He seemed like a nice guy."

"Spent way too much time with his mother." She rolled her eyes.

"A mama's boy, huh?" I was a bit of one when I was growing up.

"So, are you free?"

"Actually, no. And I have a feeling I won't be free for a long time."

She cocked her head slightly.

"You see, I have a girlfriend." I grinned from ear-to-ear. "Her name is Marie. She's got blonde hair, green eyes, and a body that would make you cry yourself to sleep."

"Oh…good for you." She didn't bother hiding her disappointment. She clearly wanted a good lay without having to do any work.

"Thanks. She's great. No, I take that back. She's perfect."

"I didn't see you as the boyfriend type…" She crossed her arms over her chest.

"I'm not," I admitted. "But this one is different. She's cute and smart…she's got the whole package."

"And other women don't?" she asked in offense.

"That's not what I said." But it's pretty much what I meant. "This girl is special. I can't really explain why."

"Well, I'm happy for you."

Bullshit. "Thanks."

"Give me a call if things go south."

I didn't like to think like that. "We'll cross that bridge when we come to it."

***

Marie was working so I decided to stop by.

When I walked inside, she was standing at the counter, snacking on a chocolate chip cookie. No one was in line, and she was slacking off. She wore a black apron that was tight around her waist, highlighting her hourglass figure.

I'd never seen anyone look so good eating a cookie.

I walked up to the register and rang the bell. "Can I get some service?"

She quickly shoved the cookie in her pocket then turned to the counter. "Shit, you scared me."

"Don't you eat in the back?"

"Well, I was bored and we've been dead all day." She came to the register then stared at me, hardly able to contain her happiness at seeing me there. "Thought you would stop by?"

"I missed you." I'd been thinking about her all day and I was going crazy without her.

"Yeah?" She leaned over the counter and lowered her voice. "I missed you too."

"I missed you more." When I woke up that morning, I had to hightail it out of the house before Francesca woke up. I wish I could just wake up there on a Saturday and lay in bed with her all day.

"Doubtful. So, you want anything?"

"Can I get you to go?"

"Do these cheesy lines actually work?"

"You tell me." I got her in the sack once, and I got her to be my girlfriend on top of that. If you ask me, I knew a thing or two.

"How about a black coffee?"

"Sounds perfect. I'm going to need it if I'm going to stay up all night." I set the cash on the counter.

"All night?" She put the cash in the register and gave me change. "I don't know. I need some sleep tonight. Didn't get much last night."

"Well, if we get rid of Francesca we can get right to it after work."

"Tempting..."

"Or you could come to my place."

She shook her head. "I don't like leaving her alone."

My sister was really cramping my style. She needed to get over this break up and move on. "I guess those therapy sessions aren't working."

"I'm not sure what would work."

"Slapping her." I wasn't kidding at this point. She completely stopped living just because Hawke lived. I didn't care how heartbroken she was. There was no real justification for that. I really liked Marie and I didn't want to lose her, but if she walked out on me I'd still get up and go to work the next day.

"We just have to be a little more patient..."

I was starting to think she would never get better. Marie and I babysat her as much as possible but that wasn't doing any good. "My patience is waning. I doubt I can put up with it much longer. If my mom were still around she'd get Frankie out of bed."

"What about Yaya? Do you think she can help?"

"I don't want to bring her into this. It's a burden no one should have to deal with..." Including Marie and I. I took the coffee and tightened the lid on it. "Thanks for the Joe."

"No problem."

"My girlfriend serves the best cup of coffee in town."

"She serves the best something else too." She gave me a playful look before she left the counter and kept working.

I froze on the spot, thinking about the specifics of what she meant.

CHAPTER EIGHTEEN

Play Date

Marie

I parked my new car in the driveway then killed the engine. It was a white Toyota Corolla and I got a great deal on it—thanks to Axel.

He parked his truck then came to my side. "She's a beauty, ain't she?"

"She is."

He nudged me in the side. "I was talking about you."

"Oh…" My mouth formed an unstoppable smile. Ever since Axel came into my bedroom and said all those pretty things everything had been different. We were playful with each other and happy. After the way he rejected me I didn't think we would ever find our way to each other. But somehow, we had.

He put his arm around my waist and walked me to the front door. "Going off-roading?"

"In a little car?"

"You could tear up the beach if you really wanted to."

"No. I need to keep that car in good shape if I'm going to sell it eventually."

He got the door unlocked and we walked inside. "You're no fun."

"I'm responsible."

"Like I said, you're no fun." He shut the door behind us and leaned in, his lips teasing mine.

I loved his kisses. They were so precise and delicious. He was never sloppy, always giving me embraces that made me lose my breath. He continued to torture me, brushing his lips past mine in a torturous way. Then he finally pressed his mouth to mine, a closed-mouth kiss.

My body shivered from the heat.

When he pulled away, his action was full of reluctance, like he didn't want to be anywhere else except pressed against my lips. "So...should we check on that worthless piece of shit?" With every passing day he was becoming more resentful of his sister.

Her behavior was extreme, but it was difficult for me to be mad. She was my best friend in the whole world. All I wanted was for her to get better. "She'll come out when she's ready." I set my purse on the kitchen table and pulled out my school stuff.

"Hey, what are you doing Saturday night?" He sat in the chair beside me with a beer in his hand.

"Axel, it's four in the afternoon."

He twisted the cap off. "It's never too early to start drinking. Now answer the question."

"I think I'm spending the evening with my new boyfriend."

"Yeah?" The playfulness entered his gaze. "He's cute, huh?"

"Oh yeah."

"Really sexy?"

"I'd say so."

"You can't keep your hands off him?"

My hand moved to his thigh. "I struggle."

He nodded, liking the course of this conversation.

"You have something in mind?"

"My office is having a going-away party for one of the partners. I want you to be my date."

My body deflated. "That's romantic..."

"I'll feel you up in the bathroom or something."

"Now that's too romantic." I rolled my eyes.

"You don't have to go but I'm pretty much stuck."

I didn't want to spend the evening with a bunch of suits but I wanted to be with Axel. The party wouldn't last forever and then we could have our own fun. "I'll go."

"You'll be my date?"

"Yep."

"Be warned. I'm gonna squeeze your ass at some point during the night."

"Be warned. Your jaw is going to be busted at some point during the night."

He chuckled, amused by my feistiness. "It'll be worth it." He set his beer down and leaned into me, his hand slowly snaking into my hair. His touches were always gentle but ignited so much heat. His thumb traced the skin around my ear and then he leaned into me, his lips coming right for mine.

I'd imagined his kiss a million times when I was growing up. I always wanted to be one of the girls he fancied, the ones he kissed in his car in the parking lot by the gymnasium. Now I was.

He pressed his mouth to mine and consumed me, taking me to a place that bordered dreams and reality. I'd been kissed by many men but none of them made me feel like this. Axel had a special touch, something about him that drove me wild.

Footsteps sounded in the hallway.

Axel quickly pulled away and grabbed his beer like nothing just happened. He looked out the window. "Yeah, and then she was like, 'I love you. You're the one.' Then I was like, 'Uh, woman. We just met.' It was an ordeal." He took a long drink to cover up his nervousness.

I had no idea what he was talking about.

Francesca walked into the kitchen and pretty much ignored us. She opened the fridge and grabbed a piece of cheese. Her clothes were several sizes too big for her, and it didn't look good. Any fat she had disappeared, but so did her muscle.

"Hey," I said. "How's your day?"

"It's okay." She picked at the slice of cheese, like she didn't want to eat it and had to force herself.

How could she continue like this? It'd been months. "I got a new car. Want to see it?"

"I saw it through the window." She walked out of the kitchen without saying another word. Her bedroom door shut a moment later.

Axel was seething in silence, his anger palpable in every corner of the room.

I placed my arm on his bicep, silently calming him. He didn't handle his frustration as well as I did. His first impulse was to come out swinging, screaming at the top of his lungs.

"I don't know how much longer I can be patient…"

"Hold on a little longer."

He stared at the window and clenched his fists, his knuckles turning white.

***

Axel whistled when I opened the door. "Da-yum."

My cheeks tinted even though I tried to fight it. I appreciated the compliments but I didn't want him to know I lived for them. "Thanks." I tucked my clutch under my arm and stepped out.

"Whoa, hold on." He raised both hands. "I want to see the whole thing. Turn."

"What is this? A fashion show?"

"A private one."

Thursday

I slowly turned around, letting him see me at different angles. When I got to my back, he took in a deep breath.

"Marie, you have one sexy back."

I was wearing a backless dress that was open until the top of my ass. It revealed everything, my spine and my shoulder blades. When I put it on, I hoped I would get this reaction from him.

"Alright. Let's go back inside." He reached for the door handle. "I need to get that dress off pronto."

I laughed and pushed him back. "We'll be late."

"Who cares? It's a stupid work party." He pressed me against the door and lowered his voice. "I'd rather eat you out than have whatever crap they're serving."

The heat flushed through my body again, burning me like I was on fire. My thighs automatically pressed together, and I suspected I'd have to change my panties before the night was over.

"Lets go back inside." He reached for the door handle again.

"How about we go to your apartment instead?"

His eyes narrowed, intrigued.

"After the party."

His eyes fell all over again. "I'd rather get fired at this point."

"Come on, the wait will make it worth it." I took his hand and pulled him to his truck.

He growled from behind me, clearly staring at my back. When we got to the truck, he opened the door for me but gave me a terrifying look at the same time. He squeezed my wrist like he couldn't control himself. "You. Drive. Me. Mad." He released me before he walked around the truck.

His words echoed in my mind long after he said them. I felt the heat reach every point on my body, burning slowly. At some point during the night the heat would smolder into an unstoppable explosion, burning everyone and everything.

***

The dinner was in a conference room at a hotel. The second we walked inside I was surprised so many people attended. I didn't realize so many people worked at Axel's company. In my mind, I pictured twenty people in a tiny office space.

Axel had his arm tightly wrapped around me, pulling me into his side with no intention of ever letting me go. "Lifestyles of the rich and the famous, huh?"

"Yeah…" It was nice but not enough to make me envious.

He pulled me to the door and got me a glass of wine.

"So, what do I need to know for this party?"

"Nothing."

"Nothing?" He wasn't going to give me a heads up at all?

"All you need to do is stand there and make eyes at me. That's why I brought you."

"As a trophy?"

"Not really. You can't feel up a trophy in the bathroom."

"Okay...now I don't think you're kidding." I wasn't letting anyone feel me up in the bathroom at some work party. Maybe one day, but not today.

"Maybe I'm not." He leaned in and gave me a smile.

"You aren't feeling up anything but yourself tonight."

He shrugged. "I've done it before. It's not bad."

I slapped his arm playfully.

He chuckled and brought me in closer to his side. "Honestly, most of the people I work with are pretty boring. Just be yourself and everything will be fine." His hand rested on the small of my back and he dug his fingers into me slightly. He pressed a kiss to the corner of my mouth, making me rethink a make out session in the bathroom.

Axel took my hand and introduced me to a few of his colleagues, including the senior partner of the company. Like Axel warned, they were pretty stiff and boring. Even with the glasses of wine in their hands they were uptight. Axel couldn't be more different from them.

At least it was an open bar.

"Hey, Axel." A brunette woman walked up to him but her eyes were on me, sizing me up.

"Hey, Alexia. Having a good time?"

"I'd have a better time if I were getting paid to be here." She kept glancing at me.

I would have to be an idiot not to notice her beauty. She had a petite frame but womanly curves. Her make up was excessive but it looked good on her. She seemed to have it all, the looks and the body.

I tried not to be jealous.

"Are you going to introduce me?" Alexia crossed her arms over her chest.

"Oh, sorry." He turned to me. "Alexia, this is Marie."

That's it? Just Marie?

She shook my hand. "It's nice to meet you."

"You too." *Not really.*

"Well, I'll see you around." She flipped her hair over one shoulder and walked away.

I knew I shouldn't blow up at Axel but I was pissed he didn't introduce me properly. Did he not want attractive women to know he was taken? Was he being a jerk right under my nose?

Axel turned to me, clueless to my anger. "She works in the cubicle across from mine."

"Yeah?" I couldn't keep the anger out of my tone.

"She and I had a fling awhile back. We even stayed at the office late and did it on my boss's desk." He chuckled like he thought it was hilarious. "We never got caught."

Why the hell was he telling me this?

He finished his glass then eyed mine. "You want another?"

I wanted to shatter the glass over his skull. I knew it wasn't the best idea to make a scene but I was beyond pissed. Just earlier today everything seemed great between us, but now he was showing his true colors. "No. And I never want another one." I pushed past him and immediately headed for the exit. I tried not to walk too fast but I was practically running. Was I stupid for ever thinking Axel could really be the man I wanted?

"Whoa, hold on." He grabbed me by the arm just when I left the conference room. "What just happened?"

I twisted out of his grasp. "You're an asshole. That's what happened."

The same blank look was on his face. "Marie, what did I do?"

He was really that clueless? "Forget about me and go feel up Alexia in the bathroom. I'm sure she wouldn't mind." I stormed off again, determined to never look at him again.

"Marie, wait." He caught up to me again and intersected his body in my path. "Does this have to do with Alexia?"

He was so goddamn stupid. "I thought when we agreed to be together you were going to get your shit together. I thought you would treat me right, not run around behind my back. You're an asshole." I pushed him back and moved around him.

This time he grabbed me by both shoulders and shoved me into the wall, keeping me stuck there like glue. "Marie, I'm honestly clueless to what's going on right now. But I know I haven't done anything behind your back so speak in terms I can understand."

"You introduced me as Marie, like I was your friend or something."

"No, I didn't."

"Yes. You. Did." I was standing right there.

"I did?" he asked in confusion.

"Yes." I wanted to punch him in the face.

"Well, she already knows who you are. It would be redundant to call you my girlfriend twice."

"She already knows who I am?" *Like I would believe that.*

"Yeah. The other day we were talking and she asked me out. I told her I had a girlfriend." His hands gripped my shoulders tightly, not allowing me to escape.

"She asked you out?" Now I was going to knock her out.

"Well, she didn't ask me out on a date," he said. "She just wanted to hook up."

And that was supposed to make things better?

"So I told her I was with you. When she and I were fooling around, she wanted a commitment, but I didn't want to give it to her. I think she was just surprised that I had a girlfriend at all."

Now I was calming down—a little. "And why did you tell me about the two of you fooling around?"

He shrugged. "Because it happened. Aren't couples honest with each other?"

Axel really had no idea what he was doing. "Honesty is good, yes. But giving more information than necessary is not. I didn't want to know that you had a thing with Alexia."

"What does it matter?" he asked. "She didn't mean anything to me."

"The idea of you touching anyone but me makes me sick."

He grinned.

I slapped his arm. "You aren't supposed to be happy."

"Then what am I supposed to be? I'm confused."

I pushed his arms down then gripped my skull. "Do I need to teach you everything?"

"You tell me."

"Just filter your words, Axel. Don't tell me stuff I don't need to know."

"But then I feel like I'm lying."

"It's not lying."

Now he looked more confused than ever. "So, if we run into a girl I've slept with, you don't want to know about it?"

"Precisely." Honestly, I could figure it out based on their interaction.

"Okay...and you won't get mad at me for lying?"

"It's not lying."

"So, you won't be mad at me?"

"No, Axel."

"Alright." He lowered his hands to his sides. "So...are you going to keep running? Or are we okay?"

It was difficult to be mad at someone when his only crime was being naïve. Axel wasn't purposely hurtful. He just didn't know anything about women—or relationships. "Yes. We're okay."

He returned his arm around my waist and guided me back into the conference room. "Okay. I won't tell you about all the other workers I've slept with."

I sighed in irritation but didn't say anything. Maybe one day he would get it.

***

We sat at a table with our glasses of wine in front of us. Some people were dancing and others were mingling. Every time I saw a pretty girl I wondered if Axel had already been with her.

Axel rested his hand on my thigh and glanced at me every few minutes, clearly checking to see if I was having a good time. "We'll stay for another hour then we'll go."

"Okay." When I looked across the room, I thought I saw someone I knew. But there was no way it was really him. I must have been imagining things, but then again, why would I hallucinate someone I hardly thought about?

"What?" Axel noticed the way my thigh tensed under his hand.

"That's not Hawke, is it?" I nodded toward the bar where a man who looked similar was talking to the senior partner of the firm. It couldn't be him. He left the firm without putting in his two weeks, and it didn't make sense for him to care that his boss was leaving.

"Uh…" Axel narrowed his eyes. "It looks like him but that can't be possible."

I waited for my hallucination to pass but it never did. Hawke was still there, his dark hair exactly the same as it used to be. His suit was a little loose like he lost some unnecessary weight. His eyes were crystal blue like they'd always been. "I think it is him."

"But why would he be here?"

"Was he close to your boss?"

"Not that I recall." He rose from the chair and pushed it in. "Come on."

I trailed behind him with my eyes trained on Hawke. The closer we got to him, the more I realized I wasn't making it up. It truly was him, standing just feet away.

When Axel reached him, Hawke halted his conversation. He turned to Axel and stared at him silently before he returned his look to his boss. "Excuse me for a moment." He stepped away with Axel while I went with them.

Hawke stopped when we were out of earshot of everyone else. He stared at Axel like he didn't know what to say or how to even begin.

"Dude, why are you here?" Axel asked. "And why didn't you tell me you were coming to town?"

"Mr. Thomas personally invited me. Since he gave me such a nice recommendation even though I left at the drop of a hat I couldn't refuse." He placed his hands in his pockets, quiet and secretive like always. "I assumed you wouldn't be here so I didn't say anything."

"Why wouldn't you want me here?" Axel asked, clearly hurt.

"It's not that I didn't want to see you." Hawke kept his voice low. "I just didn't want anyone to know I was in town..."

I knew whom he meant by *anyone.*

"I thought it would be easier if I just came and went." Hawke had an apologetic look on his face, remorse for hurting his friend. "Sorry. I thought you hated these work things."

"I do," Axel said. "But I wanted to show off my girlfriend—" He halted in midsentence when he realized what he said.

Hawke smiled, and it was one of the few I've ever seen. "I'm glad you finally went for it." He turned to me and gave me a hug. "Axel would always talk about you when he came to the city. I'm glad he got over himself and finally asked you out."

Axel talked about me? That made me feel warm inside. "Yeah..."

Hawke lowered his hand then nodded to the table. "Should we sit? They're serving dinner soon."

"Yeah," Axel said. "We have a lot to catch up on."

***

Hawke took a sip of his wine then pointed at the two of us. "So, how did this happen?"

Axel turned to me, silently asking if I wanted to tell the story.

227

I shrugged. "He's your friend. I'm sure your version is better."

Axel turned back to Hawke. "Well, you knew I thought Marie was hot as hell."

"Yes." Hawke said it in an amused way. "It came up."

"Well, we hooked up," Axel continued. "Best sex of my life." He spoke loudly, forgetting the people sitting around us.

"Shh." I placed my forefinger over my lips.

"Whatever," Axel said. "Everyone here knows what I'm like." He continued on and ignored my advice. "I started seeing Marie at the house more and more because I started spending more time with Frankie..." He faltered when he mentioned her name.

Hawke didn't react but his eyes lost some of their light at the mention of her. "I remember that too. You said you were falling for her."

He said that? I couldn't picture Axel ever saying that.

"Well, I didn't put it like that," Axel said.

"But you didn't want to sleep with anyone else." Hawke turned to me and gave me a truthful look, telling me he wasn't making that part up.

"Well...yeah." Axel seemed embarrassed by all of this. "Anyway, Marie started dating this guy and I didn't like it. I always felt sick when I saw her with him. And when I saw her kissing him on the doorstep...a small part of me died."

"Awe..." I couldn't keep the gasp from escaping.

228

Axel carried on. "We talked about it and realized it wasn't going to happen. I wasn't ready for a relationship and it would be weird for Francesca if we started dating, especially if we broke up down the road. It just wasn't working so we went back to being friends."

Hawke listened to every word he said, ignoring everyone else at the table. "That didn't last long, huh?"

"Then she started dating this other dude, a total loser—"

"What?" I snapped. "You didn't even meet him."

"I didn't need to," Axel argued. "He wasn't good enough for you. Nobody is."

My eyes softened all over again. "Awe..."

"Marie accused me of being shallow," Axel explained. "She had a thing for me in high school but I didn't notice her until recently. She had a point. All I really care about is beauty. I've never bothered to get to know a girl before..."

Hawke listened attentively, his own thoughts hidden away.

"But I noticed things were different with Marie. When I wasn't with her, I thought about her. I noticed all the little details about her, like the way her hair fell around her face when she turned and the little freckles on her skin. When I wasn't with her, I missed her. All I ever wanted to do was be with her—and I didn't want to sleep with her."

Hawke kept his fingers wrapped around his glass.

"So, I told her how I felt—that I wanted her for the good stuff on the inside and not the outside."

Hawke nodded when the tale was over. "That's sweet, Axel."

"I mean, I do care about what's on the outside," Axel said. "I think Marie is sexy as hell. I'm not going to sugarcoat that."

Hawke chuckled. "Physical attraction is important."

"And we aren't lacking," Axel said, putting his arm around my shoulders.

"I always knew you would settle down," Hawke said. "I'm glad I got to witness it."

"Whoa, hold on." Axel pulled his arm away. "Who said anything about settling down? We're just dating."

I didn't let those words offend me. Our relationship was relatively new. We hadn't even said we loved each other. But it did bother me—on some level.

Hawke chuckled. "You want my two cents?"

Axel shook his head. "Not really."

"If you haven't found a single woman you've wanted to be with until now—when you're thirty—then you know you've found the one. Maybe you don't realize it right this second but you will."

Axel remained quiet, his thoughts hidden.

"When Francesca and I...I knew." Hawke stared at his glass and didn't make eye contact with either one of us. "There wasn't a specific thing she did or said. One day you wake up and just know."

I couldn't believe he talked about Francesca like that, after he left her without looking back. He said they were never getting back together, but he talked about her like she was his one true love. It made no sense to me.

Axel didn't say anything, probably having no idea what to say.

I kept my mouth shut because I had nothing nice to say when it came to Francesca. If he really loved her he would be with her right now. They'd be happy together and she wouldn't be curled up in bed at this very moment.

Hawke stirred his wine and watched it dance. "How is she?"

It was a loaded question and I didn't know how to respond.

Axel was quiet too.

"She's great." There was no way in hell I was going to let him know what a pathetic wreck she was. He wasn't going to get that kind of satisfaction, knowing she still mourned him even after all this time. "She's excited for the semester to end and to graduate."

"Did she win that baking contest?" he asked.

What baking contest?

Axel took over. "She killed it—like always. Got a nice ribbon out of it."

It must be one of the lies he made up. "And she's seeing someone."

Hawke looked up at that statement, the sorrow in his eyes. It was only there for a moment, and then like it never happened at all it disappeared. "I see..."

Axel shot me a glare.

"Yeah," I continued on. "He's a business major too. They worked on a project together and then he asked her out. It's pretty casual right now but she seems to like him." I couldn't make it sound like she fell in love already because that just wasn't realistic.

Hawke hid his despair but he didn't hide it well enough. "Good for her…"

Even that wouldn't make him go back to her?

"I was afraid she would break down and lose herself." He stirred the wine again. "I'm glad she's living her life to the fullest. I want her to be happy because she deserves the greatest kind of happiness in the world." He stared at the wine before he took a long drink.

When he said things like that, I didn't hate him so much. Even though he left her, it seemed like he still cared about her—even loved her.

"How are you?" Axel asked.

He finished the glass before he left it on the table. "Pretty much the same as the day I left. And I'll always be this way until the day I die."

Damn, he was intense.

Axel eyed him carefully before he spoke. "It's never too late to get back together. Why don't you—"

"No." He held up his hand to silence Axel. "She's doing great without me and I'm not messing with that."

What? Did we just sabotage Francesca's happiness? "Whoa, hold on. Just because she's seeing someone doesn't mean she's over you."

"I'm sure this guy is nice and he can give her the kind of future he deserves," Hawke said. "If I walk into her life again it'll disrupt all of that. I left for a reason and I have to stick with it. It's the best for her."

Goddammit.

"Dude, if you want to get back together you should at least tell her." Axel panicked and didn't even bother hiding it. He was playing it cool just a moment ago and now all his cards were on the table.

"I'll always want to get back together with her," Hawke said. "But I can't. I have to keep moving forward. Maybe it'll get easier with every passing day. Maybe one day I'll stop thinking about her altogether...however unlikely that is." He filled his glass again, almost pouring it until it reached the top.

Axel shared a look with me, clearly unsure what to do.

Whatever problems Hawke and Francesca had would never go away. It haunted both of them.

And I would give anything to know exactly what those problems were.

***

I had no interest in fooling around after seeing Hawke. My mojo completely disappeared after that conversation. My relationship with Axel wasn't perfect but at least we understood each other.

I didn't understand Hawke at all.

What could possibly be the reason for keeping the distance between them?

Axel parked in front of the house and killed the engine.

"Do you think there's something wrong with him?"

Axel knew whom I was referring to because he'd been thinking about him himself the whole ride home. "Like what?"

"Like he has a disease or something. Maybe he can't be with her because he knows something will happen to him..." It was a far reach but I didn't have any better guesses. "Like Huntington's disease."

"Doubtful."

"What else could it be?"

Axel shrugged. "I really don't know. And I don't think neither one of us will ever figure it out."

If Francesca hadn't told me by now then she probably never would. "You're right."

We walked into the house and noticed Francesca's door was closed. She was probably asleep or hovering in her insanity. We went into my room and locked the door behind us.

It wasn't difficult to sneak around Francesca, not when she was oblivious to everything around her. She could walk in on Axel and I screwing on the couch and it probably wouldn't register.

She was that numb.

Axel tossed his jacket on the back of my desk chair then unbuttoned his shirt. "I can't believe we ran into Hawke tonight..."

"I can't believe it either." I slipped off my heels and immediately felt my feet relax in relief. I slipped off my dress and stood in my strapless bra and thong. My back was to Axel and I didn't turn around as I undressed. He'd already seen me naked but it didn't feel right letting him see me now. The moment just wasn't right.

I pulled on a nightshirt then turned around and faced the bed.

He stood in his boxers, the definition obvious in the material. He gave me a heated look but nothing more. Then he pulled the covers back and got into bed. "Your bed is comfy."

"Thanks." I got in beside him then set an alarm.

He groaned. "What are you setting an alarm for?"

"Well, you have to leave then come back."

"Why?"

"Because Francesca will know you slept here."

"Whatever," he said with a sigh. "I don't even care anymore."

"Well, I do. I want to tell her, but in a better way."

He didn't make any further argument.

I pulled the sheets to my shoulder and cuddled into his side. The second I felt his body, every stress I had ebbed away. Being with him, even in silence, was soothing. There was nothing else I'd rather do than lay together, wrapped in the warmth of each other's arms.

Axel's arm moved around my shoulders and his hand rested in my hair. He felt the strands softly, running them through his fingers. He watched me with lidded eyes, taking in my features. He didn't lean into kiss me or give any indication that's what he wanted. In that moment, all he wanted was to look at me.

My hand glided across his hard chest and stopped when it reached the skin over his heart. I felt his heartbeat, slow and steady. It was relaxed, at peace. My fingers naturally traced the area, worshipping the organ that made him so beautiful. Times like this made me realize conversation wasn't necessary. As long as we were in each other's presence we didn't need anything else. These quiet moments, when nothing exciting seemed to happen, were the most exciting moments of all.

CHAPTER NINETEEN

Day Of Hell

Marie

My arm was better and I had full range of motion. My old slings were shoved into the back of one of my drawers and my life had returned to normal. I had a whole prescription of vicodin left over that I had no use for but I couldn't toss it. Instead, I shoved it into the medicine cabinet in the spare bathroom just in case I might need it someday. There probably wouldn't be any complications with my shoulder, but it was always smart to be prepared.

Axel showered and changed in my bathroom before he visited the rest of the house, giving the impression he just came over after staying at his place. Francesca hadn't noticed anything. And if she did, she didn't care enough to say something about it.

Axel opened the fridge and eyed everything inside. "Should I even bother making breakfast...?"

Thursday

Francesca came out of her shell slightly but she was still a mess. She still had no appetite or motivation to do anything. Hawke seemed devastated but he was still up and about. I couldn't understand why she didn't do the same. "Just make her some eggs."

"Then I have to get the pan out, buffer it, wash it...it's a lot of work if she's not going to eat." He shut the door but still stayed in the same place, arguing with himself quietly.

"Then I'll make it." I felt like the good cop of this situation.

"I don't mind. I just don't want to waste my time." He was particularly irritable this morning. Last night we lay in bed together and stared into each other's eyes until we fell asleep. Neither one of us seemed interested in getting physical. Just being together was enough. Come to think of it, we hadn't even tried making love—yet.

"Let me take care of it." I guided him out of the way then scrambled the eggs before I poured them into the pan. Axel had a bad habit of screaming at Francesca and I wanted to stop that from happening. It didn't make Axel feel better ,and I knew it didn't help Francesca either.

I cooked the eggs then set them on a plate at the table. "I'll get her."

Axel stood at the counter and poured a mug of coffee.

I knocked before I stepped into her bedroom. "Come on, Frankie. Time to wake up."

She faced the opposite wall. "For what?"

"I made scrambled eggs with a pinch of pepper—just the way you like them."

"No, thank you." She pulled the sheets tighter around her.

If she didn't eat now she wouldn't eat all day. "You need to eat something."

"Put it in the fridge. Maybe I'll eat them later."

She was way too skinny at this point. Her muscle composition had waned and she hardly had any fat on her. It was getting to the point where I was scared for her health. "You better eat them later." I shut the door then walked back into the kitchen. I had a full schedule today, both work and school. I needed to get a move on it.

Axel looked beyond mad. "Is she coming?"

I wanted to cover for my friend but I didn't see how. "Her stomach is acting up…"

He narrowed his eyes.

"Must be the bug or something."

He must have known I was lying because he marched off.

Oh no.

I heard her bedroom door burst open. "Your friend makes you breakfast and you aren't going to eat it?"

Francesca and Axel bickered from time-to-time but they never had really big fights like this. It was impossible to make Axel mad, but with his sister he had a short fuse.

"I didn't ask her to." Francesca's voice was barely audible.

"You didn't ask her to take care of your schoolwork or your bills but she's doing that too. Not once have you thanked her or showed her any type of appreciation. You just lay around like a disgusting pig."

I sat at the kitchen table and prayed he would finish.

"I'm paying your rent and your car payment but I haven't gotten a thank you for that either. Frankie, it's been two months. Hawke is out screwing around and getting laid while you're moping around like a sorry excuse for a person. He's not coming back and you need to get over it. Get off your ass and grow a goddamn backbone."

Please be finished.

"I had to put up with Dad and all of his bullshit, and now I have to put up with you. I'm tired of getting the short stick all the time. You're perfectly capable of taking care of yourself but you choose not to. You're a selfish bitch that I can't stand anymore. I hate looking at you, I hate talking to you, and I hate everything about you." He slammed the door loudly behind him and stormed out the front door.

I didn't chase after him because he was too upset to see reason. And I didn't talk to Francesca either, unsure if she cared about anything he said. I grabbed my purse and prepared to walk through the front door when I heard Francesca crying from her bedroom.

Not once had I heard her cry.

I stood there and listened to it, feeling my heart break at the sound. My first instinct was to comfort her but I couldn't get myself to do it. Maybe Axel finally got through to her, made her realize she needed to get out of bed and carry on.

Maybe things would get better.

***

It was dead slow that night.

No one was stopping by because they were more interested in the new cupcake joint across the street. I couldn't blame them. I'd take a cupcake over coffee any day.

My manager sent me home even though I had two hours left on my shift. It was nice to head home early, but I knew I would feel worse when I got my small check in two weeks. If Axel weren't helping me I'd drown.

When I pulled up to the house, Axel's car wasn't there. I suspected he would stay at his apartment tonight because he was still pissed at Francesca. It was best if they both steered clear of each other, at least for a few days. Axel didn't mean anything he said, but the words were still hurtful.

I walked in the house and noticed all the lights were off. She obviously hadn't left her bedroom once that day. I tossed my purse on the kitchen table then flicked on all the lights. "Frankie?" I called down the hallway to see if she was all right.

No response.

"Frankie?" I walked down the hall and stopped when I noticed an arm laying across the floor. The rest of the body was on the bathroom floor hidden from view.

What the fuck?

"Frankie?" I ran to the bathroom and spotted her lying on the ground, her eyes closed and her breathing non-existent. She must have grown so weak that she tripped and fell.

I kneeled and held her head in my hands. "Frankie, wake up." I checked for blood but didn't spot even a drop. When I felt the pulse of her neck, I realized it was dangerously weak.

What happened here?

"Frankie?" I shook her violently, needing her to wake up.

That's when I spotted the bottle in her hands. The prescription label displayed my name and birthdate. Vicodin was written on the side.

And it was empty.

Shit.

I pulled out my cell phone and stared at it blankly. "Shit, what's the number to 9-1-1?" My hand shook as I tried to figure it out. Then it came to me in an instant. "Fuck." I made the call and listened to the operator come on the line.

"9-1-1. What's your emergency?"

"My friend needs help."

***

When I got to the hospital, I wasn't allowed to see her. I wasn't even sure what the doctors were doing. I followed the ambulance in my car and didn't arrive until minutes afterward. By the time I got there, they already rushed her off.

This was the worst day of my life.

I paced in the lobby and gripped my phone in my hand. Every time I walked past the nurses' station I eyed the one in charge and hoped she would say something to me, giving me some kind of news.

My phone lit up when Axel called me.

"Hey," he said into the phone. "You got Francesca out of the house?"

I didn't even think of calling him. I just got to the hospital and I was panicking. It slipped my mind. "Francesca swallowed my whole bottle of painkillers and now I'm at the emergency room waiting for news. I don't know if she's going to be okay. I don't even know where she is." My voice broke and the tears fell in waves.

"Oh my god..."

"I'm at the hospital."

"Is she going to be okay?"

"I don't know..." I kept pacing in the waiting room, aware of the people staring at me. I could feel their looks but I didn't care.

"Fuck. I'll be right there." He hung up.

I kept the phone to my ear because I was so numb. I continued to pace the waiting room, unable to sit still for even a moment.

***

Axel ran to me when he saw me. "Have you heard anything?"

"No." My eyes were still wet from the tears that would fall at any second.

Axel's face was paler than milk. Even his lips were white. He didn't just look scared—he looked terrified. "How did this happen...?"

"My shift ended early so I came home...and found her like that. She was laying on the bathroom floor with the empty bottle in her hand."

"How many pills were in there?"

"At least thirty..."

"Jesus Christ." He gripped his skull like it might explode.

"My manager let me go early because it was slow...but what if he hadn't. What if I got home when I was supposed to and she was already dead?"

He stared at the ground.

"Axel, I'm scared."

"Did you talk to her today?"

"No...not since this morning." I heard her crying just before I left but I didn't walk in there. I should have said something to her, consoled her.

Axel froze when the realization washed over him. He was thinking the same thing I was thinking. "It's because of what I said. It's because of me."

I crossed my arms over my chest and held onto myself tightly, trying not to shake uncontrollably. I wanted to tell him that wasn't the truth, that he couldn't be more wrong. She did this for another reason, one neither of us contributed to. But in my heart, I knew that wasn't true.

Axel collapsed into the nearby chair and leaned forward, devastated by the realization.

I sunk into the chair beside him, barely able to breathe. All I could hear were nurses traveling back and forth down the hallway. Phones rang at the desks, and the rest of the visitors in the lobby talked quietly to themselves. While I was surrounded by so many people I felt completely alone.

Alone.

***

Finally, we got some news.

"Is she okay?" Axel jumped to his feet and got into the nurse's face.

"What's going on?" I was right by his side, just as eager.

"Please tell me she's okay." Axel was just as devastated as I was, probably more so.

The nurse raised both of her hands to silence us. "The doctor is pumping her stomach now. We won't know anything for a while."

"Pumping her stomach?" I asked.

"What does that mean?" Axel asked.

"Hopefully, we're quick enough to remove the toxins before they reach her liver. If not, she could have organ failure. It's unclear when she took the pills so we can't be sure until the procedure is done."

"When will that be?" I asked.

"At least another hour."

I couldn't believe this was happening. Francesca was getting her insides pumped out because she tried to overdose. Why did I leave those pills lying around? Why didn't I realize her depression was more serious? I should have intervened. I should have done something. "Please keep us posted..."

"You know I will." She gave both of us a look of sympathy before she returned to the hallway.

Axel and I stood there, both shaken up.

"If she dies..." He shook his head, his eyes coating with tears. "I can't..."

The pain on his face made my heart break. I could feel his guilt seep through my skin. All of his regrets wrapped around me, suffocating me. I grabbed him and gripped him tightly, holding him fiercely. "She'll be okay, Axel."

He buried his face into my neck and breathed deeply. A few drops fell onto my neck and dissolved onto the skin. Without tasting them I could sense the salt. His pain hurt more than my own simply because his happiness meant the world to me.

I closed my eyes and tried to clear my thoughts. If I thought about it too much I would break down again. Right now, I needed to be there for Axel. He already lost his mother and his father.

And now he might lose his sister.

After more than an hour of waiting I asked the question I didn't want to ask. "Should we call him?"

Axel held my hand in his, his eyes on the carpet. "No."

"Are you sure…?" I would never understand why he left, but I believed he really loved her.

"He's not in her life anymore." His voice lacked any emotion. Currently, he was numb.

"Okay." I didn't want to press the argument, not right now. "Then I need to call Yaya."

"Let's wait and see what the doctor says. Then we'll know what kind of phone call we're about to make."

I think she needed to know now but I didn't press that either. It was Axel's family and I would do whatever he wanted. There was no sense in putting more pressure on him when he was about to crack.

The nurse returned and I almost jumped out of my own skin. "Axel. She's here."

Axel rose to his feet quicker than the naked eye could follow. "What's going on?"

"That girl is lucky." She crossed her arms over her chest. "The doctor was able to remove most of the toxins from her system. Some of it got through and she'll have to suffer through that on her own but she should make it."

"Thank god…" My heart actually stopped beating.

Axel covered his face and took a loud breath. "Shit."

"Can we see her?" I pleaded.

"She'll be out for a long time but you can wait in her room. Come with me." She guided us down the hall into the patient room. Francesca was lying in bed with tubes inserted every way imaginable. She was breathing on her own but she looked dead. If I didn't see her chest rise and fall I would assume the worst.

"Take a seat." The nurse shut the door behind her.

Axel and I took the seats at her bedside. All we could do was stare at her, seeing the nearly dead corpse. A ventilator was lodged in her throat, and the machine beeped every time carbon dioxide was released.

I couldn't believe this.

Axel stared at her, just as speechless.

I grabbed her hand on the bed and felt the cold skin. She was freezing.

"Frankie..." Axel approached the bed and rested a hand on her arm. He seemed to be listening for a pulse, to make sure she was still on this side of life. He stared down at her with watery eyes and a quivering lip. "I'm here."

I looked at the ground to give him some privacy with his sister.

"I'm sorry for everything that I said. Truth is, I couldn't live without you. So, please come back to me." He gave her a gentle squeeze before he returned to the seat beside me.

"I'll give Yaya a call."

He nodded.

I stepped out into the hall and made the call, grateful I had some good news in light of the bad.

***

Nearly two days later, she woke up.

Her eyes fluttered open and she stared at the ceiling for several seconds, unsure where she was or how she was alive. She didn't blink, processing the room and the tube down her throat. Her hand automatically reached for it, wanting to remove it.

Axel grabbed her hand. "Hold on. I'll get the doctor."

She flinched when she saw Axel's face. She stared at him hard, taking in every feature. Then the remorse flashed across her face. It wasn't clear if she was relieved or disappointed that her plan failed.

Axel retrieved the doctor, who removed the intubator from her throat. Once it was gone, she immediately breathed on her own. Her hand reached for her sore throat and she coughed a few times.

The three of us stared at her, grateful she was alive.

Francesca pulled her knees to her chest and stared straight ahead, not making eye contact with any of us. The shame of her actions kicked in immediately. She knew exactly what she put us through and now she couldn't handle it. She knew Axel was about to scream at her, to make her feel even worse.

Axel stood up and approached the bed. Then he took a seat beside her, his legs hanging off the edge.

She still didn't look at him.

Axel took her hand, being affectionate with her in a way he never was before. "I'm so glad you're okay. I was scared."

Her hand was lifeless in his but she didn't pull it away.

"We were all scared," he continued. "We weren't sure if you were going to make it."

Heavy drops formed in her eyes but they didn't drop into tears. Her breathing increased, her chest rising and falling noticeably.

"Francesca." He wrapped both of his hands around hers. "I'm so sorry for what I said. I was too harsh with you. I was just scared...and I didn't show it very well. I wish I could take it back."

She closed her eyes for a long time, and when they opened the tears fell down her cheeks. "Axel...I'm the one who should apologize." Her voice was so raspy she didn't sound like herself at all. But they were still her words. "I'm so sorry I hurt you like this. I was out of my mind and did something stupid...it wasn't your fault."

"It was. I shouldn't have yelled at you like that."

She shook her head. "It doesn't matter. Don't blame yourself."

The interaction was intimate and I felt terrible for being there. I wanted to walk out but I thought that would draw unnecessary attention to myself.

"Promise me you won't do this again." His voice was quiet but full of pleas.

"I promise." She looked him in the eye.

"None of us would be able to go on without you, Francesca. I hope you know that."

She nodded, more tears coming. "I'm sorry I hurt you so much, Axel. You don't deserve it."

"It's okay." He patted her hand. "You're here and that's all that matters. We'll work on making you better. I didn't realize how bad it was." He leaned in and gave her a hug, making sure he didn't touch any of the tubes still connected to her body.

I sniffed because their reunion was getting me choked up.

Axel pulled away and kissed her on the forehead.

I'd never seen him show that kind of affection with his sister. And I had a feeling I would never see him do it again.

He returned to his seat then looked at me, giving me the floor.

I sat at the edge of her bed but couldn't think of anything to say. There was too much emotion in my heart to get anything out. I looked into her eyes and felt the unbridled tears emerge.

Francesca cried with me.

"I love you." I wrapped my arms around her.

"I love you too. I'm so sorry..."

"It's okay." I felt her bones in my fingers because she was so small. She felt sickly, like a skeleton.

"I promise I'll never do anything like that again."

"I know. Once you're free to go we'll work on getting you better."

"Okay," she whispered.

Thursday

I pulled away and tried to give her a smile but I was certain it came out as a grimace. "And you're going to start baking again. The house just doesn't smell the same."

She smiled but it was weak. "Okay."

I fixed her hair and pulled it over one shoulder, cleaning her up as much as I could. "Are you hungry?"

She shook her head.

I kept staring at her.

"I mean, yes." She swallowed the lump in her throat. "Please bring all the food you can carry."

I rested my hand on hers. "That's better."

***

Yaya went home to get some sleep, and Axel had to be at the office. I blew off classes because I didn't want Francesca to be alone. Despite her suicide attempt she seemed better.

Francesca watched the TV in the corner, a daytime soap opera. "You don't have to stay with me. I know you have class."

"It's sociology class…boring." I flipped through an old issue of *People Magazine.*

"Well…thanks for keeping me company."

"Of course." I could take her home in a few days, but for now she was on observation. A psychiatrist came down and spoke to her and cleared her mental state. Whatever episode she had was over. "Frankie…what exactly happened?" I'd wanted his answer for a while, but I didn't want to hear it in front of the others.

She grabbed the remote and turned off the TV. "It wasn't pre-meditated."

"What does that mean?"

"I wasn't planning on doing it. When I went to use the bathroom, I was still in tears over the conversation I had with Axel. I just felt...absolutely numb. There was no point to anything anymore. Everything he said was true. I was a pathetic excuse for a person and incredibly weak." She shook her head slightly. "I saw that bottle of painkillers and I didn't hesitate. I just swallowed them."

I kept my voice steady and my face stoic. "So, you wanted to die?"

"No...I just didn't want to live anymore."

"Because Hawke is never coming back?"

"Yes...but not really. In that moment it was out of hopelessness. Axel painted a picture for me that I couldn't get out of my head. I saw myself in his eyes and...I didn't like what I saw."

I would never tell Axel any of this.

Francesca fell quiet, staring at the remote in her hand. "Please don't tell him I said that..."

"I won't."

"Thank you." She set the remote on the table at her bedside.

"Do you still feel that way?" In a few weeks would an episode like this happen again? Did Axel and I need to keep a better eye on her?

"No. I can't believe I put you guys through this at all. And I don't want to go back to an unbearable existence. I need to get back on my feet and move forward. I don't like who I am anymore..."

It was the greatest progress she ever made. "You can do it, Frankie."

"Right now it seems too difficult but I have to try. I miss the person I used to be."

"I miss her too."

She clenched the sheets under her tiny fingers. "I'm so sorry, Marie. I know I've put you through so much these past few months. You didn't deserve that..."

"It's okay." I would never hold a grudge against my closest friend.

"I'll get better," she whispered. "I promise."

At least something good happened in the midst of a tragedy. "I know you will."

She lay back on her pillow, her tangled hair scattering around her. She looked out the window and stared at the sunny day. Then she turned back to me, her eyes giving away the question before she asked it. "Does he know...?"

I knew whom she was referring to. Axel said we shouldn't call him, and I agreed with him. Seeing Francesca at her lowest point would make him pity her. And if that was the only reason he came back, he shouldn't come back at all. "No."

Her expression didn't change.

"Unless you want me to tell him."

She considered the question quietly, her thoughts circling in her mind. Then she shook her head. "No."

I assumed that's what she would have wanted. "You're going to get better, Frankie. Let's just take it one step at a time."

***

I stood in the hallway with Axel. He just returned from the cafeteria and handed me a coffee, the crappy kind from the vending machine. He sipped it then made a face. "How is she?"

"I think she's better."

"Yeah?" he asked. "I think so too."

"Sometimes you have to hit rock bottom before you can get up again."

"I guess." He held the Styrofoam cup in his hand, the steam drifting toward the ceiling.

"I think she's going to be okay. This experience has made her realize she needs to get back on her feet and move forward."

"She said that?"

I nodded.

"I just can't believe it came to that...did she say why?"

I'd never tell him his words were the trigger. "She just misses him..."

He looked into his cup and fell silent. "I wish they never got together..."

"I wish they were still together." I'd never seen Frankie happier than when she was with him.

255

"I guess…"

"Everything is easier from this point onward. We'll take it one day at a time, and eventually she'll be back to normal. She'll find herself again, and this time she'll be stronger."

"I hope you're right." He eyed the door but didn't walk inside. His usual vigor for life was absent, non-existent. "I really hate her sometimes. I don't mean that in a joking way. I mean it literally. There are times when I wish she weren't in my life. But…times like this remind me how much I need her."

My hand moved to his wrist.

"It's just like my dad all over again…"

"But Frankie isn't going anywhere. She's staying right here."

He nodded.

"And she's not going to pull a stunt like that again. I believe her."

"I believe her too."

I stood on my tiptoes and kissed him on the cheek. "We'll get through this together. I promise."

He wrapped one arm around my waist and held me close. His chin rested on my head and he breathed a deep sigh, letting his grief escape in a single breath.

CHAPTER TWENTY

Regret

Axel

I'd never felt so shitty in my life.

When I lost my temper, I screamed at Francesca, unsure how else to express myself. I put her down in so many ways, and this was the straw that finally broke the camel's back.

It was my fault.

My sister was always a strong person. When our parents died, she was grief-stricken but never immobile. She still carried on with school, work, and her relationships. She was more quiet than usual, but she was still around. Actually, I was the one who took Dad's suicide worse. I took it as a direct insult to both Francesca and I. To this day, I still hadn't forgiven him for the despicable action he took.

When Francesca withdrew from the world and barricaded herself in her bedroom, I should have known something serious was going on. Instead of yelling at her, I should have been more supportive. I was putting all my anger toward our father onto her.

How would I ever come back from this?

When she was released from the hospital, I could breathe a little easier. She really was back to full health and allowed to walk away. Her mental state was still broken, but at least her body was functioning.

No one said a word on the drive home. Marie sat in the passenger seat while Francesca sat in the back. I drove, my eyes moving to the rearview mirror to check on her. Every time I looked at her she was staring out the window.

We arrived at the house and walked inside. The place was messy from the way we left it. No one had cleaned anything up, and piles of books and binders were still on the kitchen table.

Francesca stood in the entryway and looked around, like it was her first time really seeing it.

Marie and I stood absolutely still, unsure what she would do.

Francesca looked at the kitchen, and after a full minute of staring she walked inside. She opened the fridge and pulled out a carton of eggs and baking soda. Then she pulled out a mixing bowl and a few pans.

I held my breath.

Francesca pre-heated the oven then quietly began to work, mixing the batter in the bowl.

This was really happening.

She was baking.

Marie looked at me and gave me a smile I hadn't seen in a long time.

And I actually smiled back.

***

Now that Francesca was up and about, I didn't sleep over anymore. It was too difficult to sneak around without getting caught. Francesca was quiet and still not eating right, but she was more perceptive.

I walked in the house with a box of pizza in my hands. "Who's hungry?"

"I am." Marie sat at the kitchen table with her school stuff surrounding her.

Francesca was in the kitchen, making more muffins. The place was littered with baked goods, more than enough to feed everyone in town. "You want a muffin, Axel?"

I was sick of muffins. I might actually throw up. "Sure."

She handed me one then returned to the kitchen.

I sat at the table and ripped off a huge piece and shoved it into my pocket. She didn't need to know the difference.

Marie gave me a smile.

After Francesca finished washing the dishes she sat down beside Marie. "What did I miss?"

Marie pushed the notes toward her. "I got this from the guy in your econ class. You have an exam on Friday."

"Alright." She pulled it toward her and began to read.

Thursday

I piled a few slices of pizza on a plate and slid it toward Marie. But then I realized my odd behavior and pulled it back, hoping Francesca didn't notice anything. "Going back to school?"

"Tomorrow," Francesca said. "I'm so behind but I think I'll pass everything."

"You should," Marie said. "We kept up with everything for you. Just try to get C's on all your exams."

Francesca nodded. "So much for graduating with honors…"

She threw that away two months ago. "You're still graduating and that's an accomplishment."

"I'm really proud of you." I took every opportunity to say something positive to her, to encourage her to keep going. With all the negativity I fed her I felt like an asshole.

She met my look and searched my gaze for sincerity. When she found it, she looked down again. "Thanks so much for being here for me. I appreciate it."

"Of course," Marie said. "We'll be here no matter what."

"Yeah," I said in agreement.

"There's one favor I have to ask of you…" She set her pen down.

"What?" Marie asked.

"I never want to speak of him again." Her voice was surprisingly emotionless, void of any kind of feelings. "I want to act like it never happened. That's the only way I'll move forward."

We didn't talk about him much anyway, so it wasn't a big sacrifice. "You got it."

"Whatever you need," Marie said.

Francesca returned her gaze to her notes. "Thank you." She flipped through the page and tried to make sense of everything she missed. Not once did she complain but she didn't look happy either.

Marie grabbed a muffin off the tray and took a bite even though she was sick of them. She broke off a few pieces and chewed, her small mouth making nearly mute bites.

I eyed her mouth and thought of other things that I shouldn't. I hadn't kissed her in so long I forgot what it felt like. With Francesca's demise I hadn't thought of anything else. My need for affection and intimacy had disappeared. But now that I watched Marie across the table those feelings started to come back.

We would have to tell Francesca the truth eventually, but I'd rather wait as long as possible. When she was back to normal, finding steady ground, then I would reveal the truth. Not being able to spend time with Marie was unbearable, but it was a small sacrifice to make in comparison to what was truly important.

***

Francesca walked inside and tossed her books on the table. She didn't say a single word but she didn't need to. Her frustration filled the air around her. It was a nice change compared to her usual depression.

"How'd it go?"

"I'm pretty sure I failed it." She slumped down into the chair. Even though she was hardly a hundred pounds at this point, her body hit the chair like she weighed so much more.

"Well, you did your best." I didn't expect her to do much better. She'd been absent for the past few months. Even if she studied every minute of the day it was impossible for her to memorize all the material.

"I guess...I'll just have to do better if I want that diploma."

I just finished making a sandwich and I placed that in front of her. "It wouldn't be the end of the world if you had to stay an extra semester and make up those classes." It would cost a lot of money and waste more time, but it was better than not getting a degree at all.

"Hopefully, it doesn't come to that."

I pushed the sandwich closer to her.

She eyed it with that usual look.

I stared her down and silently threatened her.

She grabbed the sandwich and took an enormous bite, practically rolling her eyes.

That saved me from making a speech. "People ask any questions?"

"Yeah," she said as she continued eating. "I told them I was sick with pneumonia, which led to bronchitis. I turned on my phone and my message box was totally full with voicemails and text messages."

"Because a lot of people care about you."

She paused and stared at her sandwich. Then she took another bite.

"Maybe you'll start dating soon..." Was it to soon to push her in that direction?

"Maybe." She ate the handful of chips I put on her plate.

Maybe was better than no. I had a few friends I might be able to set her up with, but they were a little older. My sister was pretty so she could get her own dates but I wasn't sure how much effort she would give it.

"What's new with you?"

"Me?" All I could think about was Marie.

"Yeah. How's work and stuff?"

"Work is pretty much the same. I'm overworked and underpaid."

"Anything else?"

Marie came into my mind again. "Not really." I'd spent nearly all my time at Francesca's place so my answer should be enough.

"Seeing anyone?"

"No." I blurted it out too quickly, my voice sounding like it belonged to someone else entirely.

Francesca eyed me with a raised eyebrow.

"I mean, I've hooked up with a few girls but that's it."

"That thing with Marie never happened again?"

Marie told her? "No, we're just friends." Friends that liked to make out.

Thursday

Francesca spread out her things on the kitchen table. "I'll have to get another job. Not sure where to start."

"The Grind won't take you back?"

"I doubt it. I never even quit. Why would they take me back?"

Maybe I could work something out with them. "It's just for a few more months anyway. I can cover your bills until then."

"You don't need to help me, Axel. I'll figure it out."

"I really don't mind. It's not a big deal."

"You've helped me enough. You have your own stuff to take care of." She opened her laptop then searched for job offerings in the area.

"I just mean, you're going to graduate in a few months and start a career. Does it really make any sense for you to find some part-time job just to quit soon? Just focus on school right now. That's the most important thing." Francesca was fairly reasonable so I knew she would respond to my logic.

"I don't know..."

"Just think about it."

She exited out of the page. "I guess I will."

***

I hadn't spent any time with Marie because Francesca was always in the way. Just a week ago I had a girlfriend, and now it felt like it never happened. I was sitting at home when I texted her. *Come over tonight.*

Sleep over?

Yeah. I missed sleeping with her. There was something oddly satisfying about having her in my arms. It chased away all the stress and gave me a strong sense of comfort. With her, I was at peace.

What am I going to say to Frankie?

Tell her to mind her own business.

Axel. The single word straightened me out.

Tell her you're seeing someone. She doesn't need to know who it is.

I just think it's strange for me to leave her home all alone. It doesn't seem believable.

Then sneak me in.

I don't know...

I was going crazy over here. I had a beautiful woman all to myself but I couldn't enjoy her. *Either sneak me in or I'm breaking in. Your choice.*

You're ridiculous.

You think I'm joking? I'd break into her bedroom window if I had to.

Maybe we should just tell her.

Let's wait a while. We can't drop too much on her too fast.

You're right.

Did that mean I was getting my way? *So...*

Come over at eleven. She's usually asleep by then.

Yes. *See you then.*

***

At eleven, I arrived at her doorstep. *I'm here.*

Hold on. A few minutes later the front door cracked open. She poked her head out and waved me inside with her hand.

I didn't make a sound as I stepped on the floorboards of the house.

Marie locked the door behind me then pulled me down the hall toward her bedroom. Just when we were halfway there, Francesca's door opened.

Oh shit.

Marie dragged us into the spare bathroom and shut the door as quickly as possible.

I locked it just in case.

Instead of walking past us Francesca knocked on the door. "Marie?"

My heart was beating so fast I thought I might die.

"Uh…yeah?" Marie gave me a hysterical look like she didn't know what to do.

"Everything alright?" Francesca asked.

"Yeah," Marie said. "Just doing my business…"

"Okay." Francesca started to walk away. "I'll wait until you're done."

Of course she had to use the bathroom. That was my luck. "Tell her to use yours."

Marie's eyes lit up in relief. "Frankie, just use mine. It might be a while."

"No, I'll wait," Francesca said.

Why the hell did she want to wait? I turned to Marie and lifted up my hands in confusion.

She shrugged back. "Why don't you just use my bathroom?"

"Because my stuff is in there. It's not a big deal. I'll just wait."

I wanted to break the mirror with my fist.

Marie covered her mouth to stifle her scream.

There was no way out of here unless I squeezed through the bathroom window. And it was way too small for a guy like me. The only way I was walking out of there was if Francesca saw me.

Then I came up with another idea.

I pulled back the shower curtain then stepped inside the bathtub.

"What are you doing?" Marie whispered.

"Flush the toilet and walk out."

"You can't be serious..."

"Just go into your bedroom. I'll meet you there."

Marie didn't like this plan one bit, not that I blamed her.

"What other choice do we have?"

She knew I was right. There was no other way besides telling her the truth. She shut the shower curtain and hid me from view. Then she flushed the toilet and washed her hands. "Alright. I'm done." She opened the bathroom door and walked out. Sorry, it took so long."

"It's cool." Francesca walked inside and locked the door behind her.

Thursday

Hopefully, she would just wash her face. Anything too awkward would strain our relationship forever. I'd never be able to look at her the same.

Her pants dropped and her bottom hit the toilet.

Ugh. This was really happening.

A steady stream hit the water then the toilet paper turned on the roll.

I tried to block out the sound as much as possible but there was nothing I could do. I couldn't make a single noise.

She flushed then moved to the sink, washing her hands then her face. She did her nighttime rituals, brushing her teeth and moisturizing.

This sucked.

She finally walked out and turned off the lights on the way.

I didn't see anything but the sound scarred me. Next time I looked at my sister I would remember listening to her pee right beside me. We were never close to begin with but now we'd never be close.

After waiting a few minutes I left the bathroom and poked my head into the hallway. Both of the bedroom doors were shut and the rest of the lights were off. I crept to Marie's room then maneuvered inside.

Once the door was shut behind me I finally took a real breath.

Marie stood there, anxiously waiting for me. She was still wearing her jeans and blouse, not getting uncomfortable until I joined her in the bedroom. "What happened?"

"What do you mean what happened?" We both whispered to one another because Francesca's bedroom was just across the hall. "She went back into her room so I came in here."

"But did you—"

"Let's just get to bed." I didn't want to recount the memory of Francesca peeing.

"Alright..."

I got undressed then slid inside her soft sheets. Her bed was smaller than mine but less space wasn't an issue when I was going to be close to her anyway. Marie undressed and joined me a moment later.

We faced each other under the blankets, and I placed her long, slender leg around my waist. I loved the way it felt hooked around me. She had the legs of a runner. They were finely sculpted with precision. I remembered the way they felt around my waist. When they were there, they felt even better.

Her blonde hair was pulled over one shoulder, framing her face in such a perfect way it didn't seem real. Her green eyes were difficult to decipher in the dark but they still glowed by their own light. Sometimes I liked just to look at her. With Francesca around again it was impossible to be myself, to cherish Marie in any way.

"She seems better."

"She does." When did we talk about something else besides my sister? I couldn't remember.

"I'm glad things are moving along. She's eating and going back to school…"

"The worst is definitely over."

"You don't seem happy."

I would always be disappointed in myself for the way I spoke to her. Francesca denied it but I knew the truth. I pulled the trigger that led to her demise. "I'm tired of sneaking around. I'm tired of attending to Francesca before anything else. I want to be with you—out in the open."

"Me too…"

"I want to take you on a date—a real one." That work party didn't count, especially when I screwed things up by mentioning what happened with Alexia. And then Hawke was there, and that was a serious mood killer.

"And I'd love to go on one."

I had a perfect idea. I was researching different things to do when I came across the most peculiar but wonderful date. Marie would probably like it, and I'd probably get lucky later. "We should just tell her. I'm not listening to her pee again."

Her face scrunched up like she was trying not to laugh.

"It was horrifying."

"It's not like you watched her."

"Listening to it was enough. How would you feel if you heard your sister pee?"

"I have."

"Well, it's different."

"Just try and forget about it."

It would take a full night of rest to make that happen. I was lying in bed with a beautiful woman but I was limp like a dead fish. Francesca was cramping my style in every way imaginable.

"Stop thinking about it." She cupped my face and ran her fingers along my jaw.

"Easier said than done."

"Think about me."

I looked into her face and concentrated my gaze on her eyes. Her thick eyelashes always made them irresistible. Sometimes when I looked at her at the perfect angle I saw different specs of color in her eyes. There were splashes of gray and yellow, and sometimes orange.

"I submitted my resume to a few places in New York..."

"Yeah?" My eyes watched her mouth, entranced by the movement of her lips.

"I hope I get a call back or something. I'd even take an unpaid internship at this point."

"Be careful for what you wish for."

She chuckled. "I know everyone has to start at the bottom and work their way up. I have long nails and I'm not afraid to use them to get to the top."

"Was that the first line of your CV?"

She slapped my arm playfully. "Shut up."

"Hey, it would have caught my attention. I'd hire you in the spot."

"Maybe if I flashed you."

"If you flashed me you'd be the CEO—under me." My hand moved up her thigh until it rested on her hip. I felt the lace of her panties and fought myself not to pull them down. She had the sexiest body I'd ever seen.

"Ooh...I wouldn't mind being under you."

"Again, be careful for what you wish for." I pressed our heads together then gave her a slow kiss. I'd never been in this type of relationship before, where it was all talking and no sex. I wasn't getting laid but I was still there. When I was alone, my eyes didn't wander, and when I was in my apartment I didn't rub one out. Marie satisfied me in a way no one else ever did. She satisfied my soul. "I'm gonna tell her tomorrow."

"You are?"

"Yeah." My fingers felt her hair, noting the soft texture. "You're my girlfriend and I want the world to know."

CHAPTER TWENTY-ONE

Progress

Axel

Francesca walked inside with her backpack over her shoulder. "I have some good news."

"You aced your biology lab practical?" I just finished packing the refrigerator with groceries.

"No...I failed that." She set her backpack on the kitchen table next to the bowl of fruit in the center. "I talked to my manager and got my job back. I'll be back at The Grind starting tomorrow."

I didn't mind paying her bills until she graduated but now wasn't the time to push it. If she was well enough to work again then that was awesome news. "Great. The Grind is lucky to have you."

"I'll pay you back for everything but it may take a while." She opened the fridge and grabbed a snack pudding. After she ripped off the foil she sat down and devoured it.

I stopped myself from jumping in joy. Seeing her have an appetite was even better news. "You don't need to pay me back."

"I insist, Axel."

"Well, I insist harder." I took a seat beside her. "I didn't mind helping you. One day I'm going to need your help and you'll be there for me."

She licked the spoon then looked at me. "I guess that's true."

I eyed my watch because I knew Marie would be home any minute. I was going to tell Francesca about us and get it over with. If my sister had a problem with it, that was too bad. Marie was a catch and I wasn't going to let her go.

"It's fine that you hang out here but you don't need to keep an eye on me anymore." Francesca finished the pudding and balanced the curve of the spoon on the end of her nose.

She would understand why I was there soon enough.

The door opened and Marie walked inside, wearing black pants and a shirt after getting off work at The Grind. "Hey."

"Hey." Francesca turned to her, the spoon still on her nose. "I got my job back."

"I heard." She patted her on the shoulder. "Good for you. And nice job with the spoon." She came to me next and automatically leaned in to kiss me on the cheek. Then she realized what she was doing and how odd it looked. Nonchalantly, she wiped off the invisible dirt from my shoulder. "You had a smudge..." She walked into the kitchen and poured herself a glass of wine. "I need alcohol after serving coffee all day."

"I need alcohol after everything," I said.

She grabbed a beer from the fridge and passed it to me. Then she took a seat across the table. Her shirt was wrinkled and her hair was pulled back, but she still looked perfect. I wanted to shower with her and lather her until she was clean.

"How was school?" Marie sat down and directed all of her attention on Francesca. "Did you nail that practical?"

"I nailed the coffin, you could say." The spoon fell off her nose and hit the surface of the table.

Marie cringed. "Sorry..."

"It's okay. I think I'll still pass the class." She picked up her spoon and kept eating.

"That was just on your nose..." I wasn't a germ-a-phob but that that was gross.

She shrugged and kept eating.

I looked across the table and stared at Marie. Silently, I told her I was going to spill the beans. Whatever happened, happened.

Marie didn't put up a fight but she didn't seem thrilled either.

"Frankie, there's something I want to talk about." Maybe it was insensitive for me to be a couple with Marie when Francesca was still struggling over Hawke's absence but I couldn't stop living my life to accommodate her. How could I give this relationship a real chance if it was a secret?

"What's up?" She finished her snack pack and set the spoon inside the empty carton.

"I know this is awkward for all three of us but there's something you need to know about Marie and I…"

Francesca's expression didn't change. She didn't catch my drift.

"Marie and I are together now," I said. "We're seeing each other."

She immediately turned to Marie. "Whoa, what?"

Marie nodded in response.

"It's been going on for a while now," I continued. "And we don't want to hide it from you. I know you'll be weird about it and object but nothing you say is going to change what's going on between us. I'm just giving you a heads up."

Francesca turned back to me. "Why would I object to it?"

"Because you have a problem with it." I didn't like Hawke dating her one bit and I made that clear.

"But I don't have a problem with it," Francesca said. "If you want to be together, be together. Who should care what anyone thinks anyway."

What? It was that easy?

"However…" Francesca turned back to Marie. "Axel? Really?"

My eyes narrowed at the insult.

Marie didn't give Francesca a look of apology. Actually, she smiled. "Yes."

"He doesn't know his nose from his ass, Marie," Francesca said. "He's probably going to drive you crazy."

"Actually, he's the biggest sweetheart I've ever met." Marie glanced at me before she turned back to Francesca. "He's different with me. He's thoughtful and kind, and there's so much more below the surface. It's not a meaningless fling. I wouldn't say it's serious but it's definitely not casual either."

Francesca digested everything, taking it in slowly. Instead of flipping out the way I did she remained calm. She eyed both of us before she shrugged. "If you're both happy, I'm happy."

Marie smiled. "I'm glad you're on board."

Francesca turned to me, but she didn't give me the same smile Marie just got. "Mess with my girl and I'll stab you in the nuts."

The insult hit me right in the chest. "We don't have anything to worry about."

"Good." Francesca rose from the table and returned to the fridge. She peered inside as she tried to find something to eat. "I'm still hungry. Anything else good in here?"

***

I knocked on the door with a bouquet of roses in my hand. It was the first time I ever bought a girl flowers. The stems had thorns and I was careful not to touch them.

Thursday

Marie opened the door wearing shorts and a t-shirt as I instructed. Her eyes took in the flowers, and her face lit up like she was truly surprised. "Awe...they're lovely."

"For my lady."

She carried them inside and prepared a vase to place them in.

Francesca was sitting on the couch painting her nails. She looked up when she saw me. "Wow, is that Axel?"

"Shut up, brat." We were definitely staying at my place tonight so we wouldn't have to deal with her.

Marie grabbed her jacket and her purse. "I'm ready to go."

"Great." I took her hand and walked out with her. Once the door was shut behind us it was just she and I.

"So, where are we going?"

"You'll see."

***

We walked onto the dock and set our kayaks in the water. The water was calm and there wasn't a single ripple on the surface. The sound of crickets and frogs accompanied us. I held a bright lantern so we wouldn't be enveloped in the darkness.

"What are we doing?"

I placed the life jacket on her. "Kayaking."

"It's pitch black."

"Don't worry. I know the area."

"Uh..." She looked around, spooked by the forest.

"Trust me. It'll be worth it."

Marie tucked her hair behind her ear nervously.

I put my lifejacket on then held onto the kayak so she could step inside. I kept it steady so she wouldn't spill any water into the kayak. I got into the spot behind her and held the lantern between my knees. "Ready?"

She grabbed the oar like she didn't know what to do with it.

"Just rest it on your knees. I'll row." I guided us away from the dark and toward the center of the lake. The water was partly freshwater and partly seawater because a channel connected with the sea. Sometimes sea creatures could be spotted underneath the water, like sea turtles and small sharks.

Marie kept her hands on her knees as she searched the darkness. "What are you going to show me?"

"You'll know when you see it." I stopped pedaling when we were far enough into the lake. We floated on the water silently, taking in the sounds of the nightlife. I stuck my oar in the water and did a dramatic scoop.

Marie watched my movements.

I moved to the other side of the kayak and did the same thing.

"What are we looking for?"

"Shh..." I kept hitting the water, hoping to find the right place.

And then I did.

Thursday

The bioluminescent phytoplankton lit up brightly, shining the blue light directly onto our faces. The water lit up like a Christmas tree.

"Oh my god…" Marie gripped the side of the boat as she stared into the water.

The microorganisms glowed, releasing their defense mechanism. And then slowly, the light faded away.

"That's so amazing. What is that?"

"The phytoplankton drift from the sea. When they're disturbed, they glow."

"Like in *Life of Pi*?"

"Exactly."

She used her own oar to churn the water, making the organisms light up once more. "Wow…"

Instead of staring at nature's miracle I stared at her. I could see her face in the light of the glow, and the smile on her face made the trek here worthwhile. Her excitement was infectious, and she reminded me of a child discovering something fascinating for the very first time.

"My father and I used to come out here—just he and I."

She pulled her eyes away from the water and looked at me.

"I've never been here with anyone else, not even Frankie."

She gripped the oar in her hands and didn't stir the water again. "Thanks for sharing it with me."

"I wanted our first date to be perfect."

"It is."

When she gave me a look like that, I felt hot all over the place. Anytime I was in her presence, the joy inside me radiated everywhere. I was rejuvenated with hope and happiness. All the darkness that lived inside me seemed to fade away when she brought the light.

***

When we returned to my apartment, we both needed a shower before anything else. The lake water was drenched into our clothes, and the smell was stuck to our skin. I turned on the shower then stripped away my clothes.

She did the same.

I hadn't seen her completely naked in nearly three months. My dick got hard just thinking about it, waiting for her bare skin to meet my eyes. Those legs stretched on for days, and I remembered the way she tasted. It was impossible to forget.

She unzipped her jacket and tossed it on the floor next to the pile I made. Then she removed everything else, her top and her shorts. When she got to her undergarments, she took her time, unclasping her bra then stepping out of her panties.

She was even more beautiful than I remember.

I felt like I was staring at a completely different woman. The one I saw before was beautiful, sexy, and perfect. But the woman I saw now was...different. There were small freckles up and down her arms, and a scar on her right knee. Her toenails were painted green and there were small tan lines on her shoulders and thighs. All the details flooded my brain, overloading it.

Now that we were together I didn't know what to do. Even now I didn't want to screw her. I used to long for dirty sex, the hard kind that happened in bathroom stalls and the backseats of cars.

But now I didn't want any of that.

Marie stared at me, expecting me to make the first move. The shower still ran, filling the bathroom with humid steam. The mutual desire to get clean left our minds in light of each other.

I grabbed my boxers and pulled them down, revealing my long cock. It was thick and swollen for her. It was a reaction I couldn't hide and I wasn't ashamed of it. She turned me on like nothing else.

Her eyes moved to my waist, staring at my size. She'd already seen me before but now she was looking at me in a new way. She studied me like I was a work of art. Her lips parted slightly like she might say something but no words ever left her lips.

She and I had a way of communicating with each other without the use of words. We reacted to each other subtly, playing off each other's moves and moods. Right now I could feel everything she felt.

Because it was exactly what I felt.

Marie took the first step and headed to the shower. She paused in front of the door and looked at me over her shoulder, her blonde hair falling down to her chest. Her green eyes lit up like the north side of trees. Then she stepped inside and stood under the water.

I followed her immediately, crowding behind her in the narrow stall. My shower was made for a single person, but she and I could make it work.

She tilted her head back toward the water and massaged the shampoo into her scalp. Her back naturally arched, her tits lifting toward the ceiling. Her nipples were hard, and not because they were cold. The water ran down her face and pooled at her lips before it fell again.

Entranced, I just stood there.

After Marie rinsed her hair she grabbed a bar of soap and rubbed it into my chest. She worked the bubbles everywhere, dissolving every particle of dirt. Her eyes were glued to her hands, watching them work my body.

I watched her every move, noting the way her tits shook when she used her hands. She was nearly a foot shorter than me but she didn't seem small. Her legs were deceptively long, giving her the height of a supermodel without the inches.

Now I wanted to wash her, to explore every inch of her body without holding back. I wanted to feel her curvy waist and her voluptuous tits. My cock was still hard and pressed against my stomach and her rib cage. Feeling her smooth skin and the warm water was getting him even more excited. I'd never wanted to be with a woman more in my life. I already had her, and even my excitement then didn't compare to what it was now.

Thursday

Unable to keep my hands to myself I cupped her tits and massaged them, feeling the soap bubbles in my fingers. They were firm and round, perfect for gripping. They were large for her petite size but that made their appearance even sexier.

My hands glided down her stomach, feeling her flat belly. Her navel was sexy and small. My thumb caressed the area before my hands moved to her hips, gripping the curves as an anchor. Our mouths and body parts hadn't touched yet, but this was the greatest foreplay I'd ever had. "You're the most beautiful woman who's ever stepped into this apartment." She made all the others look like trolls.

She didn't give me a smile but her eyes softened.

I noticed how much I changed in that moment. My life used to be centered on getting laid by as many different women as possible. There were no strings attached, ever. But now I found myself obsessed with a single woman, one that I didn't want to share with anyone else.

Her palms snaked up my chest until they reached my shoulders. She tilted her chin up, her lips aimed for mine. Even when she stood on her tiptoes I still towered over her. Instead of finding our height differences a challenge, I thought it was cute. I craned my neck down then placed a slow kiss on her mouth. Kissing was so amateur, something I hardly did with the women I spent time with, but I loved doing it with her.

I was aware of every breath she took, how excited she became during our embrace. Sometimes she would release a musical sigh, a distant symphony that made my muscles tighten. When she moaned quietly into my mouth, practically panting, my dick twitched in response. Maybe I loved kissing her because she was so good at it. Or maybe it was a different reason altogether.

***

Our bodies were still damp when we hit my sheets. We dried off as much as possible with the towels but we were both in too much of a hurry to be thorough. I lay on top of her in my bed, kissing her aggressively. Our embrace started off slow but now I couldn't get enough of her. I couldn't slow down no matter how hard I tried.

She wrapped her legs around my waist and squeezed me gently. Her moans still echoed in the bedroom, her desire for me equal to the heat I felt for her. We hooked up on this bed months ago and the sex was amazing. But it was a hit-it-and-quit-it situation. This time it would be different. I wanted to treasure every touch and every caress. I actually wanted to feel her body move with mine. I wanted to give her more pleasure than she gave me.

I wanted so much more.

I sucked her bottom lip and felt her tits rub against my chest. They were hard and pointed, giving me a definite amount of friction as our bodies moves past one another. My cock grinded against her folds, feeling the moisture that accumulated there. There wasn't any doubt she was ready for me, desperate for me.

Thursday

I pressed my forehead to hers and paused, feeling my body yearn anxiously for hers. "Promise me you'll be here when I wake up tomorrow."

Her hands glided up my chest until she cupped my face. "I'll be here—every day."

Those were the words I wanted to hear, the promise of a new beginning. This was how our first together should have been. I used her for sex and she used me, making the night anything but romantic. "Should I wear a condom?" I've never had sex without one before and now was an exception.

"No." She looked up at me with fiery eyes.

"Does that mean you're on the pill?"

"Yeah."

I was clean and I knew she would be clean too. My hands pushed into the mattress as I held myself up, and like my cock had a mine of its own it found her entrance. It recognized the slippery juice she created and pressed inside, feeling the moisture immediately.

I noticed her tightness like last time, and with every inch I inserted I felt her constrict around me. It was completely different without a rubber wrapped around my dick. I could really feel her, feel the soft flesh that molded to my size. I could feel the moisture intimately, feel it slide past me as I moved further inside.

It was the best feeling in the world.

She moaned quietly as she felt me enter her. When I inserted my entire length, she moaned even louder. She took all of me, balls deep. Her fingertips dug into my biceps, and she widened her legs to accompany my hips.

I looked into her face and stared at her reaction. I loved the way her eyes lit up for me, turning even greener than ever before. Her lips were parted, showing most of her teeth and her small tongue. It made me feel like a king, conquering a land and finding my queen.

I thrust into her slowly, making my mattress creak because of how old it was. I took my time so I could concentrate on how she felt. Our bodies rubbed together, the friction making us both pant. It was the most satisfying experience of my life—and we just started.

Her hands moved to my shoulders and she held on tightly as she rocked into me from below. She thrust her hips upwards, taking me in at the same pace. We moved together, responding to one another.

My mouth found hers and I kissed her, feeling our bodies completely combine. The moment felt right, as if we were getting a redo. Now it was more sensual and meaningful. I couldn't picture any other woman on this bed, no one besides Marie. She could have been mine all these years if I just paid attention, if I just looked a little closer.

Her fingers found their way into my hair and she played with the strands, fingering them aggressively. Her lips would stop kissing mine from time-to-time, but it was only because she was catching her breath. Then the pressure surrounded my dick and I knew what was coming next. She came last time we had sex, so I recognized it the moment I felt it.

I kissed the corner of her mouth. "Marie..."

She bit her bottom lip before she exploded, coming around my dick with a loud yell. She arched her back then dug her nails into my skull. My mouth automatically went to her nipple, sucking it as she danced in the clouds. She panted through the entire explosion, slowly coming back to earth once it passed.

I could last a long time if o really put my mind to it, but right now I didn't have the same sense of control. I got list in the moment with her, seeing her enjoy my body and soul the way I enjoyed hers.

The idea of coming inside her gave me chills. Skin-to-skin, I would give her everything I had. She would take all of me, giving herself to me in a way no other woman had before.

I panted as I rocked into her, feeling the heat burn my body in every delectable way imaginable. It felt so good I began to convulse, feeling my nerve endings explode. "Marie..." I inserted myself completely inside her and pressed my head to hers, releasing a flood.

It was the greatest sensation I've ever known. Coming inside her instead of the tip of a condom made all the difference in the world. My heart rate spiked and the sense of pleasure reached every corner of my body.

Nothing ever felt so good.

She dug her fingers into my ass and pulled me further into her, wanting every drop.

That was even hotter.

She gave me a small kiss, one with a little bit of tongue, and then she lay back and stared at me.

That was the best sex I've ever had, and now I knew there was a reason behind it.

That reason was Marie Prescott.

Thursday

CHAPTER TWENTY-TWO

Early Morning

Marie

"You're still here." Axel lay beside me, his muscled body wrapped around mine.

"Yes. Still here."

The corners of his lips rose into a slight smile. "I was gonna hunt you down if you weren't."

"Be careful when you corner a wild animal."

"Wild is the perfect word to describe you." His lips moved into my hairline and he placed a gentle kiss right on my temple. "I wish I didn't have work today."

"Me too."

He got out of bed, gloriously naked. He had a noticeable V that formed in his hips, and his stomach was tight and hard. I hadn't heard him mention the gym since we'd been together, and now I wondered when he went. "I wish I had time for a quickie but I've got to get ready."

Thursday

"We have time." I sat up, letting the blankets fall to my waist. My tits were on display. It was a great way to manipulate him, since I knew he loved them so much.

His eyes immediately went down south. "Uh…"

"Come on." I beckoned him over with a finger.

"Believe me, it won't be quick." His eyes were still glued to my chest.

"You're really going to leave me hanging…?" I pouted my lips and gave him the best puppy dog eyes I could muster.

Like a shriveled flower coming to life with a little added water, his cock hardened in seconds. I had him right where I wanted him and his body couldn't give him away. He began with a run before he jumped high and landed on the bed.

I laughed as I felt my body catapulted into the air like I was on a trampoline.

"Baby, I'll never leave you hanging."

It was the first time he ever called me that, and the second I heard it I was taken to a different place. My lips were stuck in a permanent smile and I couldn't help but adore him. "That's what I hoped for."

***

Francesca and I worked the same shift at The Grind. It was strange to work with her again, to see her do something other than lay in bed all day. She got right back into action, taking care of the café like she never left.

It was slow, so we stood behind the register and busied ourselves with some girl talk.

"You and Axel..." She shook her head and crossed her arms over her chest. "I still can't believe it."

"Yeah..." I couldn't stop smiling. After the sex we had that morning, I was good for the rest of the day.

"Like...is he romantic with you?"

That date we had the other night was pretty romantic. "Very."

"Wow...I just can't picture it."

"He's your brother. I hope not."

"But he's so...immature. It's hard for me to see him being serious—even for five minutes."

"He has his moments." I told Francesca everything when it came to romantic relationships. Even the raunchy details weren't spared. But since it was Axel I couldn't describe it too seriously. It would make her throw up on the floor, and then I would have to clean it up.

"I can't believe it's been going on for so long. How did I not notice it?"

"Well, we weren't together most of the time. We were just...I don't know." We kind of were together without a commitment. We spent most of our time in the same room, and when he wasn't around I noticed it.

"I don't know?"

"It's hard to explain..." The best example was her relationship with Hawke but I agreed to never bring him up again. "It's one of those situations where you just feel something even if neither person acknowledges it. There was something in the air every time we were in the same room together. One day it was impossible to ignore and we finally talked about it. While that conversation didn't go well, everything prior to that was real."

Her eyes became lidded, like she was recalling a distant memory. Without saying a single word, it was clear she was thinking about Hawke. She held her silence then shifted her weight, trying to forget the thought altogether. "That's crazy…"

"I was hurt he only paid attention to me after I grew into my figure. In the beginning I thought we would have some good sex and then forget about each other. In a way, that did happen. But the more time we spent together, things began to change."

"He cares about you." Francesca eyed the door to make sure a customer wasn't about to walk in. "I can tell."

"Yeah, I can tell too." When we made love last night, it was nothing like the meaningless sex we had before. There were gentle kisses, loving embraces, and so much more. It was the first time someone made love to me.

"So…have you guys did the I love you thing?"

"No." I blurted out my answer quicker than I meant to. "No, we aren't there yet."

"Okay." Francesca didn't press it further. "That would be crazy if you got married someday…you would actually be my sister."

The idea of wearing a beautiful white gown and marrying Axel was a dream come true. He was my biggest crush and now he was so much more. I lived for those smiles.

The dreamy look in his eyes always sent shivers down my spine. And his kiss...was to die for. "Yeah, I would."

"Hope it works out. That would be so cool."

"It would." The idea of marrying Axel should freak me out but it didn't. He'd always been the person I'd wanted most. If I ended up with him, I'd be the happiest girl in the world. A smile tugged at my lips no matter how hard I tried to hide it.

Francesca caught the look. "You don't love him, my ass."

"What?" I asked in mock offense. "I don't."

"You so do." She pointed her finger at me. "It's written all over your face."

"I'm just happy—that's all."

"Oh whatever." She rolled her eyes.

The bell rang overhead.

She continued on like she didn't hear the sound. "You want to marry him and have all of his babies—"

"Shut up." Axel just walked inside, wearing his suit like he just got off work. "Dude, play it cool."

Francesca spotted him then shut her mouth, but her eyes betrayed her unease.

Axel stood at the counter and eyed us back and forth. "Did I just walk in on something?"

"No." I straightened out my apron and approached the register. "We were arguing over who's cuter. Jake Gyllenhaal or Adam Levine." I put my hand on my hip and tried to act natural.

His eyes lacked any suspicion. "The answer is neither."

"Adam Levine," Francesca said. "I like his ink."

"Jake Gyllenhaal has pretty eyes," I countered.

"Well, my eyes are prettier," Axel argued. "Who cares about those losers?"

I tried not to laugh. "Are you jealous…?"

"No," he said defensively. "I just think they are both ugly and stupid—that's all."

Francesca didn't hide her laugh like I did. "Axel, you're such a girl."

"What?" he argued. "How would you feel if I was talking about other beautiful women?"

I shrugged. "I don't think I'd care…"

"Really?" he asked. "If I were talking about how hot Beyonce is you wouldn't mind?"

"I didn't realize Beyonce was your type…"

"She's not," Axel said. "I'm just saying."

Francesca laughed again before she walked into the back. "What a loser."

Axel leaned over the counter. "Why don't you go scrub a toilet or something?"

"Why don't you?" Francesca turned around and gave him the bird. Then she stuck out her tongue and disappeared into the back.

If Axel and I were going to be together for a while I'd have to get used to their bickering. "If it offends you I won't say anything anymore." The idea of him being jealous over someone I would never meet was a little ridiculous but cute at the same time.

When he didn't say otherwise, I knew he really was jealous. "When is your shift over?"

"Ten."

"Are you coming over?"

"I can't live at your place."

"Why not?" he countered.

"I shouldn't leave Frankie home alone too much…"

"She's fine."

"Even so…" I didn't want to completely ditch her the second I got a boyfriend. That's not what real friends do.

"Then I'll stay over there."

"That's just weird."

"Why?" He rested his elbows on the counter and leaned forward.

"Because you're her brother?" Did I need to go into more details? "Our bedrooms are right next door to each other. It would totally gross her out, and I don't blame her."

"Like she didn't have Hawke over."

"Actually, she never really did. Most of the time she stayed at his place."

Axel was irritated that he wasn't getting his way. "Then you come to my place. I'll make you a drawer and everything."

"How about tomorrow?"

He shook his head. "Nope."

"You're bossy, you know that?"

"I just know what I want. Totally different."

The bell rang overhead and I glanced at the door to see a customer walk inside. "You gonna order something or what?"

"I don't know. Are you gonna sleep over or what?"

"Tomorrow."

He stayed at the counter.

Since he was going to do this I had to give into him. "Fine."

"Then I'll buy a black coffee." He set the cash on the table.

I handed his drink over, glaring at him the entire time. He winked then walked away.

***

We were about to close when a guy from my ethics class walked inside. He had a friend with him and their backpacks hung from their shoulders like they just got out of class.

"Hey, Marie." Jason was nice but I didn't know him that well.

"Hey. Ready for that exam?"

"No." He pointed to his backpack. "That's why I'm getting the caffeine." He paid for an espresso then stepped aside so his friend could order.

"I'll take the same." He set the money on the counter.

Francesca came from the back with a syrup bottle. "I found an extra vanilla syrup so we aren't out after all."

The guy's eyes traveled to her, remaining glued there for several seconds.

"Cool," I said. "Now our customers won't be so pissed."

She traded it out for the empty bottle then took it in the back to toss it.

I made the espresso then rang him up. "Two bucks."

He opened his wallet and handed me the cash. "Is she your friend?"

"Who?" I asked. "Frankie?"

"Yeah."

"Yeah, she's my roommate."

"Cool." He grabbed his coffee but didn't leave. "Is she seeing anybody...?"

Hawke was out of the picture for good but she didn't seem ready to date yet. But I didn't want to make that decision for her. "No. She's single."

"Cool." He sipped his coffee then joined Jason at one of the tables.

Francesca returned to the front and eyed the clock. "Still got half an hour to go..."

I turned my back to her admirer then lowered my voice. "That guy sitting at the table over there...he thinks you're cute."

"Me?" She pointed at her chest.

"Yeah, you."

"Oh..." She looked over my shoulder. "Which one?"

"The guy in black."

"Oh…" She turned her attention back to me. "That's flattering."

"I think he's going to ask you out before he leaves."

"Oh…" It was the third time she said that.

"You interested?"

"I don't know…"

I didn't want to push her into something she wasn't ready for so I said nothing.

"What do you think?"

"What do you mean?" I asked. "He's cute."

"I mean, do you think I should go out with him?"

"Well, do *you* think he's cute?"

"Well, yeah."

"Then go out with him."

"Is it too soon…?" She crossed her arms over her chest.

Hawke had been gone for three months, and it was obvious he was seeing other people. She definitely waited long enough. "No. I think you should go for it."

"I guess one date wouldn't be the end of the world."

"No, it wouldn't." If she really agreed to go on a date with him, then that was great news. Things were taking a good turn.

"If he talks to me I'll think about it."

"Cool." I acted like this conversation wasn't a big deal at all. "Whatever." I grabbed the broom and started sweeping so I had something to do.

***

Just when we were about to lock up the guy made his move.

He walked to the counter where Francesca was standing. "Hey."

"Hi..." She stopped wiping off the counter.

"Are you new? I come in here all the time but I've never seen you before."

"Yeah, I just started today." She gave the simpler version.

"Cool. I'm excited to try your coffee. I know each barista has their own way of making things."

"Yeah...I'd say my drinks are pretty decent."

He stayed at the counter and continued to stare at her. He had light brown hair and pretty eyes that would make any girl interested.

Please ask her out.

"How about you and I get a drink together sometime? That way you can take a break."

Francesca stiffened at the question, her hand gripping the hand towel.

Shit, she was going to say no.

Don't chicken out.

"Uh..." She fidgeted as she stared him down. "Yeah, that'd be fun."

I wanted to break out into a dance right then and there.

"Cool." He pulled out his phone. "Can I have your number?"

Francesca gave it to him.

"I'll give you a call. What's your name, by the way?"

"Frankie."

"Cool. I'm Cameron." He shook her hand. "I'll talk to you soon."

"Okay. See ya."

"Bye." He walked out and Jason followed behind him.

Jason was just about to reach the door when he turned back to the counter. "Hey, Marie?"

"What's up?"

"You free Friday night?"

Was he asking me out? "I'm flattered but I have a boyfriend."

"Oh." He shrugged in disappointment. "What a bummer."

"I'll see you in class."

He waved then joined Cameron outside.

I was so happy for Francesca I could scream. She actually gave her number to a guy and she was going on a date with him. This was the best day in a long time. I wanted to squeal and dance but I kept my cool. Knowing Francesca, if I made too much of a fuss about it she would freak out and retreat into her hole.

***

"Really?" Axel asked as we lay in bed together. "Some guy asked her out?"

"And he was cute."

He narrowed his eyes.

"I'm just saying." Never knew he was the jealous type. "I'm so happy for her."

"It's a big step." He kissed my bare shoulder, his kiss warm and soft.

"Hopefully they hit it off and spend some time together. When she's with another guy, it'll help her move on."

"I'm sure." He pulled me to his chest, placing me on top of him. His hand rested on the small of my back, and his lips were pressed to my hairline. He felt like a slab of concrete, but more comfortable. When he took a deep breath, I felt my body rise with his chest. "I could lay here forever."

"Yeah?" I sat up and looked down into his face.

"You're like a stuffed animal or something." His fingers moved through my hair. "You're soft and warm."

"Did you have sex with your stuffed animals?"

He shrugged and then gave a guilty grin. "Francesca did have this rabbit…"

"Gross." I smacked him on the arm.

"What? I just hit puberty and I didn't know what else to do."

"Your hand wasn't your first thought?"

"My hand isn't soft. It's all dry and calloused." He kissed my shoulder again.

"That's disgusting." My words didn't have much conviction because the kiss of his lips was too intoxicating.

"Oh yeah?" His lips traveled to my ear. "Would you like to be my new rabbit?"

"Not really."

"Sure…" He gave my side a gentle tickle.

I swatted him away. "I'll never be your sex toy."

"Well, I'm yours." He snuggled into my side, hugging me like a stuffed animal.

I eyed the clock and realized the time. Neither one of us had dinner because we were too comfortable to move. The thought made my stomach rumble loudly.

Axel moved his hand to my stomach and grinned. "Is my baby hungry?"

It was the second time he called me that. Every time he did, I paid attention to it. "A little."

"What would you like?" His hand moved slowly up my arm, feeling every inch of my skin.

"I don't care. What do you want?"

"Well, if you want to go out I'll take you somewhere nice. But if you want to stick around, mainly in bed, I'll order a cheesy pizza."

"Hmm…I do like pizza."

He smirked as he waited for my response.

"And I do like staying in bed…"

"Pizza it is." He grabbed his phone and placed the order online. "I prefer eating naked anyway. And if we went to a nice restaurant we'd get kicked out."

"I can imagine."

He set his phone on the nightstand and turned back to me. His arms and chest were hard and defined, and I wondered if he pushed tractor tires around for exercise.

"When do you work out?"

"Usually in the morning," he answered. "But lately I haven't been working out at all—outside the bedroom."

My hand ran over his thick arm, feeling the separation in his biceps and triceps.

"You like that?"

I shrugged. "I don't hate it."

"Whatever," he said with a chuckle. "All the women love it."

I gave him a threatening look.

He quickly realized his mistake. "I mean...what women?"

"That's better." I may not be jealous of famous people he was attracted to, but I was definitely jealous of the real women who shared this bed with him. With every passing day I was growing attached to him, realizing how lucky I was to be in this relationship. Axel didn't do commitments. I was his first one. That had to mean something.

Despite Axel's ignorance about a lot of things, the thoughtful side of him always emerged. It may be difficult for him to remain serious for any given amount of time, but when he was it was a beautiful thing. I was a witness to the way he looked after his sister, watching over her day after day. Without expecting anything in return he paid her bills and kept food on the table. He even took care of her school assignments so she would still graduate on time. He didn't do that just because she was his sister.

He did it because he loved her.

I'd been watching Axel my whole life, from a distance, and I already knew all of his amazing attributes. He was honest, loyal, and caring. He might get his head lost in the clouds when it came to women and booze, but that didn't make him a bad person.

Like all people, he was complicated. He wasn't one-dimensional at all. But I liked him that way. Maybe no one else understood him, but I did.

"What?" Axel had been staring at me the entire time, noting the way I fell silent.

"Nothing." I returned my head to the pillow and got comfortable.

"You were thinking about something." His eyes lost their playful edge, and he stared at me with a different look. He was searching my face, trying to find the answer on his own.

I had too many thoughts to explain in a single sentence. "When's that pizza going to get here?"

***

Francesca rapped her knuckles against my door. "Marie. I need your help."

Axel immediately got off of me and took the sheets with him. Both panic and irritation crept into his features.

I kicked off the blankets and pulled my pajamas on.

Axel released a loud sigh. It practically came out as a growl.

I put my forefinger to my lips to hush him.

He growled again.

I fixed my hair then quickly opened the door and stepped out, shutting it behind me so quickly that it made a loud thud. I didn't want Francesca to get a peek of Axel inside. He and I weren't hiding anything but I didn't want to parade it in front of her. "What's up, Frankie?" I walked into the kitchen and pretended I needed a glass of water.

She trailed behind me with her phone in her hand. "Cameron texted me and I don't know what to do." Like it was a disgusting bug she threw it at me.

I caught it before it hit the ground. "What do you mean you don't know what to do?"

She shrugged. "I don't know...he asked me out."

I unlocked the screen. *If you're free tomorrow night, let's grab a drink. Coffee or cocktails, it's your call.*

He seemed nice. He wasn't too forward but he wasn't too docile either. "Why don't you write him back?"

"I don't know what to say." She crossed her arms over her chest, bundling her shirt in the front. Her clothes were still too big because she hadn't gained back the weight she lost. Her dark hair was pulled into a high bun.

"Well, do you want to go out with him?"

She stared at the floor and shrugged.

I missed the old Francesca. She knew exactly what she wanted and when she wanted it. Nothing intimidated her, and we certainly never had these types of conversations. "Frankie?"

"Look, I don't know." She threw her arms down. "He was cute and nice...there's nothing wrong with him."

I wish Hawke's shadow would just pass already. It'd been three months. That should be enough time for her to move on. But of course, I would never say that to her. "So, you're saying there's nothing wrong with Cameron?"

"I guess."

"Then what's holding you back?"

She didn't answer my question. All she did was give me a look.

I knew what that meant. "If that's the only reason, I think you should go out with him."

"Do you think that's fair to Cameron? I'm a hot mess over here."

"Be honest about it. If he doesn't like it he'll never call you again. Problem solved."

"I guess..."

I handed the phone back to her.

She eyed it without taking it. "Ugh...I hate this."

"What?"

"I hate dating. I already found the person I want for the rest of my life. Now I have to do it all over again." She took a deep breath that sounded painful. "It's just so much work and heartache. Is it really worth it?"

"Don't think about it like that." Otherwise, she would go crazy. "Think of it as meeting someone new. There's no pressure. Just have fun with it. If you like his company, see him again. If you don't, then that's it."

She kept eyeing the phone.

"Frankie, come on."

"What if we make it a double date?"

"A double date?" Frankie and I had never done that—not once.

"You and Axel can tag along."

Wouldn't that be weird?

"Come on," she said. "It'll make it less intimate. I don't know if I can do a one-on-one thing right now."

A double date didn't sound appetizing at all, but I would do whatever my best friend wanted. "We can do that." Axel wouldn't like it one bit but I'd convince him to get on board...somehow.

"Okay." She took the phone and typed a response to him.

"Make sure he knows it's a double date so he isn't caught off guard."

"I will." She hit the send button. "Now, I'll just wait and see what he says..."

Did I have to wait too? "Well...I'm going back to bed." Not to sleep, but that was beside the point.

Her phone lit up. "Wait. He said something."

"What?" I hid my irritation as much as possible.

"He said he's fine with the double date." She locked the screen and looked up at me.

"That's great. When are we going?"

"On Friday."

"How exciting." It wasn't exciting in the least but Francesca didn't need to know that. Once she was back in the game things would get easier.

"What am I going to wear?" She crossed her arms over her chest and tucked her phone into her side. "Nothing fits anymore..."

"We'll go on an emergency shopping spree." I gave her shoulder an affectionate squeeze before I turned back to the hallway. "Night."

Francesca stayed in the kitchen and opened the fridge. "Night."

I walked back into my bedroom and locked the door behind me.

"What the hell did that annoying piece of shit want?" When Axel was horny and unsatisfied, his temper flared.

"Boy trouble." I removed my clothes and got back to bed. "That's why you shouldn't stay here."

"No. That's why Francesca should just go to sleep and leave you alone like a normal person." He pushed me on the bed the second I was near and crawled on top of me. Despite my absence he was still hard.

"Wow..." I glanced at his impressive size.

"I found your lotion in your drawer. I carried on without you."

It should disgust me but it didn't. "That's pretty hot."

"You know what I was thinking about?" He positioned himself on top of me then shoved himself inside me.

The second I felt him I stopped paying attention to the words coming out of his mouth.

He rocked into me and pressed his mouth to my ear. "This."

***

Francesca was a total mess. "What do you think of this?" She wore a short black dress with a matching clutch. Her hair was straight with a slight curl at the ends. Her limited curves were highlighted in the fabric. Despite her lack of confidence she looked great.

"Hot as hell."

"Really?" Francesca looked down at herself like she thought I was confused.

"Absolutely."

Axel had a bored look on his face, like he couldn't wait for this double date to be over and done with.

Francesca tucked her hair behind her ear. "Okay…I'll wear this. You don't think it's too slutty?"

She used to wear stuff like that all the time. "No. My dress is the same length."

Axel leaned toward my ear. "But you can pull it off."

I elbowed him in the gut.

He bent at the waist slightly and groaned.

The doorbell rang.

"That's him." I grabbed my clutch from the table. "Let's go."

Francesca was pale in the face, like she'd been hoping he wouldn't show up.

"It'll be fine." I wrapped my arm around her shoulders. "Remember, it's your first date. It probably won't be magical or even fun but you have to do it. After this, it'll get easier." That wasn't the most consoling thing I could have said but at least it was the truth.

Francesca nodded. "Okay."

***

Francesca and Cameron sat side-by-side across the table from Axel and I. Since none of us knew Cameron it was difficult to start a conversation. Francesca sat awkwardly beside him, hunched and practically a human ball.

I came to Francesca's rescue. "Are you in my ethics class?" I didn't recognize him but the class was pretty big.

"No. I have world lit with Jason. We study together sometimes. We're both slackers so we rely on the buddy system to get things down." He wore a gray t-shirt that showed off his nice arms. He had pretty eyes and a tall stature. There was no way Francesca wasn't attracted to him—even if she wasn't over Hawke.

"Cool," I said. "Frankie and I have never had a class together—ironically." I turned to her and silently commanded her to jump into the conversation.

She cleared her throat. "Yeah...we never have."

I wanted to kick her under the table.

Cameron turned to Axel. "Where did you go to school?"

"Florida," Axel answered. "I originally went there for all the parties and chicks...but then the humidity got old."

Cameron chuckled. "I can see that."

"I came back here to keep an eye on my sister." Axel glanced at Francesca.

Cameron immediately stiffened. "You're her brother...?"

I didn't realize that might make the date awkward. "But they aren't close. He's only here because he's my boyfriend. He's not the annoying, protective type." Well, he was. But Cameron didn't need to know that.

"Good to know..." Cameron eyed his menu even though we already ordered.

I tapped my foot against Francesca's.

She looked up at me, looking like a lost dog.

I subtly nodded to Cameron, telling her to talk to him.

She eyed him before her face became paler. "So...you like cheese?"

What the hell is she doing?

Axel even raised an eyebrow.

I wanted to cover my face and die out of embarrassment.

"Uh...yeah." Cameron watched her fair face. "I put it on my sandwiches and stuff."

Axel turned to me with both eyebrows raised.

I shook my head slightly.

"Do *you* like cheese?" Cameron asked the question hesitantly, like he wasn't sure if this was a serious conversation or not.

"Yeah," Francesca answered. "But I try not to eat it too much otherwise I get backed up..." Her eyes lost their light when she realized what she just said.

Oh. My. God.

Cameron had the decency not to look revolted. "Yeah...you've got to watch out for that."

Axel pressed his lips tightly together and tried not to laugh.

"Excuse me." Cameron left the table and headed for the bathroom.

I immediately turned on Francesca. "What the hell?"

"I don't know," she blurted. "I don't know how to talk to him."

"But you do know how to talk to people, right?" I snapped.

"I'm just nervous." She bunched her hands together. "Maybe this wasn't a good idea..."

Axel took a long drink of his beer, needing to be drunk to get through this.

"Excuse me." I threw my napkin down and headed to the bathroom. Cameron wasn't outside so he must have already gone in. Without thinking twice about it I walked into the men's restroom.

He was standing at the urinal and just flushed it.

"She's super nervous. Please cut her some slack."

He nearly jumped into the air when he spotted me in the reflection of the mirror. "What the hell?" He zipped up his fly and pulled down his t-shirt. "You know this is the men's restroom, right?"

"Yes. I can see the urinal." I stepped closer to him and crossed my arms over my chest. "Look, there are a few things you should know. She got out of a serious relationship not that long ago so she's having a hard time adjusting to dating life."

He washed his hands in the sink. "I picked up on that. How long ago did this relationship end?"

"Three months."

He patted his hands dry with a paper towel. "I get it. I've been through a break up before."

"So, don't blow her off. I know she's acting like a weirdo right now but she's really not like that. She's usually confident, funny, and smart. Honestly, you couldn't find a better woman than she—when she's herself."

"I'll have to take your word for it."

"So...please give her another chance."

"Did you think I was going to sneak out the back or something?"

"No." I shook my head. "But I have a feeling you aren't going to ask her out again."

He put his hands in his pockets, a guilty look coming over his face.

"Please?" I wasn't above begging at this point.

"Maybe you should have let it just be she and I."

"She wanted us to come along. But next time we won't."

He rubbed the back of his neck like he'd been cornered. "Okay. I'll ask her out again. But only because she's really cute."

Thank god. "Great. I promise, it'll be worth it."

"If she has a girlfriend who's willing to corner me in the bathroom, then she must be an incredible person."

"Exactly."

"Or she's crazy."

"Uh…maybe both."

The door opened and Axel walked inside. He halted in mid-step when he spotted me. "Baby…what are you doing?"

"I just wanted to talk to Cameron alone." I crossed my arms over my chest.

Axel still looked confused. "In the bathroom…?"

Cameron walked passed us. "I'll see you out there." The door shut behind him.

Now that he was gone I lowered my hands. "I wanted to talk to him without Francesca knowing."

Axel bent over and peeked under the stalls to make sure we were alone. "Since we're here…" He wrapped his arms around my waist and lifted my dress. "How about a quickie in the stall?"

"Ew." I swatted him on the shoulder. "The bathroom is the most disgusting place ever."

"And you're dirty."

I swatted him again even though I liked what he said. "You're a pig."

His hand gripped my bare ass and he kissed me hard on the mouth, feeling my lips with his. He gave me a little tongue as he played with my thong and pulled it over.

His touch excited me in ways I couldn't explain. The scene of the bathroom stall and urinals disappeared from my vision. All I thought about was Axel. He kissed my jawline then moved up to my ear. When he got there, he whispered something. "Oink oink."

***

The four of us walked to the front door at the end of the night. Francesca was still tense, looking frightened of everyone and everything.

"Well, good night." I unlocked the door and Axel and I walked inside. I shut the door behind me and pressed my ear to the wood.

"What are you doing?" Axel asked.

"Shh." I waved him away.

Cameron's voice came through the door. "I had a great time tonight."

"You did?" Francesca blurted out the words like she couldn't believe him.

"Yeah," he said. "I mean, it was a little awkward but first dates can be that way."

He was being so patient with her, and that made me like him a great deal. Most guys would take off once they realized she was damaged goods.

Thursday

"I'm not normally this awkward," Francesca said. "Honestly, I haven't been on a date in a long time. I was in a serious relationship a few months ago..."

Cameron pretended that was new information. "Break ups are hard. I've been there."

"Yeah?" she asked, hope in her tone.

"Yeah," he said. "We were together for a few years then she dumped me. She never really explained why. I struggled for a long time until I finally got over her. I went on a lot of first dates that never led to second dates. It took some time for me to regain my confidence and personality."

"Oh...then you understand."

"I understand very well. So, don't beat yourself up over it."

"Thanks..." It was the first time her voice was free of fear. She actually seemed happy.

"So...you want to go out again?"

I clutched my chest and smiled because this conversation was going so well.

Axel shook his head. "You're such a weirdo."

I threw my wallet at him.

Francesca's voice came through the door. "I'd love to."

"Cool," he said. "And how about it just be you and I? Marie and Axel are nice but...I'd like to get to know you better."

"Great idea."

"Cool. I'll see you later." His footsteps hit the stairs.

"Run." I left the door and pulled Axel with me into the living room. "Act cool."

"Why?" he asked. "You were just listening to the door like a child. You're anything but cool."

"What was that?" I cupped my ear with my fingers. "No sex tonight?"

He glared at me.

"You got it."

Francesca walked inside and shut the door.

Axel leaned toward me and lowered his voice. "You want it as much as I do."

I pushed him away and tried to act natural. "So, did you like him…?" I pretended I didn't hear their conversation through the door, but it was difficult to act like I didn't know anything.

"Yeah…I think I did." A small smile formed on her lips.

This was awesome. "Great. Are you going to see him again?"

"He asked me out," she said. "I was a little surprised."

"A little?" Axel asked. "I'm shocked. You asked if he liked cheese then proceeded to tell him about your bowel movements."

"Axel, shut up." I excused him from the conversation. "So, you're going to see him again?"

"Yeah," she answered. "He said he went through a bad break up a few years ago so he understands what I'm feeling. It's nice to be around someone who gets it."

"Yeah," I said. "It must be."

"And he was nice and sweet...I'll give it a try."

It kept getting better and better. "Axel and I really liked him. You should go for it."

"I think I will." She drifted away down the hallway and entered her bedroom.

I turned back to Axel with a large smile on my face. "She's going to be okay. I can tell."

"Maybe if she gets laid she'll be back to normal."

"Don't be gross."

"I'm just saying. Sex has healing powers."

"Does not."

"You want me to show you?" He leaned in and wiggled his eyebrows.

"Is that supposed to be sexy?" When he made faces like that, he just looked ridiculous.

"You tell me." His hands wrapped around me just as they did earlier, and his fingers gripped my dress and slowly pulled it up.

"This is sexy."

He wiggled his eyebrows again.

"That is not."

He chuckled then lifted me into the air, wrapping my legs around his waist. "Believe me, I can make it sexy."

CHAPTER TWENTY-THREE

Pizza and Beer

Axel

I made the trip to New York on Friday evening to meet up with Hawke. He had tickets to a Ranger game, and we got pizza and beer afterwards. Our friendship was slowly returning back to normal. Now that Francesca was getting back on track I didn't resent him as much.

"Dude, have you ever had sex without a condom?" I couldn't get over how good the sex with Marie was. It was a million times better than that casual screw we had months ago. We were connected on a spiritual level. It wasn't just about the movement we made. It was a lot more.

Hawke was about to take a bite of his pizza but stopped when he heard my question. He gave me a dark look, like I just asked him something I shouldn't.

And then I realized what I said. "Oh right. I forgot...sorry." Enough time had passed that I forgot he and

Francesca were ever together. "Don't answer that otherwise I'll puke all the shit I just ate." I took a long drink of my beer to wash away the bad taste in my mouth.

Hawke set his slice down. "Why do you ask?"

"Marie and I don't use rubbers anymore." There were no words to describe how good it felt. Being inside her, skin-to-skin, was the most amazing experience of my life. And coming inside her was even better. I'd never gone bareback with a woman because I was never monogamous before Marie. But now she and I were exclusive I made love to her every chance I got.

"Whole different experience, huh?" He grabbed his slice and took a bite.

"It's so different. I don't think I could ever go back to condoms." I shivered in repulsion just thinking about it.

"Then it looks like you're going to be with Marie for the rest of your life." He gave me a teasing look.

"Whoa, I never said that."

"It's implied."

"I like Marie and I don't want to be with anyone else...but marriage isn't on my mind."

"Axel, there's nothing to be ashamed of."

"I'm not lying." Marie was the only woman on my mind. I didn't even check out other girls anymore, and when I slept alone I tossed and turned all night without her next to me. When I was at work, she was all I thought about. I didn't think I could be a boyfriend to anyone, but I realized I was doing a pretty good job with her. But marriage...not on my mind.

Hawke finally backed off. "You guys haven't been together very long so I get it. But when you love someone they're the only person you ever want to be around, and not just now but forever."

"Whoa, who said anything about love?"

Hawke gave me a blank stare.

"Look, I don't love Marie. I really like her and care about her. I don't want to be with anyone or anything like that. But I don't love her."

"Are you sure...?" Hawke rested his hand on his beer and gave me an incredulous look.

"Yes." I think I would know if I loved someone or not.

"I think you're in denial."

"I'm really not."

He chuckled before he took a drink. "Whatever."

"Whatever what?" If Hawke thought I loved her, maybe Marie thought the same thing.

"Nothing." He set the glass down then took another slice.

"No," I pressed. "What are you laughing about?"

"It doesn't matter, Axel."

I glared at him. "Spit it out."

"What does it matter what I think?"

"It doesn't..." But I still wanted to know.

"Love is a strange thing. No matter how much you want to deny it, it comes after you. Push it away all you want but you can never escape it. If it's there, it's there. You know what I mean?"

"No, not at all."

He shrugged then took a bite. "Why are you so determined not to fall in love?"

"I'm not. I just...I don't know."

He silently egged me on.

I couldn't tell him that Francesca tried to kill herself. I'd take that secret to my grave. "My dad was a coward. I'm afraid I'm a coward too."

Hawke gripped his beer and stared at me for nearly a minute. His eyes changed, dilating and hiding something deep within. "How do you figure?"

"When things got tough, he took his own life. He and I are very similar. I'm afraid I'm not any different. If times get tough, I'll do something stupid and reckless. I'm not reliable."

"You're making a lot of assumptions, Axel."

"I just don't think I'd be a very good husband and father. Right now, I really like where Marie and I are. She makes me happy and I can't picture my life without her. But beyond that, I don't see a future. I just want to enjoy her as long as I can."

He gave me a sad look. "For what its worth, I don't think that."

"Think what?"

"That you wouldn't be a good husband and father."

"Shows what you know..."

"You look after Francesca." He faltered when he said her name. "I know she's not your daughter but you always have her back. That's the kind of man you are."

Hawke would never understand. He didn't walk in and see my dad's brains all over the walls. He didn't see the way he closed off from us when my mom passed away. He didn't know my dad didn't even show up for the funeral. He didn't know Francesca almost killed herself too. If Francesca, the strongest person I knew, couldn't carry on then I was no different. When it came down to it, I was weak. I wasn't reliable. I was shit.

Hawke sensed my mood and backed off. "What else is new with you?"

"The internship is slowing down."

"Meaning?"

"I've learned everything I need to know. I've pretty much gotten everything out of it as I can."

"Then leave." Hawke took off to New York and got a job pretty quickly.

"I might apply for a few jobs here in the city."

"What about Marie?"

"She wants to move here anyway. So that works."

"Perfect." He took a drink. "And...does Francesca still intend to move here?"

I didn't have a clue. After their breakup I wasn't sure if her plans had changed. "She hasn't said otherwise so I would assume so."

Thursday

He nodded then took another drink. "How is she?" Whenever he asked the question, it didn't seem like he wanted to know the answer.

I was glad I finally didn't have to lie. "Really well. Almost done with school. She's seeing this guy named Cameron. He's nice. I like him." At this point I didn't care who she dated as long as she tried to move on. But Cameron was patient with her. When she made an idiot out of herself, he didn't give her a hard time about it. And he asked her out again because he knew she was nervous. If it were me, I'd take off. Obviously, Cameron was the bigger man.

Hawke stared at me in silence, the pain written all over his face.

I didn't know what to do. He was the one who asked about her.

"Are they serious…?"

"No, I don't think so. They've just been seeing each other for a while." That was a lie but he didn't need to know that. I refused to tell him how much she struggled. I had to make sure my sister looked strong in his eyes.

He nodded slowly, like he didn't know what else to do.

"Have you been seeing anyone?" I assumed he was back to his old ways, hitting the sheets with a different girl every night. But I asked anyway since he asked about Francesca.

He shrugged. "Nothing serious."

I didn't ask any more questions about it.

"I've never been so miserable in my life." He looked out the window and didn't meet my gaze. "I'm glad she's doing better than I am. She doesn't deserve anything but happiness."

When he said things like that, I became even more confused. If they still loved each other, why couldn't they make it work? I'd given up on their strange relationship. Hopefully, Francesca would settle down with a normal, boring guy. It'd make my life a lot easier.

***

I was exhausted when I came home that night. It was a long drive, and the clock on the nightstand had an unearthly hour on it. I threw my clothes off then collapsed into bed. I didn't even brush my teeth because I was so tired.

But when I closed my eyes I couldn't go to sleep.

I kept tossing and turning, trying to get comfortable in the large bed. The sheets were just washed so they were more comfortable than usual, but even then I couldn't find the right position.

Just a few minutes ago I couldn't keep my eyes open. But now my body was buzzing with alertness.

I didn't want to admit the truth, not even to myself. After everything Hawke said tonight I was even more uncomfortable. My body didn't crave a warm body beside me. It craved something much more specific. It needed that soft hair to brush across my skin, exciting me and calming me at the same time. It needed that random sigh that escaped her lips softly, waking me up every few hours without truly reaching consciousness. It needed to fight for the sheets she always stole from me. It needed the tangle of our legs when I spooned her from behind.

It needed the one woman I couldn't live without.

***

Even though Francesca was working I knew the girls still struggled to get by. Francesca wasn't working as many hours as she used to, so she was barely making rent. No one asked me to, but I still took care of the groceries. I didn't make a whole lot at my internship and I was breaking even every month, but they didn't need to know that.

I walked inside the house with bags tucked under my arm.

"You look great." Marie's voice came from around the corner.

I walked inside and set the bags on the table. "Thank you." Francesca stood in the kitchen wearing a dress with a pink cardigan.

Marie rolled her eyes. "I'm not talking about you."

Francesca eyed the clock on the wall. "He'll be here any minute…"

"Why are you nervous?" I asked. "You've already gone out with him."

"I don't know," she answered. "Still nerve-wracking."

Like he knew we were talking about him the doorbell rang.

"Shit, that's him." Francesca breathed hard and fidgeted with her hair.

"Girl, you'll be fine." Marie tucked the clutch under her arm then fixed her hair. "You look perfect. Now strut out there and flaunt it."

Francesca had a blank look on her face. "I don't know about all of that but I'll go." She walked to the entryway and opened the door. After a short conversation, they left in his truck.

Marie unpacked everything and put it away. "Thanks for the food."

"No problem." I stood with my hands in my pockets, watching her move about the kitchen gracefully. She had a steep curve in her lower back and a nice ass. Her legs were lean and toned, and her hair was always done in cute ways. I could stand there and watch her forever.

While I noticed her obvious beauty because it stared at me right in the face, I also noticed the way she shifted her weight when she walked. Her dominant foot was her left one even though she was right-handed. Whenever she was trying to solve a problem, she always scrunched up her nose and bit her bottom lip at the same time. Even though the milk in the fridge was empty and expired, she left it there and added the next carton beside it. She always did this, and I suspected she assumed it was Francesca's job to take care of it since she didn't drink milk. I noticed all of her little quirks, all the things that made her who she was.

Marie finished putting away the groceries and noticed my stare. "What?"

Thursday

"Nothing." I looked away and pretended I hadn't been staring for the past fifteen minutes.

She pulled her hair over one shoulder and she sauntered toward me, rolling her hips as she moved.

The second her neck was exposed I noticed the area. It was flawless and soft, feeling perfect against my lips. When she was close enough, my arm hooked around her waist, and I placed a kiss on the exposed area, tasting her. Her waist was the perfect size for my arm. I could hook it around her like bait on the end of the line. I gave the skin a gentle suck before I pulled away.

She looked up at me with lidded eyes, like she thoroughly enjoyed the affection. "How was work?"

"Blah."

"Blah? Is that even a word?"

"It is now."

"And why was it blah?" She snaked her hands up my chest.

"I was exhausted. Still am."

"Why is my man so tired?"

I liked it when she called me that. "Didn't get home until late last night. And when I got into bed I couldn't sleep."

"Why not?"

I knew why. "I'm not sure."

"How was Hawke?" Her tone still hinted at her hatred. She disliked him less but she would never see him in the same light like she used to.

"About the same."

"What did you tell him about Frankie?"

"That she's perfect and seeing Cameron."

"Good. No need to tell him the truth."

"Never." Francesca didn't want me to tell him, and I didn't want to tell him anyway.

"Did you guys have fun?"

"Yeah. We went to a game then had dinner."

"Is he seeing anyone?"

I shrugged. "Casually." He and I had a long conversation about my feelings for Marie but I wasn't going to tell her that.

"That's what Francesca assumed…"

"Let's keep it to ourselves."

"I couldn't tell her anyway. It would break the one rule she made."

"True."

Her hands moved to my shoulders and she rubbed the muscle gently. "How about I make sweet love to you and then we take a nap?"

My cock hardened at the question. "I'd love that."

"I'll be on top." She grabbed my hand and guided me into her bedroom.

I loved it when she rode my cock. She was so good at it. "No argument here."

She looked at me over her shoulder and gave me a playful look. "I thought not."

***

Thursday

My arm was wrapped around her shoulders as we sat together on the couch. It was ten in the evening and Francesca still hadn't come home. A basketball game was on the TV but neither one of us were watching it.

"Should we call?" she asked.

"She's fine," I said. "The later she's out the better." My eyes kept drifting to her lips. They were plump and full. Sometimes I wanted to rub my dick across them. And other times, like now, I wanted to rub my own mouth against them.

"But what if—"

I moved my mouth to hers and kissed her slowly. We already made love just a few hours ago, but now I ached for her kiss. Making out on the couch was something I used to do in eighth grade, but now I was doing it again and enjoying it. My hand fisted her hair and I slowly made love to her mouth. When her tongue touched mine, it sent an explosion through my body. I never felt more alive and close to death at the same time.

Thirty minutes passed and we kept kissing, our tongues dancing together. She was the best kisser my mouth had ever tasted and I could do this forever. Whether she liked it or not, I was sleeping here or she was staying at my place. It was one or the other.

The sound of a truck parking outside disrupted our make out session.

"I think she's home." Marie pulled away, her lips puckered and swollen. Her hair was a mess from the way I fisted it so much.

I wanted to keep kissing her. "So?"

"Let's see how it went." She left my side and placed her ear against the front door.

I didn't care how my sister's date went. All I wanted was to finish that kiss—if it would ever be finished. I came to her side and listened for a conversation.

"I had a great time tonight," Francesca said.

"Me too," Cameron said. "I'm glad you opened up a bit."

Francesca chuckled in a nervous way. "Yeah...it took me a while."

"Well...I guess this is good night."

Marie pressed her hands against the door. "Kiss her..."

I cringed.

There was a long break of silence, and that could only mean one thing.

Marie smiled the entire time, knowing exactly what was happening.

I still didn't care.

When they broke apart, Francesca spoke up. "Well, good night."

"Good night, Frankie." His voice trailed away.

Marie grabbed my arm and yanked me into the kitchen. She quickly fixed her hair and tried to act like everything was normal. "So, I was thinking we could try that new sushi place tomorrow. Everyone has been talking about it."

Thursday

I'd never seen Marie eat sushi. "Yeah...maybe."

Francesca rounded the corner, a slight smile on her lips.

"Oh, you're home?" Marie pretended to be surprised but she was terrible at it. "How was your date?"

"Pretty good," Francesca said. "I calmed down a lot."

"Great," Marie said. "Does that mean you're going to see him again?"

"I think so."

Marie almost squealed. "That's so great. I'm glad you like him."

"Yeah, he's a nice guy," she answered. "We'll see where it goes." She pulled out her phone from her clutch then headed to the hallway. "Good night, you guys."

"Good night," Marie called. When Francesca was out of sight, she did a little dance. "Yes. I'm so glad she likes him."

"Me too." It was nice to see her out and about, dating like she should be doing.

"Well, I should get to bed," she said. "Long day tomorrow."

If that was her polite way of asking me to leave, she had another thing coming. "I'm sleeping here."

"You remember what happened last time that happened?"

"I don't give a damn." If my sister was grossed out with me sleeping over then she could move on. "I either stay here or you come home with me. The ball is in your court, baby."

"Fine. I don't feel like arguing."

"Perfect. Me neither."

She walked down the hall and into her bedroom.

I walked behind her but stopped when I reached Francesca's door. "I'll be there in a second."

Marie disappeared.

I knocked on my sister's bedroom door. "Can I come in?"

"Yeah, sure."

I walked inside and saw her sitting on the bed in her pajamas. Her make up was already gone and her hair was in a bun. "What's up?"

I slowly approached the bed and took a seat beside her. I wasn't very good at these serious talks. After all this time I assumed I would improve but I never did. It was difficult being the older brother. Sometimes I wished we could switch—just for a day. "You really like this guy?"

"Yeah. He's sweet." She scrolled through her phone before she placed it on her nightstand. "Is there something you need, Axel?"

"I just...I want you to know I'm proud of you."

"For going on a date?"

"No. For moving on." I stared at her bedroom floor. "I know things haven't been easy but you're on the right path now. Seeing you get better makes me happy. I just want you to know that..."

"Axel..."

"I tease you a lot but we both know how I really feel." I stood up and returned my hands to my pockets. "Keep up the good work."

"Thanks, Axel."

I nodded before I left her bedroom and shut the door behind me. Before I walked into Marie's room I knew she would be eavesdropping against the door. I walked inside and saw her stagger back and try to pretend she wasn't doing the exact thing I knew she was doing.

She crossed her arms over her chest and acted nonchalant.

"I know you were listening."

"Oh…" The guilt came over her face. "Well…I thought that was sweet."

I shrugged and got ready for bed.

"You're a good man, Axel."

"I don't know about that," I said. "But I think I'm pretty decent."

CHAPTER TWENTY-FOUR

Family Night

Marie

I hated it when Mom texted me. Not because she was bothering me or invading my space. It was because she had no idea how to work the keyboard.

Honey, we matter you.

I eyed the text and couldn't decipher it. *What?*

Let's have thinner.

I cocked my head to the side. *Mom, just call me.*

The phone rang a second later.

"Mom, just call."

"I know everyone texts now. It's just easier that way."

"Not for you. Now, what were you trying to say?"

"We miss you," she said. "Every time I write a word it gets changed."

"Autocorrect."

"What?" she asked. "You got new auto insurance?"

I rolled my eyes. "Nevermind. I miss you too."

"Can we get together and have dinner?"

"Of course." Like I'd say no to my parents.

"How about dinner at that Italian place you love?" she said. "Your sister won't be coming but would you like to bring someone along...?" Her tone specified exactly whom she wanted to come along.

"Just me."

"Oh...there's really no one else?"

Axel already met my parents but I wasn't sure if he was ready for dinner. "Yep."

"Not even Axel? That nice man from the hospital?"

"Sorry. Just me."

"Really? Nothing happened between you two?"

How did she know? Somehow, she always knew. "Well...yes."

"I knew it." Her tone completely changed, becoming victorious. "Please bring him along. He's such good company."

I hated it when my mom spoke properly. She was a nurse, not an etiquette instructor. "I don't know..."

"Please. Your father and I really liked him."

When she pressured me like this, I didn't have a choice. "Fine."

"Great. See you tomorrow."

***

Axel remained on top of me and kissed me slowly. The clock on the nightstand said it was 3 A.M. and the time

338

was still ticking. He had work in the morning and I had school, but neither one of us seemed to care.

He already finished but he didn't slow down. He kissed me because he liked it, and I liked it too. When our lips were chapped and raw, he finally pulled away. "I love kissing you. I wish I could take those lips everywhere."

"I wish you could take my other lips too."

He immediately grinned. "My girl is dirty."

"No. I just know what I want."

He rubbed his nose against mine, an action he'd never done before, and then gave me a final peck. "Ambitious. I like it." He lay down in bed beside me and wrapped his arms around my body. We took the position we already did before we went to sleep.

"Axel?" I'd been dreading this conversation but now we needed to have it.

"Hmm?"

"Do you have plans tomorrow night?"

"Hopefully plans with you."

"Well...my parents want to have dinner and they really want you to come along."

"Me? Why?"

"I told them you were my boyfriend."

"Oh..."

"They really like you, Axel."

"That's a good thing."

"So, you'll come?"

Thursday

His hesitance was obvious even in his silence. He was tenser than he was before. I could feel it in his arms.

"I know this isn't exactly fun but my mom pestered the shit out of me. She wasn't going to take no for an answer."

He sighed.

"Is it really that big of a deal?" Now I felt hurt. He'd already met my parents before so why didn't he want to see them again? I knew we weren't getting married tomorrow but this relationship was going somewhere.

Axel sensed my unease because he held me tighter. "Of course not. You just dropped that on me."

"You've already met them so why is it weird?"

"It's not weird. It's just...I don't know."

"What?" I pressed.

"Serious," he answered. "I already met them but that was as your friend. As your boyfriend it's totally different."

"They already like you."

"I know...but it's different."

Now I was growing more insecure. "If you don't want to come you don't have to. I'm not going to force you into anything." I pulled the blanket tighter over my shoulder and focused on the clock. How could he make love to me for hours and not want to have dinner with my parents?

Axel knew he screwed up. "Baby, I want to come."

"No, you don't."

"Well, who the hell looks forward to spending time with their girlfriend's parents? It's terrifying for anyone. But I'll go. Of course I'll go."

I refused to look at him.

"Baby, come on. Don't be mad at me."

"I just assumed you would want to go...I feel stupid."

"Hey." He twisted my body until I faced him. He grabbed my chin and forced me to look at him. "I'll be there. Now stop being mad at me. I don't like it."

"You want to come?" It was never like me to be insecure, but I was in that moment.

"Yes." He held my gaze as he said it. "Absolutely."

Seeing his sincerity chased away my fears. "Okay. Tomorrow at seven."

"I'll pick you up at six thirty."

***

Axel arrived at my door wearing dark jeans and a collared shirt. His usual watch was on his wrist and his hair was done with precision. Despite his nice appearance he seemed unnerved.

"Axel, you've already met them."

"I know. But now they'll look at me differently. I've never done the girlfriend's parents thing. I'm totally clueless about it."

"Just treat them like normal people."

"Well, you know how I treat normal people. I start with a sexist joke and then I mention how big my dick is."

I rolled my eyes and walked out. "Just chill."

"You chill. How would you feel if you had to meet my parents?"

I turned around. "I already did, idiot."

"But it wasn't the same. You weren't my girlfriend."

"Whatever. They already like you. All the hard work has been done."

Francesca opened the door and stood on the stoop. "What are you guys arguing about?"

Axel turned to her and pointed at me. "I have to meet her parents tonight. Ugh."

Francesca crossed her arms over her chest. "Didn't you already meet them?"

"Thank you!" I stomped my foot.

"But not as her boyfriend," Axel argued. "Totally different."

"Axel, just be yourself," Francesca said. "They already like you so now you can just hang out."

"But you know me," he said. "I'll say something stupid."

"Just don't say anything stupid." Francesca said it like it was the easiest thing in the world to do.

"Easier said than done..." He turned around and marched to the truck. "I want the best blowjob in the world for this."

Francesca cringed then walked back inside.

"I'll do something nice for you when we get home—but not if you bitch the whole time."

He got behind the wheel and sighed. "Fine."

I buckled my safety belt. "Good."

He pulled onto the road. "Let's get this shit over with."

***

My parents were enamored by Axel. My mom paid more attention to him than she did to me, and she constantly complimented his blue eyes and his gentle nature.

Dad loved him too. He asked about Axel's internship for the investment company and his years in college in Florida. None of the questions felt like an interrogation. In fact, he seemed genuinely interested in Axel on a personal level.

My parents had never met a boyfriend before, and I always pictured it going much differently than this. I figured my family would rip into the first guy I brought around and scare him off as much as possible.

Axel was tense in the beginning, unsure how to act or what to say. But once he realized my parents were smitten he relaxed. "People think I just crunch numbers all day and sit in an office chair but it's more complicated than that. People invest their life savings with us. Our goal is to make a return on their investment. And if we don't, we don't make anything either. So, it's a win-win situation."

"Very cool," Dad said. "Do you guys invest in real estate companies?"

"Actually, we do," Axel said. "That's a hot market right now. Everywhere you look they seem to be building houses like factories. Everyone wants to own a home because of the tax benefits."

343

Thursday

"When does your internship end?" Mom asked. Her eyes were glued to Axel and she barely looked at me.

"It's only a one year commitment and I'm almost finished with my time. I only have a few months left." Axel sipped his wine then returned it to the table. "Excellent choice, sir."

"Thank you," Dad said. "I know my wine."

"Where will you go once it's over?" Mom pressed.

"I'm not sure yet," Axel said. "I'm applying to a few places in Manhattan. That place is the gold rush for investors. A lot of wealthy people live there."

"Marie was thinking of moving there as well." Mom said it like it was a new discovery and wonderful coincidence.

"I know," Axel said. "She should do it. I think she could find something good there."

A fairytale was happening behind Mom's eyes. She pictured me wearing a white dress and having all of his babies.

Thank god Axel couldn't tell.

Dad turned to me, addressing me for the first time that night. "How's school, honey?"

"It's good," I said. "Just trying to finish up."

Now that Axel wasn't in the spotlight he had the opportunity to eat some of his dinner. With perfect manners that I never saw, he cut into his food and ate quietly.

"How's your shoulder?" Mom asked.

"It's good," I answered. "Sometimes I forget it ever popped out of the socket."

"Same thing happened to me when I was young," Mom said. "I was playing softball when it happened."

"You played softball?" Axel asked. "Cool. I played baseball in high school."

"An athlete, huh?" Dad said with a proud smile. "I could tell."

Like I didn't exist again, their focus returned to him.

***

After dinner we walked out to the parking lot together. Dad walked beside Axel and talked to him about sports, something they had in common.

Mom walked beside me, lingering a few feet behind the guys. "Your father and I love him, Marie. He's smart, successful, sweet, and so good-looking."

"Yeah, I know." *Why else would I be with him?*

"He's so thoughtful and caring...he better stick around."

"That's a little out of my control." I hoped he would stick around. Our relationship seemed to grow more beautiful with every passing day. The superficial aspect of our relationship disappeared a long time ago, and now the spiritual parts remained behind.

"You love him, huh?" Mom smiled like she already knew the answer.

"Mom." I rolled my eyes.

"Awe. It's written all over your face."

"No, it's not."

"It's okay, sweetheart. I can tell he loves you too."

He does? "Just don't say that to him."

"It's so obvious in everything he does, Marie. That man is obsessed."

Just the idea made me giddy. "Mom, play it cool and don't embarrass me."

"I never would."

We reached my parents car then said goodbye.

"Thank you for dinner," Axel said politely. "It was nice to see you again."

"Of course." Mom hugged him tightly. "We loved spending the evening with you."

Axel hugged her back awkwardly, unsure what was happening.

When she pulled away, Dad moved in next. He hugged him and gave him a hard pat on the back. "See you later, Axel. Let's get together again soon."

"Sounds like a great idea." Axel stepped back, still taken aback by their affection.

Then my parents got into their Subaru.

"Uh...I guess I don't get a hug." As soon as a guy was in the picture it was like I didn't exist.

Axel chuckled. "Maybe you smell."

I smacked him on the arm. "Maybe you're a jerk."

***

"How'd it go?" Francesca asked the moment we walked inside.

"Awesome." Axel grabbed a beer from the fridge and sat down. "Dude, her parents love me. I'm like the son they never had."

"Really?" Francesca couldn't hide her surprise.

"Yep." Axel took a seat at the table across from her. "Right, baby?"

Since I loved it when he called me that my frustration melted away. "Yes, they loved you."

Axel wiggled his eyebrows. "Apparently, I'm really charming."

Francesca turned the page of the book she was reading. "Are they deaf and blind?"

"Shut the hell up." Axel kicked her under the table.

Francesca pulled her feet away before she could get hurt. "Well, I'm glad you had a great time. Now all you have to do is plan the wedding and live happily ever after." She flipped the page again.

Axel almost choked on the beer he was drinking. He coughed then slammed his hand hard against his chest. He had a cough attack right in the kitchen and struggled to breathe.

"Damn...are you okay?" Francesca watched him with both eyebrows raised.

Axel kept coughing until his throat was cleared up. By that time the beer had been knocked over and made a mess all over the table and the floor. "Sorry...went down the wrong tube." He grabbed a roll of paper towels and cleaned up the mess.

Thursday

"Are you sure you're alright?" I asked.

"Yeah, I'm fine." He tossed everything in the garbage then eyed the time. "I should get going. I have to finish a portfolio I've neglected." He gave me a quick peck before he walked to the door.

He wasn't going to pester me about spending the night? Or try to sleep over? "Okay..."

"See ya." He walked out and shut the door.

Francesca shook her head. "That dude gets weirder and weirder..."

CHAPTER TWENTY-FIVE

Uneasy

Axel

Her parents were nice and the evening went well. I was terrified of doing a family dinner because Marie and I weren't that serious yet. But it seemed important to her and I didn't want to let her down. Anytime she was upset, I felt like shit. All I wanted was for her to be happy, so I did whatever she asked.

But that marriage comment nearly gave me a heart attack.

Francesca was joking, at least I think she was. But it still freaked me out. Parents, marriage, and kids...I wasn't ready for it. I was so far away from being ready for it that I didn't even think about it.

What Marie and I had was perfect. I loved being with her and couldn't get enough of her. Monogamy was still new to me and I was enjoying it with her. Just the fact I was with only one woman was a huge step for me. It wasn't difficult because I cared so much about her. When I wasn't with her, I was uneasy. But that's all—for now.

Marie was in the same place, wasn't she? It didn't seem like she even wanted to be at that dinner. Her mother pressured her into it, and I understood why. Her parents swooped down on me and gave me their undivided attention. They were nice about it so I didn't mind. But Marie seemed bored during the entire conversation.

Now that I thought about it, she was definitely in the same place.

There was no need to freak out or have a serious conversation about it. Everything was exactly the same as it used to be. Neither one of us had a care in the world. Francesca was finally doing better so we were finally able to do what we wanted and when we wanted.

I kept my distance for a few days to recover from that dinner. I had a lot of work to do at the office, and we had a big client that just signed on with us. My internship was coming to an end and I wanted to go out with a bang. I already had a few resumes to submit to investment agencies in the city, thanks to Hawke. He knew who was looking for new talent and who wasn't. That would definitely give me an edge.

After a few days of space, I got over the dinner and the comment Francesca made. I missed her too much to stay away. My apartment began to feel like a small island far out to sea, and I never felt so lonely.

I texted her. *I miss you.*

Her message popped up immediately. *I miss you too.*

I didn't explain why I hadn't been around much. Maybe she noticed. Maybe she didn't. *Can I come over?*

How about I go over there instead?

That was even better. *Sure.*

I'll be there soon.

***

She walked inside with her overnight bag hanging on her shoulder. "Hey."

"Hey." I wrapped my arms around her and kissed her. The second my mouth was on hers I realized how much I missed those lips. They were soft like honey, and just as sweet. No other woman made me light up like this, like someone plugged in a string of lights that happened to be wrapped around my body like a Christmas tree.

I pulled her bag off and shouldered it before I pulled her into my bedroom. "What have you been doing?"

"I had a term paper I totally forgot about. I even called in sick to work to finish it."

"You should have had Francesca help you."

"She did, actually." She undressed and kicked her shoes aside. "Even then, I barely got it done in time."

So, she was too busy to notice my distance. That worked out in my favor. "All that matters is you got it done."

"I can't wait until I'm done with school." She pulled back the covers and got inside. "I just want to work, do what I love."

"I know what you mean." I got into bed beside her and cuddled with her. I missed sex but I missed this more. Just holding her gave me a sense of satisfaction. I loved it when her hair grazed my shoulder, and I loved it when she released beautiful sighs as she fell asleep. All the little details never escaped my notice. Now that I had her in my arms again I never wanted to let go. I shouldn't have freaked out over the dinner with her parents, and I shouldn't have cared when Francesca made that comment. None of it mattered anyway.

Only this did.

***

Marie wore skin-tight jeans and a black tube top. She always looked good in black. Her petite shoulders were rounded and chiseled, and her stomach was flat with a slight amount of definition from her abs. Marie had the perfect body, the perfect face, the perfect everything.

And she was mine.

The four of us sat together at the bar while the loud music played overhead. Our drinks sat in front of us, most of them empty. It was weird going on double dates with my sister. Even when she was with Hawke that never happened.

Francesca and Cameron seemed to get along better now. Francesca wasn't so tense and awkward. She made jokes from time-to-time, being herself. Cameron was warming up to her. I could tell he liked her more as time passed.

Marie moved her hand to my thigh under the table. "They're cute, huh?"

"Who?"

She nodded to Cameron and Francesca, who were holding hands on top of the table.

I shrugged. "I guess." I didn't pay attention to that sort of thing. I was just glad Francesca was seeing other men and moving on from Hawke. It seemed like Hawke still loved her but he was sleeping around again. Francesca shouldn't waste anytime hoping he would come back.

"I think they're cute." She leaned into me and kissed me on the lips.

Like always, my body grew hot. Any time we were physical together it always led to home plate. She turned me on like no other woman ever had. I'd had sex with her dozens of times, maybe even a hundred, but I still wasn't tired of it. I didn't crave something new with a different woman.

I only craved her.

"Be careful." I pulled away and broke our kiss. "Otherwise, we're going to barricade ourselves in the bathroom stall."

"I'm kinky but not that kinky."

"If you gave it a try you might actually like it." The possibility of getting caught always made it hotter.

"I'd rather wait until we're in bed. We can take our time and really feel each other. I can savor every stroke you give me and every kiss you press to my skin. And I can scream as loud as I want."

353

Thursday

My dick hardened in a nanosecond.

Marie smiled before her hand glided up my thigh. She reached the bulge in my jeans and gave me a squeeze.

"Can we go home now?" I blurted.

She chuckled then pulled her hand away.

Now all I could think about was Marie underneath me, enjoying everything I did to her. She was so good in bed. I loved giving it to her good.

Cameron pulled Francesca onto the dance floor. They moved together, laughing and having a good time. The fact Francesca was moving at all, especially in front of people, was a miracle.

Marie turned back to me. "I'm so glad—"

I sealed my mouth over hers and kissed her hard. All I wanted to do was suck her lips until they were raw. I wanted to feel her small tongue dance with mine. My body yearned for her in a desperate way. She was the most beautiful woman in the room tonight. Actually, she was the most beautiful woman in every room.

Marie turned her mouth away. "That's a little too affectionate for the public."

"Then let's go in the hallway by the bathrooms." This double date was stupid anyway. Cameron was a nice guy but he was boring. And I saw Francesca all the time. The only person I wanted to be with was Marie—and that involved a lot of kissing.

"Axel—"

"Come on." I grabbed her hand and pulled her with me. We moved through the crowd until we entered the deserted corridor that led to the bathrooms and the back of the bar. I pressed her back to the wall then kissed her again, my chest against hers. One hand fisted her hair and I kissed her the way I wanted, not caring if anyone walked by and saw it. She was the best kisser I've ever had, and while she satisfied me I always wanted more.

"They're going to wonder where we went..."

"Who cares?" I kissed her neck and felt her up discreetly. We could just go home and hit the sheets but I loved kissing her. Somehow, it was my favorite thing to do. I loved feeling her pant into my mouth with deep breaths. I loved it when her fingers cut into me.

I loved every moment.

***

We carpooled together so we ended the night at Marie's place. To our surprise, Francesca invited Cameron inside. But instead of going into the bedroom they sat on the couch and watched TV.

Marie and I could head back to my place but that would take too long. We'd have to drive and waste precious time. Besides, I wasn't sure if I should leave Francesca alone with this guy. She might rush into something she wasn't ready for. I decided to stick around and headed into the bedroom with Marie.

"Maybe we should just go to your place."

I grabbed her shirt and yanked it off. "It'll be fine."

Thursday

"But it's—"

"We'll be fine." I gave her a kiss before I undid her jeans and pulled them off. When she was just in her panties, I picked her up and carried her to the bed. Spending the evening making out and feeling her up got me harder than a nail. I wanted to make love to her slowly, to taste every inch of her and to fall deep into a different reality.

She slowly undressed me while she lay underneath me, kissing me and keeping her legs tight around my waist. She pulled my shirt off then felt the muscles of my chest and stomach. Then she moved for my jeans and boxers, pulling them off until my dick popped out.

My dick was so hard it actually hurt.

I kept my eyes glued to hers as I inserted myself. I loved watching her reaction to me. It was always sexy as hell. Her nipples always hardened and she released the sexiest noises. Her lips formed an O before she bit her bottom lip, loving every inch of me as it stretched her open.

The slickness of her pussy was too good to be described. I loved feeling her like this, noting the warmth and the sensation. And I loved the fact I was the only man who'd been inside her like this. Everyone else had to wear a condom—but not me.

I was special.

I inserted myself completely inside her then paused, letting the sensations wash over me. Her legs were over my shoulders and she was pinned underneath me, entirely mine to enjoy. Her tits were voluptuous and round, and every time I moved they shook.

"You're beautiful." The words flew out of my mouth without any further thought. The second I thought it, I said it. She really was the most beautiful woman I'd ever been with. She made everyone else look like a troll. And she was beautiful on the inside as well as the outside.

"Axel..."

Despite my built up sexual need I took it slow. My hips rocked gently into her, giving it to her slow. We hadn't fucked in a long time but I didn't miss it. I loved it when we made love like this, taking it slow so we both could experience every touch.

I paid attention to the way she breathed. It was deep and raspy, full of pants of desire. I noticed the way her green eyes darkened based on her arousal. Instead of looking at my chest or stomach she looked into my eyes.

I loved that.

I always looked into her eyes, wanting to be connected in the most intimate way possible. Eye contact was always awkward during sex and I avoided it as much as possible. My eyes were usually glued to the ass or the rack. But with Marie I always looked into her eyes. She was too beautiful not to.

My hand dug into her hair like it usually did. My fingers always fisted the strands like an anchor. Long hair was sexy on a girl but I didn't touch it as much as I touched Marie's. My fingers were always getting tangled in it, clamping onto it like l owned it as well as her. My hold was so strong she couldn't leave even if she wanted to.

She was mine.

I pulled one leg down and pivoted my body further over her, deepening the angle and getting an extra moan to come from her lips. Instead of coming like I wanted to I held on because I wanted her to finish first. Whenever we were together, that was my main focus. With other women I didn't really care. If she came, great. If she didn't, I didn't lose any sleep over it. But with Marie it was different. I gave her the best customer service because I wanted her to keep coming back—and not go anywhere else.

Her hands glided up my chest, her nails scratching the skin. She grinded against me from underneath, taking me in over and over. Then her hands moved to my ass where they gripped me tightly, tugging me further into her. She panted louder, loving everything I was giving her.

I got lost in the moment and didn't think about anything else. All I paid attention to were the sounds we made together and the sensation of my dick sliding in and out of her. Her body was wrapped around mine so I could get as much access as possible. We desperately clung to each other, needing to give pleasure as much as receive it.

Her hands glided up my chest until they moved passed my neck and face. They dug into my hair and fingered the strands, her pants becoming louder and sexier. She held my gaze then brought my forehead to hers.

I felt more than just pleasure in that moment. I felt a connection that was surreal and unbelievable. I'd never felt my mind sync with someone else's so well. I gave everything I had to this woman, and I wished I'd done it sooner. What if we got together long before? We would have had so much more time together. We would have made love a thousand times by now and we still wouldn't be tired of it.

"Axel..."

I loved it when she said my name. It usually meant she was on the verge of coming. Her pussy was tightening around me and my dick was feeling even better with every thrust. "Baby..." I never called a woman that, and I couldn't recall when I started calling Marie by that nickname. It just came out and I didn't think twice about it. I kept using it because I liked it.

"I love you."

Everything stopped. My thrusts died out and my ears started to ring. Her words echoed in my mind long after she said them, but I still couldn't believe what I heard. The ground shook beneath me and I couldn't find my footing. Like a lightning storm, I was struck—a thousand times. Fear gripped me by the throat and my mouth went dry. My tongue felt too big for my mouth. My heart pounded painfully in my chest, causing an adrenaline spike.

What did she just say?

Marie knew she said the wrong thing. All the pleasure left her look and she stared at me in embarrassment. Her hands left my hair and returned to her sides. She breathed hard out of fear. "Axel...I shouldn't have said that. I was just in the moment and—"

I got off of her then moved away, still panting. No one had ever said those words to me in my life and I wasn't ready to hear them now. First, we had dinner with her parents and then the marriage joke...and now this. I wasn't ready for it. I didn't think we were that serious.

I moved again but ended up falling on the floor.

"Axel?" Marie moved to the edge of the bed.

I got to my feet again and hastily pulled on my clothes. "I've got to go." My shirt was on backwards but I didn't care enough to fix it. All I knew was I had to get out of there. I didn't mean to mislead Marie into something serious, but I thought we were in the same place. I couldn't fall in love and get married. I didn't have the guts and the strength. I didn't have the balls to be a good man to anyone. I never meant for her to get hurt but somehow it happened anyway. "I'm sorry. I have to go." I reached her bedroom door and opened it.

"Axel, hold on."

I stopped at the doorway but didn't turn around.

"You can't just leave. Let's talk about this."

"I...I don't want to talk. I have to go."

"Axel—" I walked out and shut the door behind me. Everything after that was a blur. I walked passed the living room and ignored Francesca and Cameron. I wasn't even sure what they were doing or if they noticed me leaving. I ran to the truck and got it started but couldn't remember turning the key. I got onto the road and drove home but couldn't remember the drive. By the time I got into my apartment I collapsed on the couch and stared at the wall. The paint was white and a few coats old. I concentrated my thoughts on that—nothing.

It was the only thing that comforted me.

I hoped you enjoyed reading THURSDAY as much as I enjoyed writing it. It would mean the world to me if you could leave a short review. It's the best kind of support you can give an author. Thank you so much.

Is that really the end of Axel and Marie? Or is there still hope? Find out in the next installment of the series FRIDAY.

E. L. Todd

Want To Stalk Me?

Subscribe to my newsletter for updates on new releases, giveaways, and for my comical monthly newsletter. You'll get all the dirt you need to know. Sign up today.
www.eltoddbooks.com

Facebook:
https://www.facebook.com/ELTodd42

Twitter:
@E_L_Todd

Now you have no reason not to stalk me. You better get on that.

Thursday

I know I'm lucky enough to have super fans, you know, the kind that would dive off a cliff for you. They have my back through and through. They love my books and they love spreading the word. Their biggest goal is to see me on the New York Times bestsellers list and they'll stop at nothing to make it happen. While it's a lot of work, it's also a lot of fun. What better way to make friendships than to connect with people who love the same thing you do?

Are you one of these super fans?

If so, send a request to join the Facebook group. It's closed so you'll have a hard time finding it without the link. Here it is:

https://www.facebook.com/groups/1192326920784373/

Hope to see you there, ELITE!

Printed in Great Britain
by Amazon

83851796R00210